Escape from the Legion

Escape from the Legion

A Novel by

Jacqueline A. Granström

Strategic Book Publishing and Rights Co.

Strategic Book Publishing and Rights Co.
12620 FM 1960, Suite A4-507
Houston TX 77065
www.sbpra.com

ISBN: 978-1-62857-569-9

ACKNOWLEDGEMENTS

To the whole of my family who have been very supportive and patient whilst this book was being written and also to "Tom" without whom there would be no story.

CONTENTS

PROLOGUE

The ten of them, as well as the infamous Mr Z, were lounging on the five opulent and very comfortable large sofas, upholstered in the softest of brown leather, high up on the tenth floor in one of the exquisite new buildings in the centre of Paris. It was 6 o'clock in the morning, a meeting time that happened to suit all members of the group.

Unlike many old areas, this particular arrondissement of Paris had been one of the most dilapidated and rundown areas in the whole of the city. Now, with all the rubble having been removed, this area of the 21st had been redeveloped to become the most luxurious and unique part of Europe. People came from all over the world to view and admire the outstanding Rococo architecture, which was distinguished from other styles by its carvings and decoration.

The creation of this masterpiece was the work of a Greek adventurer who had been roaming around Europe looking for a special spot for his very fertile imagination. Arriving in Paris soon after the Second World War, he had come across this hidden, but very large, district. The buildings had been completely obliterated by the German bombs that had rained down upon this magnificent city. With the arrival of the Allies in 1945 and the end of the war, it was fortunate that only a small part of Paris had to be rebuilt. This elusive site was forgotten until Nikolas Socrates rediscovered it, and with prices at their lowest ebb was able to buy this large piece of land for a song. No expense was spared. When the designs had been drawn up, the plans laid down and, of course, permission granted, he ordered the most expensive materials from all regions of the world to be shipped into Paris, together with the most skilled workers, such as, builders, plasterers, plumbers, electricians, and landscape gardeners. When all of these had been brought into the city the work began.

It was a fantastic endeavour, Mr Socrates' workforce never ceasing to work on this sensational creation until the whole enterprise was completed within a period of ten years. People passing by would stop and watch the continual hectic buzz of activity.

The astonishing sight of this new mini city was unveiled in October 1955. Nobody was prepared for the splendour that greeted their eyes on that momentous day. It looked as though it had come out of a picture book, the gold and silver buildings glowing brightly in the darkness of the night. The only difference in this modern-day city was the height to which the skyscrapers had been built. By the 1950s architects had begun to explore different ways of creating very tall buildings by using the latest technology and incorporating the material du jour, reinforced concrete.

This small metropolis was mostly a business centre, with all the main banks of the world having offices there. There was also a social centre, with every opportunity to indulge oneself in the casinos as well as being able to participate in every Western sport. The golf course had the most beautiful greens, but only the most influential business executives were able to join.

Being located a fair distance from the Seine, a canal was built through the city centre to give the atmosphere of a Venetian environment. It was possible to take a gondola on a warm and starry night, minstrels singing romantic songs to the lovers perched upon the seats at their feet. Little wooden chalets surrounded by yew trees and cascades of brightly coloured flowers grew up on an artificial hill for the "aristocrats" of the region. There were 50 such chalets in all.

Its shares quoted on the CAC (the French stock exchange) rose to the highest level that had been seen in years. For most of the population in France life seemed pretty good, and a very high standard of living was enjoyed by many of the 65 million that inhabited this beautiful and wealthy country. As the years went by, the country flourished – and so did the underworld. The wealthy became wealthier and used the 21st arrondissement as a means to further their already nefarious activities.

It was in the middle of the 1960s that a group of businessmen hired a suite of rooms on the tenth floor in a sumptuous building on the east side. Nobody knew who they were; their very intention was, of course, to be as anonymous as possible. Mr Z had rented these large rooms by placing an advertisement in the paper, "Rooms Wanted." The required payment for these rooms was sent to a numbered account in Switzerland. Their main business interests were in the trading of drugs, human trafficking, and the unusual occupation of shanghaiing young and able-bodied men into the French Foreign Legion. They had been doing this for a number of years, their profits from this being extremely lucrative.

The quorum, which consisted of ten men, came from all parts of the world; their real names being kept secret to conceal their existence, they were identified only by the first letter of their country. They were: Mr A from Afghanistan, Mr B from Bangladesh, Mr E from Egypt, Mr F from France, Mr G from Germany, Mr I from Italy, Mr J from Japan, Mr K from Kazakhstan, Mr L from Libya, and Mr M from Morocco. Each man was given a small tiepin with his letter on it so the others could see who was who. They were advised at the beginning of the first meeting to memorize from whence each of their fellow associates originated, as the names of the countries would not be mentioned again. After a very short time, of course, they came to know each member of the quorum and his native country but nothing else. All the information on their backgrounds was locked away in a vault, again in Switzerland, for only one person to see: Mr Z.

At this particular monthly meeting at the Sampson Building Mr Z rose after the minutes had been read to advise the members of their next assignments. The original ten were still part of this group, but Mr E from Egypt was starting to have doubts about this organisation. The iniquitous activities that they all participated in were beginning to give him nightmares; and even more, a conscience! It would be dangerous, he knew, to bring this to anybody's attention, for most likely his assassination would then be imminent. His nightmares were mostly centred on the trafficking of human cargo, many of the enormous trucks laden with men, women and children being transported in airless containers from the more populated areas of Bangladesh. Mr E had a young family of his own and the horrors of this happening to them gave him untold fears that they might also be included if anybody knew of his plan to bring down this appalling quorum.

Mr E had a friend in the police force who knew nothing of the business that he was involved in and whom he could trust. They had got to know each other through their respective children, who were at school together. Apart from having similar interests, Mr E thought it would be extremely beneficial to have a friend in an occupation that was law-centred while he himself was at the other end of the spectrum. If he could glean certain information from Yves Marchand, it could help in the enhancement of his shady business dealings for himself and for his notorious companions.

One evening soon after the latest meeting in Sampson House, he called on his friend Marchand to ask how he was. He did not at first allude to the reason for his visit, feeling that he needed to test the waters before coming out and telling him about the notorious business he was tangled up in. That meeting passed without any incident and without any mention of the reason for his visit. Marchand was somewhat perplexed at Mr E turning up unexpectedly, and also at such a strange time of night. He had never done this before. In fact, they usually arranged a leisurely lunch during working hours or to meet up at weekends with their respective families. It was the first time that Mr E had shifted from his normal routine, and this in itself was disconcerting.

Not one of the ten had ever caused Mr Z to doubt their allegiance. They had followed his instructions to the letter ever since it had been set up, but he knew it would not last forever and there would be at least one or two of them who would step out of line. A surveillance team was always in force, and through them he was able to observe the strange behaviour of Mr E on that particular evening. He arranged for one of his "plumbers" to visit Marchand to check up on Mr E's visit, but nothing untoward turned up.

Perhaps it is nothing, he reflected, but until I know for sure that he does not intend to betray me I will continue to keep tabs on him. Nevertheless, it was somewhat unusual for him to be visiting his police-chief friend in the middle of the week and a little out of character. These facts led Mr Z to wonder what his intentions were.

Mr E had a bout of influenza very soon afterwards and was laid up in bed for a week. His arranged holiday was due soon after his recovery and he and his wife and children went to Egypt to meet up with other members of his family. He had a very happy time, and to some extent forgot his intention of exposing Mr Z and the company to the police. Since the quorum was due to meet at the end of November he would be back in time to attend it. Again the horror of what he was planning to do appalled him, so just before the meeting he thought he would visit his police friend again and this time alert him to the horrors. He was prepared for a long term in prison, but not before the destruction of the group.

The night he returned from holiday he again turned up at his friend's house, only to find that he had just gone out and would not be home for quite a while. He asked Marchand's wife whether Yves would have a moment to speak to him when he returned home. "Of course, he would," said Chantelle. "He will be very pleased to see you. Why don't you come in and have a cup of coffee and wait for him?"

He paused before replying, "That is very kind of you Chantelle, but Suzanne will be waiting for me at home and I need to let her know that I will be coming back here in about 2 hours' time."

"I understand. I will let Yves know as soon as he returns that you will be calling in to see him later on."

Mr E thanked Chantelle and returned home, totally unaware the he was being followed. One of Mr Z's surveillance team was again watching his movements but drew a blank when he saw Mr E leave the policeman's house after a few minutes and return to his own home. The tracker felt it was no longer necessary to continue with the surveillance that night, for it was getting late and as there was nothing of any significance to report to his boss. He decided to return home and call it a night. Unknown to the tracker, however, Mr E did return to his friend's house a couple of hours later and began to tell him about the terrible crimes in which he and the quorum had been taken part during the past 8 years.

Yves Marchand listened in silence, his face drawn like mask. He and his colleagues had been looking into this criminal syndicate for some time. (He did not tell Mr E of this, as they had not come up with anything of significance.) It was an innovative organisation masterminded by a brilliant criminal intellect. Mr E did not know who Mr Z was but was able to describe him as a tall, dark, swarthy individual aged around 40 who probably came from somewhere in South America, but he was not certain. Marchand recommended that Mr E go home and write down every tiny bit of information with facts, figures, rendezvous, activities, nationalities of the men, etc., and send a copy to him and another to a PO box number (the whereabouts of Mr E's choice) with implicit instructions for it to be opened only if anything should happen to him. In that way his back would be covered. The man tailing him noted that he had stayed much longer at Marchand's house than he usually did, and on passing the information back to Mr Z it increased the doubt as to his motives. Mr E delivered the details to Marchand the next day, as well as placing a copy in a PO Box as proposed and sending the key to the Prefecture of Police. Mr E was still unaware that he was being shadowed. A little later Mr E was asked by the boss if he would come and see him after the scheduled meeting. Knowing that his actions had been discovered, he excused himself from the meeting as soon as he could, saying that he had a terrible migraine. Grabbing a lift to the ground floor he managed to exit the building without being followed. Despite these prompt actions, Mr Z's bodyguard was waiting in preparation for his exit. At his boss's expressed instructions he shot Mr E in the head as he opened his car door. No one heard the shot, as a silencer had been used; the assassin stepped behind a bush and slipped away unnoticed.

Later on in the day Mr E was identified by his wife Suzanne, who was devastated and naturally bewildered by his murder. Marchand did not enlighten her about her husband's illegal activities and had no intention of ever doing so. He was aware that it would be wiser to remain silent and not approach Mr Z regarding the murder, for he was hopeful that Mr Z would not then immediately leave his present premises and find another one, which could result in his group being lost to the authorities for a number of years. By keeping quiet Marchand would have a slightly better chance of surveying this iniquitous team from a distance and compiling a more complete dossier on the organisation, building on and fleshing out the information that Mr E had given him before he was killed.

Hearing nothing from the police, Mr Z relaxed a little but had devised alternative plans in case he needed to decamp to an unknown destination at a moment's notice. Activities continued. Soon after Mr E's demise another member was presented to the team. He was introduced again as Mr E, but this time he came from Ecuador. It made it much simpler to keep the same letter and up to that time nobody had been introduced to the quorum from South America except for Mr Z himself, who had never informed his organisation from whence he came. The second Mr E, Mr Z felt, was a great asset to the team and complemented the group extremely well.

A couple of months after the first Mr E's assassination they were all sitting comfortably on the leather sofas on the tenth floor of the Sampson building, waiting to be given their various tasks. On this particular occasion, Mr Z instructed his team that he wished them to focus on the third strand of their activities, shanghaiing. He gave all of the members localities from which they could source some of the finest young men for the French Foreign Legion. The team was informed that it was acceptable to employ an accomplice, either male or female, if it was absolutely necessary, to assist in the implementation of the assignment.

Mr G from Germany chanced to join this criminal organisation through falling into serious debt at the gaming tables in Monaco. With his ready smile and charming ways, this tall blond, muscular young man of about 30 was considered a perfect candidate for this task. For his assignment, on this occasion, Mr G employed an actor who sported a moustache and wore the famous *Képi Blanc* to suggest he was a respected member of the Legion. Mr G not only covered Germany but also Austria, all of Scandinavia, including Finland, and some of the Slavic countries. He set off the next day, going from country to country in search of suitable candidates for the Legion. Thus it was that while sojourning around Sweden and checking up upon the recruits who were doing their national service, he encountered Tom.

A perfect candidate, he thought; this one will be worth a great deal. He did not find any other suitable individuals in Sweden on that occasion and moved on to Romania the day afterwards. Checking up on this latest prospective candidate, he carefully laid his plans. He just had to wait.

CHAPTER 1

Leaving Sweden

It was one of those days when nothing seemed to go right. Tom fell out of bed far too late on this particular Saturday after having had one too many drinks the night before, only to find that the barracks were strangely empty and silent. He had been dreaming about having his favourite breakfast of bacon and eggs, and of course the delicious velvety smooth coffee that he usually drank. The imaginary smell of the bacon and eggs and the aroma of the coffee penetrated his befuddled brain, which woke him up with a start. He jumped out of bed with a happy grin, his expression changing to extreme disappointment when he realised that that there was nothing there. He was not in the familiar surroundings of his home in Eskilstuna, which was quite a distance from the parachute company in Halmstad, but actually in the barracks, which was an enormous building where they all slept. There was never any food there but just beds and cupboards for their clothes. They obtained all their food from the canteen, which was 5 minutes' walk away. If he quickly threw on some clothes he might just get there in time before it closed. He was so hungry he knew he had to eat something before one of his splitting headaches kicked in. If only he had eaten something the night before and not only liquid refreshment. He would never learn.

He sprinted to the canteen which was only open from 07.00 to 08.30 hours, hoping against all odds that it would still be open. There was always masses of food for all of the 200 recruits that were housed in the Halmstad barracks, but on this Saturday morning, as most of the rookies had returned home for the weekend, everything was quiet and they had shut the canteen 5 minutes earlier than normal, believing that nobody else would be coming. He was not happy.

Tom was placed in a parachute regiment, which he had thought would be exciting. Halmstad was a small town in the county of Halland in the south of Sweden, a long way from his home, but since he especially loved the south of Sweden with its beautiful beaches, he was very content to have been posted there. With only 2 more months of service to run, he had no idea what the future held for him: something different, but what? Tom was an A-class recruit who exceeded all his objectives and excelled in everything he did, but somehow never seemed to feel sufficiently challenged. Why was he so restless?

He had been invited to a 21st birthday party of a good friend of his that evening and had been very much looking forward to it. He was taking his girlfriend, Eva, whom he had been dating for about 18 months, but having become gradually disenchanted with her was looking for a way to end the relationship. It was not going to be very easy, as he knew she was quite enamoured with him. There again, there was nothing wrong with her – she was a good-looking and very pleasant girl – but he now needed to focus on his future and did not need any unnecessary distractions.

Two months later, after having completed his National Service at Halmstad and breaking up with Eva, he returned to Eskilstuna, still not having any clear answers about what he should do next.

It was a miserable day in early December. Everything looked dull and grey, the rain splattering against the windowpanes, and the grey clouds lying low in the sky. It was very cold. Tom stared out of his bedroom window of his parents' home, which looked over a beautiful lake. He had lived there for the past 22 years. He spent time reflecting on what lay in the future. He had been very content living in such a warm ambience; it was time to go forward, but he was still restless, unsure, and a little anxious about his future. He was a cheerful young man, full of life, warm, clever, but a little impulsive and lacking in thought from time to time.

"Go on holiday," his father said, "but find somewhere where you are not going to get into any trouble, somewhere that is civilized, where there are decent hotels, running water, no bugs and where people speak English or French, and finally where your passport and papers are not going to be pick-pocketed."

Tom left Eskilstuna early one morning in the middle of the cold dark winter, his father very happily driving him to Arlanda, Stockholm's International Airport, from where he was booked on a flight to London Heathrow. He was determined to go to a place where it was warm, regardless of the endless and boring advice that his father had tried to give him. Morocco would be a haven at this time of year, with plenty of pretty girls, and for the foreigner sufficient beer to lubricate entertainment. Being a tall, dark-haired and well-built young man with a perpetual twinkle in his eye, he thought he would have no problem wherever he went.

Unknown to Tom, a tall blond muscular-looking man, around the age of 30, was watching his every movement from an unmarked car as he followed Tom's father's BMW on the way to Arlanda. His task was to locate any reasonable and presentable young man who had few ties and introduce him into the French Foreign Legion. Mr G and his colleagues always researched the young men who had completed their national service in the hopes that they might be suitable candidates for the Legion before falsely luring them into it. It was a very successful and remunerative past time, and one that had been implemented on many occasions by Mr Z's group.

Arriving at Heathrow Airport, Tom moved to gate 21 to await the departure of his plane to Morocco, his passport safely ensconced in his jacket pocket. With high spirits he almost ran up the gangway in anticipation of what was going to be, he felt, the holiday of a lifetime.

Another unidentified and dubious character was also silently scrutinising Tom. He was a smart-looking gentleman dressed in khaki uniform, tall, straight-backed, middle-aged, sporting a moustache and Képi *Blanc*. He ascended the gangway just a short way behind Tom. Luckily for him, as none of the seats was numbered, he was able to seat himself in the same row in the aeroplane as Tom, asking him politely if he had any objection. With his usual good humour he assented. The neatly attired gentlemen took the middle seat next to Tom, who had chosen the window seat. Tom was extremely intrigued by this unusual traveller, but the smart-looking stranger reclined his seat and seemingly went off to sleep, as per his orders: minimal conversation with the target individual. Tom, therefore, had no option but to amuse himself. When a pretty young stewardess moved down the aisle with the trolley of drinks, he eyed her with pleasure, observing her colourful uniform, closely fitted to her slim but curvaceous figure; her rich chestnut hair was piled neatly in a chignon on top of her head. He examined her beautifully chiselled fingers and manicured nails as she handed him a beer.

Tom was quite unaware that his quiet neighbour was watching him from under nearly closed eyelids. When Tom's head was turned for a second a very strong sleeping drug was slipped into his beer. Without realising that his drink had been tampered with, he downed it with relish and quietly and suddenly fell into a deep sleep, almost, it appeared, in the same mode as his companion.

When the plane landed 3 hours later, both gentlemen appeared to still be asleep. To the rear of the plane, the muscular blond-haired man came forward. Without preamble, he picked up the sleeping young man and carried him down the steps of the plane, explaining to the crew on board that the young man had probably had had too much to drink, and that he had promised his mother that he would look after him. Just prior to this, the uniformed man had surreptitiously slipped out of his seat, disembarking and disappearing among the throng of passengers heading for the Arrivals Hall.

Had the crew of the aeroplane given much consideration to this incident and reflected on the strangeness of it, they might have become suspicious and heard warning bells. Being so occupied with the departing passengers and the aircraft, however, this scene was only given a passing thought. Only later on did they realise that something very strange and forbidding had taken place!

A wheelchair in preparation for this clandestine operation was awaiting Tom, who was gently placed into it and wheeled to passport control. His passport was discreetly removed from his jacket, and with Morocco being a developing country it was relatively easy to get through Immigration without raising any suspicion. Mr G picked up his own case as well as Tom's and was able to pass through Customs without a hitch. A dark maroon saloon car with tinted windows was waiting for them at the airport exit. Pushing the wheelchair to the rear of the car, the blond man removed Tom, who was still heavily drugged, and gently slid him over the black leather seats to the other side of the car. He clambered in himself, the car moving slowly away from the curb. The wheelchair was left abandoned on the pavement outside the airport doors for somebody to pick up. Though still unaware of what had transpired or what was awaiting him, Tom's nightmare was just about to begin.

No conversation was uttered as the car sped towards the Moroccan border at Ceuta. Mr G and the driver, the actor who was wearing the *Képi Blanc (and who had drugged Tom),* both knew what was expected of them. A wiry individual dressed as a fisherman was waiting by the water's edge as they got out of the vehicle. His role finished, the driver returned to the airport while Mr G and the fisherman-cum-skipper carried Tom aboard a small fishing vessel, rendered inconspicuous by its size and general wear and tear. The acting colonel, who was already sitting in the boat, smiled and greeted Mr G as the rope tethering them to the bank was cast off. Their destination was Marseilles, a distance of at least 4 to 5 days travelling at approximately 15 knots. There was no need to hurry this trip, for any strange manoeuvre or behaviour on the part of the skipper would cause untold problems if it were discovered by the coast guard that that a shanghaiing was taking place.

CHAPTER 2

Arriving in Marseilles

The fishing boat slowly sailed out of the harbour towards Marseilles, heading northeast. The Mediterranean was a stunning blue, so beautifully clear that one had a view of some of the marine life, with flashes of brightly coloured fish that were swimming near the surface of the sea. Tom was still out cold after being given the sleeping drug in the plane. To ensure that he would not discover his destination or be able to identify his captors, he was injected with a sedative. This was to be topped up on accession so that it would last until he arrived at Marseilles. At the same time, he was carefully monitored so that nothing untoward happened to him. He was a valuable piece of cargo that needed a round-the-clock surveillance.

On the second and third day they passed the Balearic Islands of Mallorca, Ibiza and Menorca, which were favourite holiday resorts for tourists who sojourned to these islands throughout the year. The fourth day started with a beautiful dawn, crisp and cool, with only a whisper of a breeze coming from the Mediterranean. Marseilles, situated on the southeast coast of France, greeted them with screeching gulls, a cacophony of hooting and booming from the many different types of boats and tankers moored in this, the largest commercial port (and the second most populated city) in France.

Once again, a car with tinted windows was awaiting this clandestine group, the next port of call being Aubagne, the Quartier or camp of the French Foreign Legion. It is here that recruits learn the basic requirements of this notorious organisation. On arrival Tom, who had now completely awoken, realised that his so-called wonderful holiday had turned into a nightmare. Where was he? What day was it? Why had he been brought to this camp full of untidy, dishevelled and scary-looking men, who apparently had been issued with dirty denims without buttons, held together with string? He suddenly realised that he, too, was wearing these disgusting blue denims and old shoes. When had this happened?

His captors had disappeared while the drug had loosened its hold on him and he had no idea what he was doing in this place. Finding himself alone, he put his hand in his trouser pocket to find some papers signed by him purporting to be a signed document for his entry into the French Foreign Legion for the next 5 years. Now he was beginning to remember the uniformed soldier who sat next to him on the plane and the strange dreams he had of rocking in a boat. He must have been drugged all this time. Not knowing where he was or what to do next, he approached a fairly senior looking person in a uniform he was unfamiliar with and asked him, as politely as possible, where he was and what he was doing there. He received the abrupt response: "Are you speaking to me? One only speaks French in the Foreign Legion so cease your foreign chatter and go and stand over there in line with the others." Not understanding what was expected of him, he didn't move. The sergeant punched Tom in the stomach and shoved him over to where a group of men between the ages of 20 and 40 was standing. Winded by the assault on his person, a very outraged Tom had no option but to line up with the others and try and reason why this was happening to him. Unable to speak to anybody until the drill was over and hoping to ask for some explanation, Tom bided his time. Before he was able to find out anything more, however, he was called across to the sergeant's side. This time the bully, taking his papers and quickly assessing the possibilities, realised that this young man could be a useful and valuable recruit for the Legion. "You have now enrolled in the French Foreign Legion, Fredriksson, for the next 5 years. Your signed papers indicate this. Make the most of this and become an exemplary soldier. Go and stand over there. Everything will be explained in due course."

This time he spoke to Tom in English, a language in which Tom was fairly proficient so was able to understand the full meaning of his dilemma. His clothes had been removed, as well as his passport and any identification that he might have had. His signature must have been forged on the document he had had in his pocket in order for him to be forced into this situation. With a horror and dread that he had never experienced before, Tom realised that if he was ever to get out of this hell-hole he would have to be very careful to play his cards exactly the way any dutiful soldier should.

Though it was an undercover operation, most of the Legion was aware of the nefarious activities of shanghaiing unwilling recruits. It was only later that he realised that this particular sergeant had no idea that he had been shanghaied for it was, of course, totally illegal and the guilty person or associated persons would be seriously punished if it came to light. In any organisation there are always crooks that will try to make some easy money, especially if they know that recruiting a candidate of Tom's high calibre will earn them generous compensation.

The military compound in Aubagne near Marseilles was an enormous white building with high fences from which nobody could enter or escape, with sentries guarding the exits. After his initial shock at being abducted and knowing there was no hope of breaking out, he pretended to acquiesce, knowing that rebelling and being argumentative would only aggravate his plight. It would alert his superiors and he could be targeted as being an unruly and undisciplined novice. Since he had, with full knowledge as far as the Legion was concerned, signed the alleged form to join up, his so-called cooperation had to be genuine.

For the next week he was in a dream, not believing that this was actually happening to him but instead to somebody else. There were about 600 candidates, perhaps not all of whom were willing, who were being trained in different capacities. It was required for all the applicants, who were a mishmash of different nationalities, to apply themselves to the menial jobs that would keep the compound in impeccable condition. Tom gleaned that about 50% of the recruits had absconded from their countries and had entered the Legion to escape the many crimes they had committed. It was a place where their dubious pasts could not catch up with them and where they would be exempt from prosecution. Many of these individuals were given an alias so they could not be identified. He had been given the name Fredriksson, although he had not committed any crime.

***

A thorough medical examination was undertaken for all recruits. If a soldier was not in pristine health his application would be turned down, which could be disastrous for someone who was trying to escape the law. After all the aptitude tests had been taken and selection had taken place, the recruits were allowed to remove the filthy gear that they had been given to wear when they first entered the Legion's compound. These garments were then replaced by clean tracksuits and new trainers.

After 4 weeks in Aubagne, the recruits were sent to Castelnaudary, a small town near the Pyrenees. Castel camp was absolutely immaculate, extremely modern and well equipped. It was really most surprising. This was the venue where the recruits really began their training and indoctrination started. Tom began to realise that this was the place where they would all lose their freedom and the French Foreign Legion would become their complete masters, owning them body and soul. In a very short while he came to the realisation that decision-making was discouraged and he was no longer an individual but a clog in a very large wheel. From 05.00 hours in the morning until 23.00 hours at night, the recruits studied. They had to learn the songs of the Legion and how to slow march (88 paces a minute compared to the usual 120 in other armed forces). It was extremely difficult to keep to the exact rhythm and to learn the low and true songs that were being taught. Some managed but others were not able to keep up. The punishment for not trying hard enough was to have to crawl on their stomachs, resulting in their knees and hands being scraped on the hard tarmac until they were shredded. The upshot of doing this for 10 minutes improved the group to such extent that their marching skills improved phenomenally!

Activities continued: running, marching, climbing or rock-climbing. After 4 months in Castelnaudary the trainees moved on to the Farm, still in the Pyrenees but markedly different from the camp in every way. The Farm was a very cold and dilapidated building, and primitive. This, he presumed, was to remove any illusion that they were in for an easy ride, for there the training was cranked up several notches and became even tougher than it was before. They stayed at the Farm for about a month, after which these rookies returned to the camp, where to Tom's delight he received the Legion hat. Even though he had been forced into this captivity through unscrupulous means, he was surprised to find that he was beginning not to enjoy, but to be proud of his own achievements. He had never been subjected to such toughness and brutality in his life regardless of his experience in the Swedish Air Force, but he knew that it was the making of him and he would never again be so fit. His father would have been so proud of him.

His life had been turned around in such a drastic way that he was extremely confused and ambivalent as to what he should do next. His return to Marseilles after a short sojourn in Castel was the key to his future, and having gained the famed hat he was now informed that he was being sent to Calvi on the French island of Corsica to commence his training as a parachutist. Calvi being the training ground for the Legionnaires where the 2nd Parachute Regiment was housed, Tom was extremely pleased. He had done a fair number of jumps in Sweden and had become fairly proficient at it, but knew that he still had a lot to learn and that it was going to become much tougher.

The elitist group of parachutists was taken by bus to the airport in Marseilles, the plane then flying on to Ajaccio Airport in Corsica, and then on to Calvi. The next part of his ordeal was about to unfold.

CHAPTER 3

Corsica

As the plane approached Corsica, Tom saw, far below, a high wall of white rock that resembled the White Cliffs of Dover in Kent, southern England, which he had visited with his parents when he was a young boy. The vista was breath-taking. The aircraft landed at Ajaccio Airport, where an army convoy was awaiting to take the group of new recruits from the Cours Napoléon, the main street that stretches from Place Général-de-Gaulle northwards, towards Calvi. This was the headquarters of the French Foreign Legion, situated on the northern coast of Corsica, and home to the only airborne parachute company in the Legion.

Although Tom was still in a great state of distress over his abduction, he found the island of Corsica enchanting (notwithstanding the fact that every piece of knowledge regarding the island could be of use to him). The island had almost a thousand miles of coastline with soaring granite mountains that stayed snow-capped until July. The isle had been ruled by several different peoples dating back from 7000 BC, invaders such as the Iberians, Ligurians, and Phoenicians, Etruscans as well as the Romans, the Vandals, the Genoese and the people from Pisa.

The bus continued winding around the picturesque lanes towards the outskirts of Calvi. Tom was filled with trepidation and fear, wandering what on earth was going to happen to him next. The other recruits seemed fairly relaxed, but they had chosen this path and although apprehensive were not as fearful as he was. The barracks of Raffali, set on the outskirts of Calvi, consisted of a whitewashed building with red roof tiles that majestically faced the sparkling blue Mediterranean Sea. Exotic plants surrounded the building, together with the most elegant pine and palm trees on the island. Everything was kept in the most immaculate condition. There was a beach lying very close to the main gate, but this was out of bounds and was constantly guarded.

The recruits regarded their new abode with pleasure, and grabbing their belongings headed towards the building. They were greeted with the same kind of edifice that they had left in Marseilles: a cold grey stone structure that did not inspire any great emotion, though Tom should not have expected much else. That said, the island was beautiful, the climate very comfortable, and the wine and cuisine were excellent.

Lined up against the wall were several metal beds with straw mattresses and metal lockers beside them. Their kit, they were informed, had to be folded item-by-item and placed in the open locker; shirts, trousers, vests, etc., all stacked on top of each other to form a perfect rectangle. A white scarf needed to be folded down the front with a piece of cardboard behind it for stiffening purposes so that all that would be visible would be a neat square panel. The bed itself was made up of three different parts, which had to be dismantled and cleaned every day. Each bed and locker was to be scrutinised by a sergeant every night at roll call, or "appel", for the slightest speck of dust. Some of the sergeants were quite brutal, and Tom would come to take the brunt of this from time to time. On his arrival, however, he needed to survive and concoct an escape plan, though he was still unsure as to what he really wanted and how he was going to get it.

He had managed, surreptitiously, to telephone his family collect very soon after his arrival in Marseille to let them know of his abduction. Unfortunately there was nothing that they could do, he informed them, for as far as the French Foreign Legion was concerned he had signed the legal documents accepting the conditions and he would be unable to leave for 5 years unless, of course, he attempted desertion. Apparently this and stealing were two of the worst crimes a Legionnaire could commit and the repercussions of being caught were horrendous.

After an excellent supper in the refectory that night he did manage to fall into a dreamless sleep only to be woken up at 06.00 hours. His first day as a real Legionnaire had begun. After a quick breakfast their instructions as new recruits commenced, their destination, a 24-km trek over the hilly terrain with a rucksack of heavy rocks on their backs. Not even one of the new recruits managed to complete this assignment. As this was their first day they were not penalised but were warned that should the task not be completed next time their hides would be at the mercy of the sergeants.

After returning from the rolling hills of Calvi, and after having grabbed a quick lunch of bread rolls, butter and corned-beef, the recruits had to stand to attention for the next step of their training. Sergeant Major Dupré was a brutish French-Swiss compatriot with a large round head, tufts of hair sticking out of his ears, and beady charcoal eyes that glittered with icy contempt at the newcomers. He seemed to enjoy the discomfort his presence was causing them. He was just one of the many non-commissioned officers who enjoyed inflicting pain and fear upon his subordinates (one of the many "tin-gods" that exist in today's society).

Everyone's feet were sore and swollen after their trek through the rough terrain. A few of them of them were not as trim as Tom and certainly not fit enough to be able to cope with the demands of this sergeant. It was no wonder that the sergeant had it in for them! Barking his orders with delight he assigned the recruits to some very unpleasant but necessary tests, such as running with a sack of sand on their heads, rope climbing, press-ups, abdominal exercises, knee-bends, hurdles, springs and crawling under barbed wire.

It was early days and Tom knew from past experience that it would only get worse, the training getting harder in order for them to become exemplary legionnaires.

"Cleanliness is paramount in the Legion," the platoon sergeant informed all the recruits. "Everything has to be immaculate. Every one of you has to have two pairs of denims, which need to be washed and ironed every day, as well as spotless shirt collars that are be inspected for any dark and dirty marks. Teeth and behind the ears are also inspected. Boots have to be absolutely black so a kind of thick grease is to be put on them to soften and to make them waterproof." Tom took all this in hoping against all odds that he would not be pulled up for not adhering to these important rules of the Legion.

***

Tom had learnt at the beginning of his incarceration that only French was allowed to be spoken and had noticed that some of the younger soldiers had been very badly beaten for relaxing into their own language. Tom was not prepared to be caught out in that scenario. Everyone for whom French was not the first language was given a bonhomie who was a French-speaking rookie. The bonhomie stayed close to his special "foreign" rookie until he became fluent in the language, or at least competent. Tom's bonhomie was called Luke, who taught him every-day and idiomatic French. Luke was very interested to learn Swedish, so every so often Tom used to give him a Swedish lesson. With Luke, who was a very nice guy, Tom's French was improving rapidly and so soon he would no longer need such assistance.

The Legion was famous for its songs, its soldiers marching to the wonderful tunes wherever they went. Tom took great delight in their music and their wonderful singing, and within a very short time had become familiar with all the words and melodies.

Occasionally Tom managed to telephone and write to his parents, but there was very little contact with the outside world, as all television, newspapers, and radio were banned.

CHAPTER 4

The whore house

It was a great milestone in Tom's life that soon after his arrival, while doing one of the most exacting drills of all, he encountered an Englishman from Staffordshire who was to touch his life. With both heads and faces almost obliterated by the thick mud, they both managed to slither like snakes under the barbed-wire fence, just missing the sharp spikes that had been built into the ground to encourage any stupid ass to tear himself to pieces. Macey was a rough diamond that had come from a tough neighbourhood where illiteracy was normal and manners unknown. He had, however, been brought up by a very loving couple (not his parents) who had given him not only all the love in the world but ethics and standards that would stand him in good stead for the future. He was, however, the complete antithesis of Tom, who was a gentleman from a good family and was very comfortably off. Little did Tom know that it would be this tough English northerner who would be his saviour and friend for life! They exchanged names, but Tom was not yet prepared to trust anybody with how he had become a recruit of the Legion. As his name had been changed to Fredriksson from Sandberg, he wondered whether Macey's name had been changed, too, but since Macey had volunteered and had no hidden agenda there was no need for him to have an alias. He remained Macey to his friends and superiors throughout his time in the Legion.

On one particular evening, a couple of weeks after their arrival when they had some time off and with a week's pay in their pockets, they decided to peruse the local whore-house. Neither young man was particularly au fait with the workings of such an establishment, nor were Tom and Macey especially sure that they would undertake to go the "whole hog" with a female of dubious character in a foreign country. On surveying this questionable house of disrepute from the outside, however, they threw caution to the wind and walked in through the open door to ask what services there were on offer. Unwisely they were still dressed in their uniforms. The brassy looking girl at the desk studied them with interest and rather liking the way they looked, especially Tom, ushered them into two separate rooms. Macey had the smaller of the two rooms, which had elaborate furnishings and a comfortable-looking medium-sized double bed. The room appeared to be fairly respectable and relatively clean. Tom, who was presented to the prettier of the two teenage girls, was given a larger room with a king-sized bed and fine linen sheets. Since neither of the young men saw the other's room, they had no idea that they were being set up. Tom was pleasantly surprised at the attention that he was being given. It was suggested that he should remove his clothes and lay them on the chair, which was standing in the corner of the room. Unused to having sex with a strange female he was hesitant to do the girl's bidding, but after being given a large whisky – which unknown to him had been drugged – he relaxed and fell into a deep sleep.

Jeanne, the pretty teenager, had no interest in having sex with Tom. She only wanted his money. Drugging her more elite clients and stealing from them was far more remunerative and an easier and quicker way of getting rich and improving her lifestyle. Usually the client was unaware that anything toward had happened until after the event, and by then there was nothing he could do.

She mistook Tom for one of her richer clientele, thinking that he had more money on his person than he actually did. Realising that she was not going to collect on this one she became enraged and decided on another approach. While Tom was in a drug-induced sleep the girl tore at her clothes and scratched her face with her long manicured nails in order for it to look as though she had been attacked and he had forced himself upon her. This would undoubtedly besmirch his name and that of the Foreign Legion, which most of the natives disliked being on the island. She also knew that Louis, her jealous lover, would not believe her if she just handed over the small amount Tom had in his pocket. She hoped that the scene in the room would make her look like the victim and disguise her error of judgement. Jeanne, knowing that Louis could enter the room at any moment (his being one of the regular heavies there), prepared herself for his arrival.

Though not liking Jeanne's lifestyle, Louis did like the money. Hearing him coming into the room she sat on the floor with her head in her hands in preparation for her performance.

"What are you doing, and why are you in such a mess?" Louis shouted at her.

"I did as you said and put a potion in his whisky, but before it took hold he turned rough, tearing my clothes and scratching my face."

With disbelief Louis asked, "How exactly was he meant to have done that?"

"He was very strong," Jeanne retorted.

"He must have been if he could do that to you when half drugged. Did you manage to get the money?"

She said that he had hardly any on him. Jeanne knew that she had to try and convince Louis.

"I don't believe you. These soldiers and specially the Foreign Legion ones have plenty. Just look at them. They are rolling in money, with their fancy dress and big ideas about themselves."

"I promise you, he had very little on him," she pleaded.

"Listen Jeanne, you have done this before. You know you don't cheat Louis. Give the money to me. That's what we decided." Jeanne suddenly felt a little braver, "It may be what you decided but it is not what I had in mind. After all it is my body." In a rage, Louis slapped her across the face throwing her to the floor and hitting her over and over again before running out of the room in panic.

***

Tom awoke some time later to find two policemen standing by his bed. This was the second time Tom's drink had been spiked since leaving Sweden, and being duped a second time did not help his usually equable temper. Unable to answer the questions the policemen bombarded him with, and still only having a basic grasp of French – besides only having just woken up from a drug-induced sleep – he challenged their presence. He asked why they should be in his room and where was the girl who had administered this opiate? Of course the police were just as ignorant of English as he was of French, and after ordering him to get dressed they pinned his arms behind him, bundled him into a police car and drove him off to the police station. Tom was still unable to understand what his crime was when the young girl was brought into the station. With great horror he saw that she had been beaten up very badly, for large welts had come up on her arms and legs. She also had a black eye and a broken nose. Who had done this to her? Was it the police? He could not believe they would use such force on a woman. There would be no other reason, and he himself had never hurt a woman in his life, but there were no witnesses to prove otherwise.

Macey, who had been waiting outside the whore house for his friend, had heard the incident with the police and luckily understood a substantial amount of French. Although he could not believe Tom would do this, he still had not known him long enough to be absolutely sure. However, the least he could do was to go to the police station and see what it was all about. By this time Tom had been relegated to the cells, so being unable to speak to him and still not being able to get any more information Macey ran back to the barracks and sought out Colonel Ziegler, one of the toughest but fairest of the officers.

It took Macey well into the night before he could locate the Colonel, and though it was unacceptable to speak English he hoped that Ziegler, a German subject who was fluent in English, would understand his dilemma and help Tom. The Colonel listened quietly, without any interruption, to the difficulties that Tom had somehow got himself in, and with a nod of comprehension at what Macey had reported strode off to the police station in his full uniform, a most dashing and authoritative figure.

The Colonel had been watching Tom from the side-lines, noting the disciplined body and the strong mind that went with it. Being a good judge of character, he too felt it was unlikely that the young man had done these terrible things. Although a Colonel in the Legion, however, he was still a foreigner himself in this country. It was fortuitous, though, that as well as being a high-ranking officer he was also a lawyer. Macey could not have chosen a better man! He ordered Macey to return to his barracks, giving him strict instructions not to say anything to anybody. An incident of this type with the local police did not bode well for the French Foreign Legion, and the sooner this incident was closed the better.

On arriving at the jail he, like Macey, was told that the prisoner was not allowed to see anybody, and that a lawyer had been allocated to Tom for the next day. Colonel Ziegler, bringing himself up to his full height of 6ft 5ins, informed the policeman in charge that every Foreign Legion soldier is assigned a Foreign Legion lawyer and suggested that the allocated civil lawyer should be discharged from his responsibilities.

"I expect my client to be decently clad and in a healthy frame of mind and body when I visit him tomorrow." Colonel Ziegler, having made his point and making ready to go, turned back to the constable in charge, Constable Moreau, and with a passing comment added, "I would appreciate your telling my client that I will be here at 08.00 sharp. If I find that you have mistreated him, you will be sued and the wrath of the French Foreign Legion will be upon your head."

With a salute to the constable, he marched out of the door. Constable Moreau was dumbstruck. He had never been treated in this manner before. He was an inveterate bully and was slightly anxious about the consequences of his actions, for he himself had taken more than a few swipes at the young recruit with a couple of his lackeys as back-ups and had taken a lot of pleasure in beating him up, believing that no-one would be any the wiser. Now he was in a tight spot and was rather concerned as to how he could disentangle himself from this dilemma. Handled badly he could lose his badge! Could he get away with blaming one of his junior constables? After a second pondering, he thought better-of it as he knew the incarcerated recruit would dispute such an accusation. He decided instead to play the defence card. After all, Tom was looking increasingly responsible for the girl's injuries. It would not have seemed so farfetched, therefore, if Tom had been the first one to pull a punch. Moreau knew it was more likely that it was the girl's infamously jealous lover, -Louis, who had been responsible for Jeanne's brutal beating. What Moreau was sure about, however, was that he was not going to take the fall for looking after his own.

At 8 o'clock promptly the next morning, the Colonel arrived at the police station wearing the army regalia and of course the *Képi Blanc*. He was ushered into Tom's cubicle; a low-roofed room of about 25 square feet. On the left-hand side of the cell was an iron bed with a mattress, a pillow, and a blanket. In the corner was a latrine with a sink next to it. There was one chair and a small locker beside the bed. The room was damp and airless.

Tom was sitting on the bed as the Colonel entered, his face and torso a mass of cuts and bruises. Gone was the immaculate outfit that he had been wearing on that fateful night. It had been replaced with a charcoal-grey pyjama-like suit, the uniform of a prisoner.

As Captain Ziegler entered a look of horror passed over Tom's face, which hitherto had been expressionless and bland. He had not been given the message from Constable Moreau that Colonel Ziegler would attend his cell the next day, so was naturally shocked and bewildered by his arrival.

Regardless of his physical discomfort and pain, Tom immediately stood to attention, a look of enquiry in his eyes.

"At ease Fredriksson. Do not be alarmed. Young Macey asked me to help you, so here I am. I actually happen to be a lawyer, so the sooner we get started the better. First of all I want you to reflect back and give me every minute detail of your experience in the whore house."

Tom painfully gave a detailed description of his night at the house of disrepute, describing the luxurious room he was given, as well as a description of the girl, the drugged whisky and waking up in horror to find two policemen standing beside his bed. He had not seen the girl since she had been brought into the police station in a terrible state. He had then been charged with this assault, which he, of course, denied. As no one had listened to anything he was saying (he was still having difficulty with the language), he had been thrown into the cell that he now occupied.

"Has a forensic specialist been here to ask you about the incident?" the Colonel enquired.

"No Sir. Nobody has been near me except the Constable, who beat me up, and the person who brought me some food and water, which was put through the grill."

The Colonel pressed on. "Did you retaliate when the Constable hit you?"

"No, I couldn't as two of his men pinned me down as his fists came raining down upon me."

"Can you describe your assailants?"

"No I can't for, they were wearing balaclavas."

The Colonel contemplated Tom's answer. What a strange thing to happen in a crime-prevention establishment. "Did Constable Moreau wear one too?"

Tom's recalled Moreau's determined grimace when he laid his first punch. "No, he is far is too arrogant to hide his face behind a mask, and would not think for one moment that he'd ever be prosecuted for beating me up."

"Well now he will be," said Ziegler, sternly. "No law enforcement officer should ever be allowed to operate in this fashion.

"But first things first. I have arranged for a doctor who specialises in forensic medicine to visit you later on today, not only to look at your injuries but also to check on your hands and knuckles and to see if there are any tell-tale skin signs under your nails.

"If your hands and knuckles are without abrasions it will prove that you did not beat-up the girl, nor were you the aggressor in the fight with the chief of police. It will be recommended that Moreau be checked for abrasions on his hands and knuckles as well, though he will undoubtedly deny everything. Regrettably we do not have much proof of his doing it except for your word. This will not mean much in a civil court of law. It is important for you to avoid having any contact with water, either to wash or to shower, for the evidence could be compromised if you do. If there is no compromising evidence that links you with the prostitute you are off the hook, so to speak, as well as proving that you were not the aggressor in Moreau's attack. In case of a further attack upon your person, I have arranged for one of my sergeants to stand outside your cell to prevent any unwelcome guest visiting you in the stealth of the night who might, perhaps, cause you untold damage or aim to erase any evidence that we might have had."

With a quick salute Colonel Zeigler left the cell, giving Tom more hope than he had ever thought possible. He was so appreciative of Macey's help in locating the Colonel and for his sound judgement and support.

CHAPTER 5

Forensic evidence

The next month went past in a blur. The forensic evidence proved that Tom had not touched the girl or the constable, and he was released without the incident even going to trial. He returned to his unit and to the routines of the French Foreign Legion almost as though nothing had happened.

But there was much that did happen. The girl's ex-lover was prosecuted on the evidence of the prostitute. It took quite a while to persuade her that unless she did so, her ex-lover might very well repeat the assault and would possibly kill her the next time. She also admitted that Lois and the Constable had put her up to using Tom as a "scapegoat" to the detriment of the Foreign Legion, for which she was very sorry. She also admitted that she had stolen from her elite clients on occasions. Being so young and contrite, she was let off with a caution and returned to her parents' home and continued with the studies she had hitherto left because of the lure of the big city.

Constable Moreau was imprisoned for 10 years for his regular assaults on prisoners for his clandestine involvement with a local drug cartel, which was uncovered while his behaviour was being investigated. He was a most embittered bully who threatened to get even with Tom when he got out. It was recommended that he should never been given bail and hopefully Tom would be long gone before he did.

The thugs who helped Moreau were also let off with a caution. When a new Constable was appointed they became exemplary police sergeants and never put a foot wrong again.

CHAPTER 6

Macey

One cold dark winter's morning in a small town in Staffordshire in the early 1950s, a small bundle wrapped in a thin cotton shirt, shawl and nappy was thrown into a dumpster. This was before the abortion laws had become legalised. The girl had found herself in the unfortunate position of being pregnant out of wedlock had been dumped by the amorous man who had been responsible for the situation the moment that he discovered she was with child. The young woman, finding herself in this predicament, had not then been able to return home or ask her parents – especially her father – for any help or support.

She often had to change lodgings and supported herself until the day of the birth. It was on this particular day that Eloise, just 16, gave birth to a little boy. Without any fuss and without much thought either, she decided to solve her problem by abandoning the child where it would not be found. So very quickly and quietly she found a large, fairly full dustbin and threw the infant into it, hoping that nobody would find him. She wanted this episode in her life to be over. She knew that never again would she succumb to a man's charm.

Without even glancing back to the rubbish bin where she had discarded the child, she made her way back to her lodgings, where she promised herself that a new life would be in front of her. Perhaps she would return home, even if it were just to see her mother, but having very little affection for any other member of her family she doubted that she would see any of them again.

Meanwhile the abandoned baby, almost freezing to death, let out a high pitched wail that by some chance was heard by an old tramp passing by looking for some food early in the morning. Initially thinking it was a mouse, he made to pass by. However, some instinct told him that it sounded more like a human cry and turning back to where the noise came from and rummaging among the rotting food waste and empty cartons found himself grabbing at something that felt warm and moist to the touch. To his horror he came upon a small bundle among the rubbish. Pulling it out he was shocked to see this mite of a baby dressed in the scantiest of clothing, cold but alive. What a miracle! Who knows what would have happened if he had not found the baby when he had? He bundled the shivering child under his old and worn but thick overcoat, and headed towards the corrugated hut where he had set up home.

The old tramp, whose name was Jo, lived with another friend in this dilapidated abode. It was warm and contained the essentials on which to live. Jo knew that it was not the best place to bring up a child but what option did he have?

"What should I do Fred?" he asked his mate. "I can't look after this child on my own and of all places here! If I get found out, who knows what they will do to me and who knows what will happen to this little blighter!" Fred was a good chum and had quite a lot of common sense for an old codger.

"You could always put it outside a hospital so it could be found, though the child might freeze to death." Thinking this through, Fred shook his head solemnly. There was an alternative. "I know you have had no contact with your daughter for a long time, but this is the time to make bygones be bygones and heal the rift. She has always been a fine and very kind lass and might very well welcome a little one, especially as she and her husband, Stan, haven't managed to have one of their own. I do not think there are going to be too many questions asked, as these incidences of unwelcome births are pretty common nowadays. What do you reckon?"

Jo, with some trepidation, walked to his daughter's house, which lay in a built-up area a couple of miles away. Like lots of places in Heron Cross in the 1950s, the houses were built close together with a two up and two down layout. The smoke from the nearby factories blackened the buildings and clogged the air, which was thick and putrid. Many of the youngsters who lived in this area had asthma or breathing-related illnesses. Jo really did hope that he was doing the right thing by bringing the child here.

Knocking at the door at this fairly early hour did not prevent it being opened immediately by a very sweet looking woman of about 22. She gasped with surprise as she opened the door to her father. "What are you doing here, Pa," she asked, "at this time of the morning?"

Jo, very shyly, handed over the little bundle. "I have a little present for you," he said. "I found him on a rubbish heap this morning and thought you might be happy to have such a lovely little chap. I also want to say sorry for being such an irritating and stubborn old fellow, especially as I know you have always wanted the best for me."

The woman, named Cheryl, whose mouth reminded her father of a cherub, burst into tears and ushered her father and the baby into her front room, hugging them both as they came through the door. Regaining her composure, she first of all took the little mite out of his thin clothes and wrapped him in warm clothing, which she had bought for the child she had lost the year before. Throwing on a coat, and leaving her father to mind the baby, she rushed to the local corner shop that was only 5 minutes away and opened early to collect the day's newspapers to buy some powdered milk for the infant. Mixing and heating up the milk in a bottle on her return home, she fed the infant until his cries lessened and he fell into a wonderful slumber, child and surrogate mother clinging to one another in the most unexpected of situations, fulfilling a need in each other that only they, themselves, would ever understand. Thus Macey, who was given the name John, came to be the beloved son of Cheryl and Stan. He grew up to be a strong and sturdy boy, was full of fun and life, and a great joy to both of them.

The years went by happily but, like many adolescent boys, John on entering his teens became restless and dissatisfied. He had the most concerned of parents but there were few opportunities in that part of the world for a young man of his capabilities. It was pottery country and most youths left school at 15 to join the throngs of young people who entered these factories. He needed to move away, but to where, and to do what?

He was doing well at school, his teachers sending back good progress reports of his achievements. Though extremely competent in both sport and academic subjects, he was still unable to pinpoint which area would best suit his talents. At his present school there was no counselling to help students plan their careers. As John's father, Stan, was bent on his son following him into the building trade, he had no one with whom he could talk with or ask advice from.

Walking back from school one winter's evening he decided to take a different route home by way of the back streets of Heron Cross. He knew from time to time that there could be unruly gangs who would waylay any unsuspecting person, male or female, and rob them of any valuable items they had on them. Removing any evidence of his birthday watch and hiding the money that he had saved from working in the local garage in his shoes, he walked sedately through these back streets, almost hoping he would be accosted. He did not have long to wait, for within 5 minutes of entering this backwater a group of five boys ranging in ages from seven to 13 years old attacked him from all sides, pulling his satchel off his shoulder and throwing it down in disgust when they did not find anything of interest in it. John, having religiously visited the local boxing club for several months, was able to fend off his attackers without too much difficulty, until all five of them were lying dazed and bruised on the hard ground. Dusting off his school uniform and checking that it was intact with no tears or damage, John picked up his satchel and walked home, totally unperturbed by what had just happened.

Now he knew what kind of career he would be best suited to. He would join some combat force, the army, but as yet he did not know which one. He was only 15 years of age after all.

It would take him a few years before he was able to put his plans into action, and much to the chagrin of his parents he packed his bags one winter's day and set forth for Marseilles to join the French Foreign Legion.

CHAPTER 7

Djibouti

It was now about a year since Tom's kidnapping and he had had enough, but there was no way out apart from deserting. Things did not get better. Sergeant Major Dupré capitalised on Tom's so-called misdemeanour in gaol and made his life most unpleasant. It was a regular occurrence for the contents of Tom's locker to be turned upside-down and for unexpected blows to rain down upon him for no apparent reason. Dupré enjoyed tormenting his charges. The other officers seemed to turn a blind eye when this happened, which Tom could not understand. He supposed it was what happened when one became a real soldier.

One day Tom found out that they were off to Africa, to Djibouti, one of the hottest places on earth. It lay on the Red Sea, sandwiched between Somalia and Ethiopia. The Republic of Djibouti spans approximately 34,000 square miles and has a population of just fewer than 500,000, many of whom are nomadic people.

Despite his earlier elite parachutist training, the time leading up to the posting was taken up with hours of training: learning about parachutes, how to pack them, carry them and put them on. The Legionnaires would swing on wires and cables to simulate being under a parachute, and had in-depth lessons on all the technical aspects of jumping. Tom and his fellow recruits were rigorously trained to use the issued weapon, the FAMAS, a 5.56-calibre assault rifle made for the French army. It was necessary to know how to assemble and disassemble the rifle in seconds, which during the final bout of training was done with their eyes closed. The Legionnaires' physical and mental endurance were pushed to the limit in preparation for their arrival in Djibouti. The training had been harsh but necessary. Survival was of the utmost importance. There were tropical diseases to be aware of, not just the symptoms but how to minimise the risk of getting them. Hepatitis, malaria and blood poisoning were rife. On aspects of sexual health, they were informed that consorting with prostitutes was not one of the ways to enhance one's health or love life, and was not to be recommended.

***

The Foreign Legion tropical kit included regular-issue sunglasses, a huge khaki headscarf, shorts, lightweight shirts and canvas boots. As they made their way to Djibouti, Tom began to realise that going into this God-forsaken land was not going to be "a piece of cake". It was a place that Europeans would find most unpalatable, with the extreme heat, high level of disease, hard work, ill health, and dust. He ran through ideas in his head as to how he could get out of going, but came up blank.

One very dark and moonless night the action began. The small group of soldiers parachuted down into the wilderness of the Danakil desert, hoping against all odds that they would land safely and not get caught on any of the prickly bushes that grew in that part of the country. They had practised enough but jumping down onto this rough terrain without light and without a clue as to where anyone was going was still quite a feat. One of the recruits landed in a bush, scraping his shins and tearing his uniform, but luckily he was not badly hurt and managed to disentangle himself. Being the first time any of them had set foot in this barren land, they felt extremely apprehensive. Having been trained as the most efficient soldiers in the world, however, they set out with the knowledge that despite this they would succeed in their mission: to put down the rebellion against the French occupants in the country.

Their first job was to find a location about 5–10 miles from the drop and erect tents for the 4 days and nights that they were going to be there. The shooting began early the next morning, around 0600, but though the recruits returned fire they were unable to see the targets.

The camp moved again, this time to a denser part of the desert where they were hidden by the dry prickly large bushes, which made up the only greenery in that part of the country. The greenery did not provide shadow or make it more comfortable. The heat was unbearable, and like all the other recruits every part of Tom's body was soaked to the skin with sweat within 5 minutes of landing in the desert. It was a little cooler at night, but when the sun came up there was no reprieve: it was about 29°C at night and 36°C during the day. It was cooler in the first few months of the year.

Just a few days after their arrival, the Legionnaires all went on a mission to try and target the enemy, who were based on the other side of the hill. The initial sortie crawled on their hands and feet up the dry and brittle surface of the slopes with a shot-gun in one hand and a grenade in the other. The other Legionnaires were just a stone's throw behind, with the younger ones trying to emulate the more experienced. A single shot rang out and a soldier, who was only about 18 years old, fell to the ground clutching his foot and screaming with the sudden and excruciating pain. He fell backwards down the hill but luckily his injury was not serious. After the skirmish, the soldier was picked up and seen by the trained medical staff that was always on call for any emergency.

CHAPTER 8

Desertion

Whenever Tom and Macey obtained a pass they would walk into the town and have a beer with the locals. They would also speak to the migrant Bedouins (whose language was mainly Arabic, but who also knew some French). From time to time the young recruits would be invited into the Bedouin tents, which were made of goats' hair panels, which the women had woven on their narrow ground looms and stitched together, to drink the local coffee and smoke shisha. These wandering nomads were a gentle and hospitable people, and Tom and Macey spent many pleasant hours with them discussing life in general.

Tom noticed that the Bedouins had very few medical supplies and were always seeking out medicines, as the child mortality rate among them was very high. It was during one of these visits that a plan began to form in his mind as to how he might escape. Tom realized that in formulating his escape plan it was imperative that if Macey were to be questioned it would be better if he could honestly answer that he knew nothing.

First Tom had to find the keys to the medical cupboard and remove the medicines that Tom deemed would be useful to the Bedouins. He would be unable to carry too much in his rucksack as he also needed to take a rolled up mat on which to sleep, some tinned food, 2 or 3 litres of water, a commando knife and sun cream to prevent his being burned to a frazzle in the burning sun.

He had already discovered how to get into the medical cabinet, which was in a large cupboard just outside the hospital. There were three keys: one held by one of the doctors, one by the matron and the third by a duty officer whose key hung in a box in his office. The duty officer's office was often open to anybody who wanted to meander in or out. At 02.00 hours one Tuesday morning there was not a sound to be heard. Tom quietly walked into the office and with great ease removed the key from the box. He then silently and stealthily moved to the medical cabinet, removing some penicillin, ether, gauze, aspirin and morphine. He then returned to the key to its box, and wiped away any trace of his fingerprints. He did not want this to lead back to him.

With his rucksack over his shoulder, Tom slipped out into the night, making his way to the Bedouin camp, which was approximately 8 miles out of Djibouti City on the outskirts of the Danakil Desert. The Bedouins planned to leave for Berea the next day. Tom had researched the route the day before and discovered that it was absolutely perfect for him; for once he reached Berea near the Red Sea he could catch a lift at a trading post. This would hopefully take him to Somalia's capital, Mogadishu. In Mogadishu he would be able to enlist the help of the Swedish Embassy, which he knew was still open to Swedish nationals because Sweden was a neutral country.

He was dressed in the darkest clothes he could find. With no moon hovering in the sky, everything was dark and deathly quiet. It was still stiflingly hot and Tom was perspiring, half with nervous anxiety and half due to labouring under the weight of his backpack.

Reaching the Bedouin camp, Tom decided to spend the remainder of the night a short distance away from his allies, who were sleeping soundly in their tents. Any unwelcome person would be considered an enemy in that territory. Tom noticed that some of the camels who were fenced a little off were sleeping, though there were others who preferred to eat at night and were happily feeding on the prickly desert plants. The camel has especially thick lips and so is able to eat these plants without injuring itself. The man on guard was asleep, snoring contentedly, so Tom was able to slip past him and make a bed for himself on the mat he had brought with him, just a short distance away from the entrance. Nobody heard or saw him.

At dawn a group of female Bedouins began to surface. The women wore long, beautifully coloured dresses woven from goats' hair, the traditional material from which they used to make fabric. As the women milled about completing their morning chores and ablutions, Tom could hear the waking cries of small children and babies echoing around the camp. There was very little water in which to wash and it was normal to clean ones' hands and faces with sand.

Tom opened his left eye to see if he had yet been spotted. Lying not far from the entrance he observed how the Bedouin tent was divided into two parts: one side for the women and children and the other side for the men. From the smells that wafted through the tent, he surmised that the women did all of the cooking on their side while on the other side the men used their area for entertaining.

As one of his Bedouin friends sauntered out in the early morning sun, he saw Tom laid out on his mat nearby. He looked at him quizzically. "Good morning Tom, what are you doing here at this early hour?"

"*Soo maal Eludi*," Tom replied, rather pleased with his pronunciation. He had always found the origin of this salutation rather interesting, given that essentially the greeting was a way of offering a guest the opportunity to milk an animal, thereby enabling the guest to drink at the same time.

His friend smiled, "I am impressed, but Tom you are in trouble. What is it?"

"I have deserted," Tom blurted out, realising that as he did so that the look on Ludi's face was not one of approval. Ludi was confused. He was not able to comprehend Tom's reason for deserting, especially as he, himself, had such a high regard for the Legion and the loyalty that went with it. Tom treaded carefully and continued in a whisper. "I was just unable to soldier for the Legion any longer. I never chose it. These so-called colonels, masquerading as officers, shanghaied me into their organisation by drugging me." He went on to outline the story of how he had ended up a member of the Legion in Djibouti.

Ludi was shocked. "How could this have happened Tom? I had no idea that this is how they recruited their men. And it happened to you?"

"No Ludi, I do not believe that this is the normal way the Legion recruit its men. Only a very few are press ganged into this combat force and to date I do not know any others who have experienced what I have."

Ludi paused for thought before replying. "I can understand your distress and anger when this happened approximately 18 months ago, am I right. But surely you have become accustomed to it by now. After all, the Legion is a legendary force and famous for its wonderful work at keeping terrorists and rebels at bay. We could not manage without them! I thought it would be an honour to be enlisted in such an organisation."

Tom was most disturbed by his friend's response. This kind and hospitable Bedouin friend saw only the good side of the Legion. He had no idea of the bullying, the cruelty, the unfairness, the everyday life that most of the recruits found, at times, almost unbearable. Ludi's impassioned feelings about the French Legion made Tom realise that it was now going to be impossible to barter his stolen medical supplies for the accommodation that he was hoping to receive in return. They would be horrified, and stealing in the Arab world was a terrible crime. He would be seriously punished regardless of his stealing from another place. He decided to keep quiet about the supplies and would produce them only if an emergency was to occur. It would also be unwise to undermine the Legion, for its members did carry out wonderful and courageous acts. Criticising them would only alienate Tom from the tribe.

Ludi gestured to Tom to enter the tent. "Please come in Tom and have some coffee with us while we talk about it."

Filled with anxiety Tom entered the tent. Ludi, locating a place for them to sit on the Arabic rugs that covered the floor, offered him a cup of coffee and asked him whether he would like to share a shisha. Tom was most appreciative of his kind hospitality. While Ludi was preparing the shisha and pouring Tom a cup of coffee, Tom realised that he had not really thought through this escape plan very well. While knowing that he could count on Ludi for his friendship, he was not particularly conversant with the Bedouin customs and laws. They were Arabs. They were Muslims. They had a very different code from Westerners, sometimes being much fairer in their treatment of the rebel but much harsher in others.

These people had a number of unusual ways with which Tom was not familiar, for example the camel not only provided transport, but also meat and milk. Fuel was extracted from its dung, which was also used for lining nappies. Camel wool was used to weave ropes and clothes. The camels' urine was used medicinally, cosmetically as a shampoo for washing women's hair, and for the tanning of leather. Tom recalled, during one of his occasional visits, seeing young girls by a herd of camels, often screwing up their eyes against the bright sunlight while holding a container ready to rush forward to catch the camels' precious urine. This sometimes took hours. He knew that the camel was a very economical animal to keep, given it only needed to drink once a week, though it could down 46 litres in one drinking session. It could also go without food for several months. It had all the physical attributes to withstand the harshness of the desert, and was usually a gentle and docile animal when treated well. It could, however, be stubborn and angry when ill-treated!

Like any culture, you have to live within it for years before you can truly integrate yourself into its ways. Tom knew he had to tread carefully.

Ludi looked directly at him. "Tell me Tom, what you think you will gain from running away. Do you really think that you can escape the Legion and create enough distance between you and them in order not to be captured?"

"I heard that you were going as far as the deep sea port of Berea. I was hoping to pick up a truck at a trading post there and travel to Mogadishu, where I would then be able to enlist the help of the Swedish Embassy and finally return to my own country."

Ludi considered Tom's response.

"Yes, that is a feasible plan. We do hope to reach Berea and trade our sheep and goats with another tribe or tribes, but nevertheless it could take several months and many things could take place en route that could shatter your plans.

"This is a dangerous world and the desert is not an especially hospitable place. It is a way of life that only a few embrace. We have been a nomadic people for thousands of years, but a non-Bedouin might find it difficult to do without the water he normally has plenty of, as well as the normal luxuries of life in the West. There will be some in our tribe who will rally with the others against your inhabiting our tent and embracing our life style.

"However, I will do my best to appease my fellow Bedouins and convince them it will be for a relatively short period of time, that you wish them only good will and will adopt any and all of our traditions. You will need to be as accommodating as you possibly can. As I can speak English, which I studied at the University of Cairo, and some French, and you have knowledge of English and French and limited Arabic, you might still survive the difficulties ahead. It will be entirely up to you. If you fail to comply with these conditions you will be asked to leave."

"Our women folk live differently from yours, and though we do have some Western traditions regarding the fair sex, ours are still treated dissimilarly, mostly out of safety and respect. You may be friendly and polite but do not initiate conversation with them, unless there is a special reason like danger or accident, for example. If you do, it could bring a lot of problems for all of us."

Tom realised that Ludi was going out of his way to accommodate him. "I really appreciate your helping me in this way, and I cannot thank you enough. I will follow your wishes in every aspect and hope in the ensuing months that I will not give you any cause for you to ask me to leave. It will be difficult to follow some of your rules, especially as far as water is concerned, but having lived in Djibouti for some time now I have become aware of the shortage of water in desert countries."

Having said all that was necessary, Ludi gave Tom the everyday colourful clothing – a galabeya and a shaali to protect his head from the sun and cold winds – which he would wear while travelling with them. He also showed Tom where he could carry out his ablutions.

A little while later he remarked that they would be leaving at sunrise the next day. Ludi outlined the expectations and aspects relating to Bedouin lifestyle that Tom was expected to comply with.

"Before we set off we shall start the day by facing Mecca and saying our morning prayers to Allah. We do this usually five times a day. A prayer area consisting of a circle of stones is set up whenever we change camps."

"Of course you may not follow our religion, though we are praying to the same God, but I would wish you to join us anyway like a good Muslim. You must not be different in any way. The purpose of prayer for a Muslim is to take time out of his busy day and worship God. I do not think the average Westerner does that!"

He went on to say: "Our livelihood, as you know, is to produce as many herds and flocks as possible. We use the animals as food, wool and more, and also as a means of selling and buying from other tribes. We rely on our women to produce the food and to make our tents, clothes and ropes.

"In case of an attack by a monsoon, which is an on-going hazardous phenomenon in the dry season, the animals are safeguarded by a corral, which is a circle of thorny bushes: this circle protects the livestock."

"Unfortunately we are always on the move, for as soon as it is realised that the pastures on which the animals are grazing have been stripped of the scant vegetation that there is in the desert, we need to journey to another place."

CHAPTER 9

Life among the Bedouins

Tom gradually became acclimatised to this new way of life among the people in the Bedouin camp. They slowly wended their way south to Berea, stopping and starting, the tent being erected and then pegged down again. Tom had not appreciated what an incredibly difficult existence this was, but kept his own council on such opinions. He realised that unless there was enough pasture for the animals, and of course water, they would all die.

After 5 weeks the Ludi's camp reached a very large oasis, 50 miles from Djibouti City. This oasis was a meeting point: there were the tribes who had just left en route to another city or oasis and some who had just arrived. It was a most beautiful place, the palm trees swaying gently in the breeze, with lush and plentiful green grass for the animals, and an abundance of water.

Everyone was pleased to have arrived, but with all the many goats and sheep hurling themselves at the verdant green grass it was chaotic. Disputes and arguments among the tribes were rife but were gradually sorted out by the sheiks of the tribes, who were chosen for their diplomacy. Ludi was the sheik in Tom's group.

In the evenings the Bedouins visited each others' tents and enjoyed the delightful hospitality that they are famous for. The delicious fresh bread made from rice and flour was a favourite among them. Music was a social pastime, there being several Bedouins who played the drums and the samsomeja, which is not dissimilar to a Western guitar. Tom very much enjoyed joining in during these musical gatherings, having played the guitar and sung when he was younger. After a month in the oasis delighting in the food and water, the cool breezes and greenery, and having satisfactorily negotiated various exchanges and purchases, Ludi's tribe started to pack up their tent and belongings and to move south again.

One day, early in the afternoon after having left the oasis, Tom heard a scream on the other side of the tent. No one, it seemed, other than Tom heard this high pitched sound. Propping himself up on his elbow he was unsure as to what he should do. He had been forbidden to associate himself with any of the women except in an emergency. Another scream pierced the quiet of the afternoon. As everybody was outside dealing with the animals and as he himself had been lying down suffering from a migraine (he had them infrequently nowadays) there was absolutely nobody to ask for help. He rushed out of the tent to see if there was anybody outside but no one seemed to be around. He had to do something.

He quickly moved into the women's side of the tent where the sound was coming from and saw a young and pretty woman lying on her mat crying copious tears. Tom went up to her with some urgency, being very careful not to touch her. "What is the matter, what has happened?"

Through her muffled tears, she wept. "Someone tried to rape me." Tom was horrified. "What?" He looked around, almost expecting to see someone trying to escape from the tent. "I can't see anybody nearby."

She continued: "No, he ran away when I began to scream. I don't know where he went. He was not of our tribe."

Tom knew it was pointless but asked her nonetheless.

"Can you describe him?

With some clarity she responded, "No it was far too sudden. He came into the tent through a flap, which is seldom used, so it caught me completely unawares. He jumped on top of me with such force that he took all the breath out of me and at the same time tried to rip off my clothes."

Tom was not sure he wanted to hear this.

"Did he succeed?"

"Luckily not." Tom let out a quiet sigh of relief while the woman continued her story. "I kicked him so hard in the balls that he groaned with pain and ran away."

"But you screamed." Tom was trying to piece it together. "Did you scream when he tried to take off your clothes or did you shock him into running away when you began to scream?"

"I really do not know. It was all so quick."

Tom was beginning to become suspicious. There was no sign of a struggle, the clothes that she was wearing, as well as the mat on which she had purported to have been lying on, were completely unruffled. She did not have a mark on her and there was no one in sight except some small children. What reason did she have for calling rape?

"I will go outside and check for footprints to ascertain from where he was coming and where he disappeared to."

The woman became a little flustered.

"I am sure he has long gone and you will see nothing."

Tom headed towards the exit.

"I will check anyway."

But just as Tom was leaving the tent a gale-force wind hit the tent with such a fierce impact that he was completely knocked over. The gust disturbed much of the contents of the tent, yet the woman remained in the same position beside her mat swaying to and fro, clutching onto the tent's central pole but still managing to stand upright. The small children who appeared to be hers were playing quietly a short distance away and, being startled by the strong wind, began to cry in fear. Their mother rushed over to them and picking them up comforted them. The presence and proximity of the children made Tom doubt the woman's story even further. How could this woman call "rape" and allege to have been attacked by a strange man when the children themselves were completely unperturbed by her screaming and wailing and the supposed attack on their mother. Yet the children were frightened by the strong wind that surely they must have experienced on many an occasion. Is this how the Bedouin woman behaved, he wondered? He very much doubted it. There was something ominous going on.

The wind, having picked up so suddenly, was still howling and did not lessen its strength. Tom picked himself up from the ground and ran towards the men who were now trying to tether the animals firmly to a strong post. Saving the animals was their first priority, and with the dust rising into an invisible and impregnable blanket the men were hardly able to see their hands in front of them.

All the vegetation in that area disappeared, becoming dark and sinister shapes. It seemed that the wind was starting to tear it from its roots and fling away. Tom was horrified. He had never experienced a dry monsoon in this part of the world. Such a monsoon would manifest itself between the months of December and April. It was devastating to health and to man's livelihood. Although there were always a number of these calamities, it was a frightening phenomenon and the repercussions were enormous. This fierce sand storm did not abate until the next day, and by that time the camp site had been ravaged, many of the animals having been blown away and the remaining ones bereft of anything to eat and very little to drink.

Ludi, in his capacity as leader, gathered his tribe around him and counselled them as he usually did.

"Be calm my family," he said, in his usual reassuring way. "We have had many of these destructive sandstorms and have always managed to get through them and survive. This calamity is no better and no worse than before. Our biggest concern is for our small children, who will suffer the most. They are not as strong as we adults are, and without enough water and nourishment it will be harder for them. I do beg you, my brothers, to be patient and help our women and the little ones. I believe, Abdulla, your wife Sara is expecting your first baby at any moment?"

Ludi turned to one of his cousins, a young, slim and bearded man who was anxiously looking towards the women's side of the tent. "Go to her and see what you can do to make her more comfortable," he encouraged him. "She is probably very frightened and needs your care and attention."

Ludi continued, "Since we are short of all the basic necessities, the sooner we move on the better, and preferably to an oasis. Regrettably we are about 15 miles from the nearest water hole but it is the best and only course of action to take. If there is anybody with a better solution, I would be happy to listen."

A lot of murmuring voices rang out among the men, but they did not have anything further to offer so, with a quiet sigh at the magnitude of the situation, Ludi returned to his favourite area in the tent and sat down and wrote out an inventory of what they had and what they had lost. Even though he had minimised the damage caused by the situation, they had in fact suffered much more than at any time in the past. They had lost three-quarters of their sheep and goats. Very luckily their life-saving camels, having become used to the desert and all its idiosyncrasies, had stood valiantly against the elements and survived. Only one camel, which had not been tied firmly enough inside the corral, had been driven away by the storm.

After the tribe had cleared up the debris and mess in the tent, which had been ravaged by the winds, they congregated together to discuss their fears and concerns. Too many of the tent's flaps had been opened when the storm began, which accounted for the large amount of sand and small stones that had infiltrated their comfortable abode. The women's area was a little better, for they were always conscientious about the safety of their children. Since the storm had hit the area without any warning whatsoever, even their domain was in disarray; nevertheless their greatest consternation was the abundance of sand that had perpetrated the eyes and mouths of the little ones. There was no water except for a small urn that was kept for emergencies, so they were unable to rinse the grit out.

There was sometimes the slight possibility of obtaining water by being scraping out holes in the sand to a depth of 5 or 6 feet. This very difficult and arduous job was usually allocated to the women, but on this occasion all the men were put to work as it was a matter of life or death. Even if water was to be found, it would only trickle into the hole very slowly. Another possibility of obtaining liquid, albeit slim, came from the chance that a camel would urinate. Three young girls who were the last effected by the sand were sent out to the cordoned off area where the camels lay. They had to persuade them to stand up before they could attempt to extract the vital liquid, which had medicinal properties. If they were successful it could alleviate a little of the danger of eye problems, diarrhoea, dehydration and respiratory diseases that were rife following stand storms.

For several hours the men kept on digging into the sand but only managed to accumulate a few drops of precious water. The same results were obtained following the girls' efforts to collect urine. Tom dug along with the men but felt that his skills could be better used elsewhere. He could still delve into his medical supplies but would have to be cautious.

Because of the excellent insulation of the tent (cool in the summer and warm and cosy in the winter), Tom still had not used his tightly secured water bottle that he had filled up in the oasis. Instead he had placed it in the coolest place in the tent, together with the medical supplies.

He approached Ludi, whose face was white and drawn with the worry and fear he had for his people. Only he, Ludi, knew the disastrous effects of this latest monsoon could have and he was at his wits' end. He needed to start moving, but there were still particles of sand blowing through the desert, and these prevented the Bedouins from packing up, mounting the camels and moving on. Though visibility was better, they would still be disadvantaged. The biggest concern was that they were unable to move the children, many of whom had become ill with the influx of sand in their eyes and mouths.

"What can I do to help, Ludi?" asked Tom, interrupting Ludi's train of thought. "I have a fair amount of medical knowledge, as we are all trained in survival techniques and how to help our fellow soldiers. We secure boundaries and keep rebellion down in so many inhospitable countries that it is absolutely imperative that we are very well instructed in other areas. My mother is a midwife and I often used to accompany her and have learnt about the care of babies. My dream is to train as an obstetrician when I leave the army."

"Oh Tom, please go and help Abdullah's wife, Sara, as she has gone into labour and that is an area I know nothing about. Here is a note. Give it to Abdullah so that he knows I have given you full authority to do what you can."

Tom nodded. "I need a clean gown Ludi. Do you have one?"

"Yes I do." Ludi answered appreciatively. "Abdullah will know where they are kept. Thank you Tom."

Tom moved to the women's area of the tent, his medical supplies in his thick canvas bag. Abdullah was standing by a flap looking scared. He did not have a clue what he should do. Unfortunately all the women were looking after their own children and help was not at hand. Usually they would all rally round and help, but there were too many sickly children in need of their mothers' ministrations.

Tom handed Abdullah Ludi's note and was directed to where Sara was lying, her body writhing in the throes of labour. She had never been taught what to do as her own mother had died giving birth to her. She was petrified by the prospect that history might be about to be repeated.

Tom set about calming Sara down, checking her pulse and teaching her the gentle breathing exercises that would help her with the pain and control her movements.

Hour after hour went by, with still no sign of the baby. Still having a lot to learn, Tom wondered whether the baby was finding it difficult to get through the birth canal. Checking her abdomen he felt no head. Though one can never be sure and without being able to X-ray the woman, he could only assume that it was a breech presentation and that the baby's bottom was at the base of the uterus. Sometimes one can use obstetric forceps to ensure a smooth emergence of the head. Tom did not have the correct tools. As the poor girl was beginning to lose consciousness from the heat, dehydration, exhaustion and pain, he felt the only option was to bring the baby into the world by caesarean section.

One of the medications he had taken from the medical cupboard was ether, which would enable him to put Sara to sleep without her feeling any pain. He was aware that presenting this could be his downfall, but either he looked after his own hide, or the woman and baby would not survive. He did not want that on his conscience. He had never done an operation of this magnitude but he knew what needed to be done as he had witnessed more than one operation of this kind in the hospital his mother worked in. Instinctively he knew that he would need to make a vertical cut in the abdominal and uterine walls just above the pubic bone.

He put the colourless ether on a gauze mask and placed it over Sara's nose and mouth. She soon lost all consciousness. With help from Abdullah (who was horrified by the procedure), Tom correctly made an incision into the abdominal wall, the baby being delivered through the cut in the lower part of the uterus. The actual delivery only took 4 to 5 minutes, although the whole procedure took much longer. The umbilical cord was then cut and the afterbirth removed. Regretfully Tom did not have an injection of ergometrine, which would have made the uterus contract and stop any internal bleeding. He was, however, able to sew up the uterus and abdomen with small and neat stitches.

"Here is your new son, Abdullah. Congratulations," Tom said handing the infant to the bewildered new father. "Omar. His name is Omar," Abdullah said looking into his son's eyes.

"Sara is still under the anaesthetic and will be out for a while. It's very important that you do not disturb or move her. I do not have all the medical tools that would be used in the West and she still may not make it unless the internal bleeding stops. I shall administer some antibiotics to prevent any infection that might occur. In addition to this, I have some water in my bottle. Please give all of it to her and the baby."

Abdullah, taking the full bottle of water with surprise, proceeded to gently wipe Sara's face and neck as well as little Omar's body, as he had not yet been cleaned up and still had streaks of blood and white creamy substance clinging to his skin. Omar was subsequently placed on Sara's breast to receive his first taste of life-saving milk. What a wonderful sight it was, the baby starting to suckle more or less immediately.

***

Ludi was in a dilemma. What was he going to do? He could not move the women and children for at least a week. By that time a lot of the animals could become so dehydrated that they would not be able to travel to the oasis across the desert. His family had just sufficient water to survive for 7 days but the there was none for the animals, and without the animals they, themselves, would not survive. The spectre of death was around the corner unless a solution could be found.

Tom let himself out of the women's side of the tent knowing that if his instructions were to be followed, Sara, being young and strong, would most likely survive. He walked around to the men's side to let Ludi know what had taken place. He was tired, but relieved that everything had gone well. He would, however, need to return at regular intervals to check up on them both.

He found Ludi in his special place looking desolate and incredibly anxious.

"Sara and little Omar are doing well, but Sara needs to rest for a week," Tom uttered in a matter of fact way. Ludi's demeanour lifted slightly at hearing mother and baby were alive. "That's marvellous Tom but I cannot wait a week. The animals are on their last legs already. We have to move now."

Tom, reflecting for a moment, suddenly came up with an idea. "Why don't you take your animals with you, leaving a sheep and a goat behind, and with a few of your single young men go to this oasis you suggested. That way, at least, the animals can recoup, take their fill of water and delicious green grass, and you alone can return home as soon as possible. You will probably need 2 days to reach the oasis, but only a day for your return journey as you will have fewer obstacles and you will then get back much more quickly. You won't have all the tribe to take care of either. I will remain as well as the other fathers, if that is all right with you, as I have to look after the sick and especially Sara and Omar. If you are away a week, everybody will survive as we still have a little water left as well as food. We can always slaughter the sheep if necessary."

Ludi began to relax as he processed Tom's suggestion. "That is such a good idea Tom. I shall start making the arrangements and leave early tomorrow morning. I will call a meeting this evening to put the motion to the family and hope they will agree. I must be tactful and not make it seem that you have come up with this plan, as you are only meant to be a visitor."

Tom understood. "I quite agree. Putting me in the foreground would be most unwise. I had a very strange experience with a young woman two days ago." He went on to explain the incident of the woman calling "rape" when Tom was resting from his migraine and all the others were outside with the animals. There was no evidence that anything untoward had happened to her, no intruder, no cuts and bruises or tearing of clothes or any footprints. "I have a feeling that there could be ill-feeling towards me and jealousy of our friendship. Calling 'rape' at any time could put someone like me in a great deal of trouble and I am aware of the penalty for raping a woman."

"That is possible. I am so sorry. Who is this woman?" Ludi asked.

Tom considered Ludi's question but thought better of answering it. "It is better that I do not tell you for it might get her into trouble and more antagonism would ensue. However, if she does create another such disturbance or commotion I will let you know."

"Thank you. Now let's call the meeting and see what the men have to say."

The married men with children were in accordance with Ludi's plan to stay and protect their families, while those with wives but without children wanted to go with the unmarried men. Ludi addressed his people. "I am very pleased that you concur with my plan for I very much need your help, but I shall also need some of you to return with me to help pack up the tent and lead the camels back to the oasis where our other animals and the young single men will be waiting for us."

With everything organised, Ludi left early the next morning with the young single men, the men without children, and all the animals minus a sheep, a goat and all but one the camels (which was used to carry food and other supplies for the men's journey). It was a fairly large entourage and Tom was concerned that it would take much longer to arrive at the oasis than hoped and would not return within the allotted time. A week was the very longest they could be away and then death would come slowly. Tom was left with a terrible sense of foreboding. He was alone with the women and their husbands, whose responsibilities were for their families.

***

Tom continued to visit Sara and little Omar and was treated with great respect and admiration by Abdullah. The young woman who had called "rape" kept her distance, so Tom hoped that it was the end of the subterfuge. He was retrospectively glad he had mentioned it to Ludi.

Two days passed, and all was quiet in the camp. Sara's strength began to return as she took short walks around the tent. The little boy was surviving on what milk his mother was able to give him, as well as the milk from the goat.

Antibiotics were administered to the small children who had developed an infection from the filthy sand during the monsoon, and they initially showed signs of recovering. This recovery was short-lived, however, as the shortage of water caused dehydration and digestive problems and there was absolutely nothing Tom could do about it. On the third day a little girl of three died. Everyone was devastated. It was the parents' only child. On the fourth day a little boy of five succumbed to dehydration. Tom felt powerless and only wished there was more he could do. There were still 3 more days before Ludi and his entourage were due to return. Were they going to lose anybody else? He was aware of the terrible child mortality that occurred among the desert folk and it distressed him knowing that unless they changed their lifestyle completely the deaths of small children would continue. There was a shortage of nutritious food and a great lack of water, which resulted in growth disorders and in many children being underweight. At least half of the children who came into the world were way below the normal weight of a European child and a good proportion died at birth. Half of infants around the age of 6 months suffered from anaemia.

On the fifth day everything and everybody was subdued but there were no deaths. The quietness among the clan was more frightening than the noise and wailing of an enormous storm, and the rattling of the poles that supported the tent.

On the sixth day it was even quieter, except for the hushed sounds of a family crying for their beloved grandmother whose heart had given out, the and the determined Sara, whose footsteps could be heard as she paced the tent to ensure she would not develop thrombosis. Little Omar continued to survive.

A week after Ludi and his men had left a loud noise was heard outside the tent. Wonders of wonders, Ludi had returned with the camel laden with water and food. A great ring of joy peeled out from the families, save from those who had lost loved ones.

***

Even having journeyed back the day before, Ludi knew that it was imperative to pack up as soon as it was feasibly possible. The water and food would only last a couple of days, and being the monsoon period the sooner they were safely ensconced in this nearby oasis the better. It was not quite the direction that Ludi wished to go, and their journey to Berea would take longer than planned, but at least they would all be safe. Added to this, the sooner they were able to restock their herds the better.

Knowing the debt Tom owed the Bedouins, especially Ludi, and having saved his last lot of wages (the Foreign Legion paid better than they used to) for emergencies, Tom was able to give Ludi a substantial amount of his hard-earned money to help towards replacing the group's losses. Ludi was overwhelmed by Tom's generosity, as well as his invaluable help as a medic during the crisis. He had never had such a wonderful friend and found it fortuitous that Tom had joined them at the beginning of their journey from Djibouti.

Their tent packed up again, the clan depleted but determined, started wending its way towards the green pastures of the nearby oasis.

CHAPTER 10

Journey to Mogadishu

With their herd having been replenished at the oasis and with the clan having recovered from their ordeal, Ludi and entourage set forth south to another town. It would take them a month to reach it before returning to Djibouti.

Tom bade farewell to Ludi and his family at Berea, and made his way to a trading post just outside the town. He was sad to have to say his goodbyes, especially to Ludi, but was content in the knowledge that Sara and Omar were thriving and were getting stronger by the day. Even though he had regretted taking the medical supplies at the beginning of his journey, he was relieved that he had been able to use them when in a tight spot to save lives. Ludi was extremely grateful for everything Tom had done and made a mental note to inform the officer in charge of Tom's abilities and kindness, should he fall foul of any the authorities during his onward trek. He knew that Tom was entering dangerous territory and would find the journey extremely challenging as there was many unscrupulous individuals who would willingly inform the authorities about a white man who appeared to be deserting if he or she thought they could gain from it. Tom would only be out of danger when and if he reached the Swedish Embassy.

On arriving at the trading post, Tom found a small but fairly clean boarding house where he could stay the night. He was tired and could not think of anything better than having a decent meal, a cold beer and sleeping in a comfortable bed. There were three trucks leaving for Mogadishu in the morning and Tom was hoping to catch a ride with one of them. He approached a large Volvo truck, asking the driver whether he could have a lift with him into the capital. The man, a large and attractive looking Somalian, seemed receptive to this request. "My name's Pete. Where are you headed for?"

"I am just visiting some old friends who live near the Swedish Embassy in the city." As soon as the words were out of Tom's mouth he regretted it, for it could be interpreted that he was seeking asylum and wanted to get out of the country.

Pete seemed interested. "How long have you been away from your country?"

Tom tried to sound vague. "A while."

He pressed Tom further. "How is it that you have landed up in this part of the world?"

Tom regained his composure. "I have always been interested in Africa, especially the eastern region."

The driver seemed baffled. "I cannot understand why you would want to travel in this part of the world. It is made up of mostly desert and we always seem to be at war with each other, resulting in famine, hunger, poverty and death."

Tom felt that this conversation was going nowhere, and changing the subject asked him what time he would be leaving tomorrow. Unfazed, Pete answered Tom, saying "I shall be leaving around 6 am I will leave promptly so please be ready."

Tom agreed and thanked Pete. He then returned to the hotel, hoping that despite the comfy bed awaiting him and lack of alarm clock that he would wake on time. If he was late the he could expect difficulties as Pete wouldn't wait and he would have to try and catch a lift with a different trucker – if there were any who would listen to his plight. Despite Tom's concerns he overslept and tumbled out of the hotel at 6.30 am the next morning. All the other trucks had left except the Volvo.

"You're late mate. Get in, we have about 600 miles to Mogadishu, quite some distance, which could take about a week or more depending upon the road and the traffic, for this is the only road that leads to the capital. Perhaps you would like to contact your friends to say when you will be arriving."

Tom was confused. "How can I do that? Are there any phones in this part of the world?"

Starting the engine, the man amused by Tom's question answered, "Not that I am aware of, but I you Westerners are full of brilliant ideas and will always manage to get a message relayed across any difficult terrain!"

Tom hesitated, not understanding where this driver was going with this comment, but curiosity got the better of him and he asked. "Do you think they might have a telex machine at the next trading post?"

"Yes, I think they might have."

"Good, then I might be able to send a telex to my friends."

There was silence. Tom had an uneasy feeling that the Somalian was playing cat and mouse with him. He did not know whether Pete had plans to hand him over to the authorities or to pirates for ransom or whether it was just his particular brand of humour.

The truck travelled on towards Mogadishu, stopping at various small towns on the way. The first one was Boosaaso, a fairly large settlement by the coast where they stayed the night. Despite being the area's commercial capital, there were no telephone lines to be found. At Eyl they found a very comfortable place to stay where the food was delicious. Although the amenities were comfy, technology was scarce. There were no telephone lines to be found in Eyle either.

Tom was beginning to feel a little calmer and more at ease with his companion, who was always very cheerful and friendly. His confidence was growing with the thought that he might actually be nearing his destination. Escape to Sweden seemed to be a more realistic possibility.

Tom should not have let his guard down, however, as apart from being a trucker – which was his main occupation – the "friendly" Somalian was a bounty hunter whose "job" took him all over the eastern side of Africa. It was a most lucrative pastime. He had a dingy office in Mogadishu where he had a number of pictures pinned onto his wall of all the men who had deserted from the various armies. Pictures were sent around the various capitals of Africa, alerting any bounty hunter who would be willing to capture and return such deserters to their platoons. When Pete had seen Tom at the trading station he recognised him from one of the pictures. Knowing that these Legionnaires were very strong and resourceful, Pete decided to cool his heels, hoping that there would be an occasion when he could overcome Tom.

Before they reached Hobyo, the next town, Pete began to form a plan. He had a mate who worked closely with him in the bounty stakes whom he knew would be pleased to share in the prize money. On arrival, Pete and Tom again booked a room at a cheap boarding house, which had a fairly good kitchen and decent beds. It was cheaper for them both to share a bedroom, for they were fast running out of cash, particularly Tom as he had given most of his money to his Bedouin friend. Pete sent a telegram to his friend.

They walked into the restaurant and ordered hamburgers and French fries. During the meal Tom excused himself to go to the gent's. Pete followed him, glancing at his friend, who at his request lived locally and was dining at the same restaurant so he could assist Pete in jumping Tom when he was most vulnerable. Tom was totally unprepared for the onslaught of the two large Somali men, who grabbed him by the arms and handcuffed his hands behind his back. He did not have a chance to defend himself.

Once they had Tom safely secured, Pete addressed him. "You are a deserter from the French Foreign Legion and we will be returning you to your platoon at first light. I have been watching you ever since you arrived at Berea. From the photo of you on my office wall, I had no doubt that it was you."

Tom had nothing to say. After all these months and planning he was a captive again. He would not be able to escape from these bounty hunters. They were very tall and strong and would brook no nonsense from him. They wanted him alive but were not against roughing him up if he caused them any trouble. A pretty unpleasant reception awaited him in Djibouti anyway, so Tom was prepared to await his fate in good condition rather than turn up looking like a beaten up chunk of meat.

It took several weeks to travel back to Djibouti. Each night Tom was handcuffed to the bed, the handcuffs only being removed when he went to the bathroom. He was always guarded, either by Pete or by his friend. On arrival, Tom was handed over to his superior officer and thrown into a cell where he awaited retribution. Pete and his pal received 350,000 Djibouti francs for bringing this particular deserter back to the company. They would have preferred American dollars, or even Somali shillings, but were given no choice.

***

Ludi, who was continuing his journey, felt uneasy about Tom, having heard nothing from him. He had various friends in the cities whom he could contact, though it would take a while. They would be able to check up on Tom's whereabouts and let him know. Several weeks later, Ludi received the alarming news that Tom had been picked up by bounty hunters and returned to the Legion.

"They will do untold damage to him," he thought. "I must get news to the officer in charge and hope the extenuating circumstances that I'll present to him will lessen the extreme punishment that he will receive."

Regrettably the missive only reached the officials at the end of Tom's long and brutal treatment. It did, however, alert the commanding officer about Tom's humanitarian effort in the Bedouins' home, which ensured that he was given the greatest care and medical treatment in the hospital.

CHAPTER 11

Punishment and retribution

Tom considered his situation as he awaited his punishment for deserting as and stealing the valuable medical supplies from the French Foreign Legion. Taking the lift with Pete was a big mistake, he reflected, but now it was too late to regret anything. Perhaps the bounty hunter felt that it was his duty to uphold the law and to book a deserting Legionnaire as well as returning a defecting soldier. He probably kidded himself into believing that by doing this he was doing the honourable thing: defending the Legion's values and beliefs. Mainly, of course, he was interested in lining his own pockets!

Beaten up by two of the Italian corporals, the following day Tom was stripped of all his clothes and cast headlong into another cell. It would be solitary confinement for him for 28 days. He had been absent for several months and the longer a deserter is away the longer the punishment.

The days were spent sweating on a concrete floor, being taken out to the courtyard for exercise in the afternoon and made to carry a heavy rucksack of rocks on his back. For 4 hours in the hot sun he had to trot round the concrete jungle in circles and figures of eight.

After the 28 days were up, he still had another 40 days of hard labour, which was the punishment for deserting. He was moved to another filthy and cell with two other deserters, whom Tom noticed were in a worse condition than he was. He still had to receive a further punishment for stealing the scarce medical supplies for the Bedouins.

Tom was aware that the corporals were concocting a most unpleasant penance for his offences. The fear and terror of this impending chastisement gave him the most terrible nightmares. He knew, too, that this was part of the psychological torture that was meted out to offenders who disobeyed the League's unwritten rules.

Three and half months after being caught, the most brutal of all the corporals, Corporal Reinhardt, strolled into Tom's cell one morning ordering him out onto the beach, without his boots, for a snail's pace 5 km walk across the jagged volcanic rocks. Tom was horrified. There was a strong possibility that this would shred his feet and it was doubtful whether he would be able to walk normally after this ordeal. He had seen other deserters being given the same punishment and they had been left hobbling, even after the wounds had healed. A pistol prodding his ribs gave him no alternative but to comply. The pain was so excruciating that every part of Tom's body called out in agony as his feet were cut by the rocks, which tore at his soles and ankles. He did wonder whether his toes would still be intact after he had completed the 5 km.

Corporal Reinhardt, someone that Tom had always tried to avoid, looked on with a smirk on his face, enjoying every moment of this most tortuous exercise. Half stumbling, but determined not fall down, Tom managed to manoeuvre himself over the razor-sharp rocks, his resolution and willpower stretching beyond his normal physical endurance. Finally reaching a sandy spot, but with the butt of the gun being prodded into his ribs, Tom, with sweat falling in rivulets down his face, remarkably still managed to keep himself erect. He arrived at his prison cell without collapsing. Reinhardt thrust Tom with great force through the cell door. The young man fell onto his back. He found that he could not move; the agony from his tortured feet was vibrating through every fibre of his body. "What have I done to deserve this?" he thought. "I did not choose this way of life."

None of the corporals or colonels had any idea that he had been shanghaied into this tough and inflexible organisation. They probably would not have cared if they had. Perhaps they were "all in it together" and were pleased that their coffers were being filled up by recruiting eligible new blood, by whatever means.

Despite the physical agony he was in, Tom fell fast asleep on the floor where he had been thrown. The last few days in anticipation of this agonising treatment had taken its toll. Tom was exhausted beyond anything he had ever experienced or would ever experience again.

***

Tom was woken up several hours later by someone coming into his small cell with some rice cakes, soap and water. Whatever the Legion was, they certainly did not want a death on their hands following punishment meted out by one of their own. Even though the hierarchy never intervened when a recruit was punished, they were aware of the merits of each rookie, and Tom had always proved that he was of a far higher calibre than most of them. He had never squealed or begged when his punishment was given, nor had he faltered during his most recent ordeal. He did notice that he was treated differently, though he never knew why.

The two prison guards picked Tom up gently, and placing him on a stretcher took him to the local hospital. There he was treated like royalty and given the greatest care and attention. He found it difficult to comprehend. Why, when he had been mentally and physically tortured for so many months, ending with the ultimate punishment, would he now be treated so humanely? Tom wondered what they had up their sleeve. Was he to be brought back to health only to be tortured again? Confused and sceptical he was uneasy about this treatment.

Nothing happened. With excellent food and care in the hospital, Tom recovered completely and within a month he was flown back to Corsica to prepare for his next assignment. What a wonderful homecoming he received from his fellow recruits. He had no idea that he had become so popular! He was relieved to be back in one piece and very pleased to see his mate, John Macey again. Macey was overjoyed to see Tom, having felt sick to the stomach in the belief that his very good friend was dead. While Macey naturally had been questioned, as he had never been involved in Tom's scheme to escape he was totally oblivious of what had actually happened to him. As such, after being grilled he had been released.

CHAPTER 12

The island of Mayotte

On settling down in Corsica again and recuperating after his ordeal, which accounted for only a couple of weeks, Tom was sent to his commanding officer.

"Fredriksson, we are giving you a new assignment. This time you will have no chance of escaping. We have some problems in the Comoros Islands, our main island being Mayotte, which is situated in the Indian Ocean, the archipelago between the eastern coast of Africa and Madagascar. The Comoros islands consist of three volcanic islands, numerous coral reefs and uninhabited islets. Mayotte is the most southern island and remains a French dependency.

"We are sending a platoon of our very best recruits to the island to resolve some of the disagreements, which have created political unrest and instability. Though you have disgraced the Legion by your defection, you are still one of our best recruits and I hope you will do the honourable thing and help resolve the problems that have occurred and bring the island to peace and harmony."

The commanding officer went on to explain the reason for the political unrest. "The population has increased quite significantly over the years and there are very few natural resources, which is creating a problem among the inhabitants. The island relies heavily on imports of some of the basic necessities, which are often paid for by foreign aid. However, their main export is spices, which have proven to be fairly profitable. Tourism is another key way in which they can raise revenue, though this has not been exploited to its full potential as yet."

The commanding officer who was now handing out the orders was a pleasant enough fellow, but Tom could not understand his reason for singling him out. He had replaced Zeigler, the previous commanding officer who had assisted Tom out of the tricky whore-house situation soon after his initial recruitment into the Legion. Tom had proved, as far as the Legion was concerned, to be quite dishonourable and not to be trusted. Little did Tom know that news of his exploits had drifted across the desert and had been logged in the archives of the French Foreign Legion. The Legion had always admired an intrepid soldier of initiative and enterprise.

A week later a platoon of 14 young recruits flew out from Ajaccio in Corsica to Mayotte on an aeroplane owned by Air Corso, flight AC 1234. The other two islands of the Comoros were Grand Comoro and Anjouan. The plane was a twin-engine, short to medium range narrow-bodied airliner and was carrying 90 passengers, excluding the crew of six. According to the pilot, the journey of 1,695 miles would take 8 hours 52 minutes. They would be landing at Dzaoudzi Pamandzi International Airport, the only airport on Mayotte.

As the plane flew out from Ajaccio in the early evening light, Tom gave a quiet sigh, the beauty of the island never ceasing to give him pleasure. It was June and the temperature was a comfortable 20°C, but they had been warned that the Comoros Islands were experiencing cold and windy weather and the flight could be a little uncomfortable. The plane, cruising at a height of 30,000 ft, flew gently southeast towards the Indian Ocean where the Comoros Islands lie. At 2 am the seatbelt sign came on, the stewardess announcing that there would just be another half an hour before arrival at Mayotte's airport.

As the aircraft began to descend there was a rattling noise that seemed to reverberate throughout the whole fuselage. Everyone was strapped into their seats except for the two stewardesses, who started moving around the plane trying to pacify the frightened passengers. The parents were unable to calm their children, their own fear being felt by the small children who began to scream at the top of their voices. As the clattering of the aircraft increased in strength and velocity, the lights dimmed and finally went out. For an instant they were all in darkness.

The emergency lights flickered on. With a calmness of voice that Madeleine, the stewardess who was located by the cockpit did not feel, she suggested that everyone remove their life jackets from under their seats and put them on before helping the children with theirs, as there was a technical problem and there was the possibility the pilot would have to make an emergency landing. At the same time the oxygen masks dropped down from the overhead racks. There was hardly time to don the life jackets and masks to protect the passengers, however, as the plane was rapidly losing height, as one of the engines burst into flames, and heading towards the Indian Ocean at approximately 375 miles an hour. Nevertheless, at the very last minute the Air Corso pilot managed to regain some control and level out the plane as it crashed into the ocean. Out of the 90 passengers only a handful managed to escape, as the fuselage shattered on impact. The sea was carnage, the debris having scattered in all directions. Most of the passengers who had been thrown by the impact of the crash did not have a chance of surviving. It was a tragedy of enormous proportions made worse by the fact that the nation did not possess any sea rescue facilities, which might have rescued those not killed when the plane broke up.

***

It was 2.30 am when the aeroplane crashed into the Indian Ocean just 1 mile from Grande Comore, the largest of the three Comoros Islands. The inhabitants were already on high alert, their rescue services stretched to full capacity. Grande Comore is made up of an irregularly, gently sloping plateau and secured by two volcanoes. At the island's highest point Mount Karthala, an active crater, had started emitting fumes and shaking the earth a couple of hours earlier. Lava had started pouring down the mountain side, the ash flying everywhere and starting to blot out the landscape.

This was a natural and regular occurrence, but always a frightening one, the islanders now needing to prepare to make their escape to the next island, Anjouan, which was the nearest landmass to them. The subjects of Anjouan, the second largest island of the Comoros, were always diligent in monitoring each others' volcanic movements. They had sent over a great many of their own motor boats which were already lying in the harbour in Grande Comore in preparation for such an eventuality. The other side of Grande Comore was not affected, so only a couple of hundred inhabitants needed to escape the hot lava that was streaming down into the sea. They were petrified, having no idea as to what their houses would be like on their return, or in fact whether they would still be standing. They were a poor people, not expecting a lot out of life, just hoping that the existence they led would offer them the basics to look after their families.

In the dim light all that could be seen were flames on the water surrounding the debris, which was bobbing up and down in the choppy sea. Madeleine, the French-speaking stewardess, was one of the lucky ones, having been thrown clear of the plane and landing in the cold water. She was barely hurt; just a little bruised with some minor cuts. Having been top of her class in the swimming team, she was able to reach a large piece of a broken wing and hang onto it. It was bitterly cold but she was determined that she would come through this. She had no idea what had gone wrong. Perhaps all would come to light when the black box was found. At least it would give the authorities an idea as to what was going on in the cockpit at the time of this disaster. She could not see anybody else as she tried to manoeuvre the piece of wing towards Grande Comore. "Am I the only survivor?" she wondered.

Madeleine thought she saw a red light in the distance and hoped that somebody had seen the crash and that a rescue party was being organised to come and help them. But nobody came. Little did she know that the light was coming from the lava spewing forth from the erupting volcano. As the piece of wing she clung to floated very slowly towards Grande Comore, she felt something bump into her. Startled she noticed a body lying over the side of an inflated raft, which had probably originally been attached to the door of the aeroplane. Though her legs were tired and her body cold,

Madeleine managed to propel herself to the side of the raft. She made a grab for the rope hanging over the side and used the last of her strength to haul herself in, praying that she wouldn't overturn the raft while doing so. By pure chance this did not happen.

She lay down beside the body, her lungs sucking in air and her legs and arms shaking from the cold, exhaustion and shock. After a few minutes, she sat up and considered the body. It was a man. She wondered whether he was alive. He was not moving and looked as grey as death. There was a large gash on his forehead and his eyes were shut. In an almost abstract manner, she noted that he had a good strong jaw line. She supposed him to have been be quite handsome prior to the crash and tried to picture where he had been seated in the plane and whether she had served him. Feeling for a pulse in his neck, she was relieved to find a fairly strong one. Putting her arms around his middle she pulled the man into the raft and curled up against him in order to give them both as much warmth as possible. Sheer exhaustion took over and she fell fast asleep.

***

A couple of hours later the man awoke, astonished to find the pretty French-speaking stewardess with her arms wrapped around him. "What a lovely feeling," he murmured. He had not been held like that for a long time. "Am I in heaven?"

Madeleine peered shyly at him when she awoke a couple of minutes later, finding herself looking into the warm brown eyes of John Macey. "Not yet. I thought it would help, help us both if I lay close to you for bodily warmth. Did I do wrong?"

"No," Macey was quick to respond, "It's just that I have not had a woman close to me like that for quite a time. It was wonderful." Cheekily he told her: "Feel free to put your arms around me again."

Madeleine flushed, "I think we should check where we are and what we are going to do."

Macey sat up a little straighter to appear to be in control. "I've been trained in survival skills so this should really be my department. I should be thinking and planning the next move."

Confidently Madeleine offered her hand. "Shall we begin by introducing ourselves? My name is Madeleine Marten. I am a Corsican air stewardess living and working on the island. I was one of the two stewardesses who were serving on Air Corso A1234."

Macey looked at her with renewed interest. If he had been able to see through the gloom he would have noticed a blush spread across her cheeks. "Yes, I remember. You were the pretty one I noticed."

"That is very kind of you to say. Now your turn."

"I am John Macey, an Englishman, and a recruit of the French Foreign Legion."

"What are you doing here?"

"Fourteen of us were recruited to come here to help with the stabilising of Mayotte, which is a French Protectorate, and to try and resolve the disagreements that have created unrest and instability on the island." Macey stopped in his tracks, the horror of what had happened suddenly hitting him. Were they the only two alive? Where was Tom? What had happened to him?

He, Macey, had been knocked unconscious when the plane crashed so had not witnessed the scene unfold around him. How had he got into this inflated raft? It was a mystery. He had to go back to look for Tom. Macey turned to Madeleine. "I have a very good friend who was also on the plane. We met in Corsica when we joined the French Foreign Legion two and a half years ago. I must return to the crash site and look for him."

Although exhausted, hungry and thirsty, the two of them turned back towards the area where the plane had gone down. With two pieces of debris that they had found floating in the water, which they used as paddles, they made their way back to where the sinking plane had been. All they saw on returning to the scene of the accident was a lot of debris, suitcases, clothes and some bodies floating on the surface of the water. There appeared to be no survivors. The odour of diesel was unpalatable, but Madeleine and Macey were beyond being concerned about the smell and concentrated on looking for a tall dark-haired legionnaire, probably either floating in the water or hanging onto a piece of the aeroplane. They searched up and down the area of water where most of the bodies had been thrown, but did not see him anywhere. Macey was becoming frantic. Even though most of the passengers and crew had been killed, he was sure that Tom would be alive. Tom had already proven that he was indestructible.

A new day arrived as they searched, the sun poking its head over the horizon. With it came warmth that he and Madeleine lapped up, after having been chilled to the bone by the cold air and freezing water. All was quiet as the sea was calm. There was still no sign of Tom. Even if he had been killed, Macey was sure that he would have located his body by this time.

Macey and Madeleine paddled around the area one last time, checking rather grimly every dead body as well as every body part, and looking at every piece of debris to see if there was anybody hanging on. There was nothing. Everything was deathly quiet after the chaos and disaster. The only thing they could do was to paddle back to the nearest island, hoping they could get more information and freshen up. By the time they had reached the spot where they had first become acquainted they were exhausted and extremely hungry and thirsty.

To their horror, on approaching the island of Grande Comore they were welcomed by a terrific heat and were enveloped by a cloud of ash. The air was putrid and seemed to lack oxygen. Macey could not believe their bad luck. "We must get away from here as quickly as possible. This is one of the volcanic islands of the Comoros, which if I am right erupts on an average every 11 years. Not an especially comfortable island on which to live!"

Just as they were about to turn around to avoid the fine particles of ash being thrown out by the erupting volcano, a large motor boat shot by nearly colliding into them. Macey was too dumbfounded to recognise his good friend. "Look out, you idiot," shouted Macey, "you nearly ran us down."

The pilot of the motorboat slowed down and with an enormous grin on his face called back. "Macey, it's me, Tom. You are alive! Thank God you are still in the land of the living." Macey returned the sentiment with an equally happy smile on his face. "Yes, I am fine, only a few cuts and bruises but I'll live! I also have the lovely stewardess, Madeleine, who was with us on the plane." Macey then glanced into Tom's boat. "Where are you going with these people?"

"I am helping to steer them to the next island. Maybe you can come with us. There is very little room in the boat, but as most of these good people are fairly slight we might be able to squeeze the two of you in as well. I doubt very much if you and Madeleine would survive on the raft all the way to Anjouan."

Macey laughed, "I don't think so either."

With great difficulty Tom steered the motorboat alongside the raft. With the help of two of the male passengers, Macey and Madeleine were pulled into the cramped, overloaded boat. "Thank you very much. We so appreciate your help and sympathise with your awful dilemma!" Madeleine looked around at the concerned faces surrounding her. Macey agreed and started explaining their situation.

Although Grande Comore was not a French Protectorate, many of the passengers on Tom's vessel, though not having French as their first language, were actually French speaking. They were therefore able to understand Macey's sensibilities.

The boat moved on slowly towards Anjouan, Tom piloting the vehicle through the ash fog, hardly seeing anything but using his instincts and a compass to direct them. Macey did not ask him any questions, knowing it was not the right time. It was a difficult task Tom was undertaking and Macey wandered how on earth he had become involved with these people and with such speed. The plane had only gone down a few hours before. But Tom was an extraordinary fellow, always getting involved in difficult situations and always managing to extricate himself as well.

The motorboat powered on. Saying a big prayer, Tom hoped he was not going to crash into any foreign bodies but remain afloat as he had volunteered and promised to look after these people and take them to safety.

Being one of the very few to have been thrown clear of the plane, and since he was a very strong swimmer he was able to locate one of the inflatable rafts attached to the doors of the aeroplane before it sank, climb onto it and paddle towards Grand Comoro. He was aware that the island was in the throes of a volcanic eruption and understanding that the inhabitants would be scared for their families and homes, as well as their lives. He floated towards the coast where he could see masses of people trying to flee the angry eruption that was making headway down the mountain. With his innate understanding of and concern for others and an air of authority, Tom was able to calm people assemble them in an orderly fashion. He and several islanders organised the inhabitants into groups of 25 and placed them in the waiting motor boats Anjouan had supplied for emergencies, which were tethered in the harbour. The women and children boarded first. Some of the men, at the request of their families, clambered aboard the vessel that Tom took control of. He was relieved about this as he was not sure he would have been able to cope alone if any unsuspecting incident had occurred. The islanders were relieved to have somebody to direct them, and within 15 minutes of Tom arriving on the beach all 200 people were safely ensconced in the boats and were on their way. It was not possible for them to take any belongings with them beyond blankets, food and drink for the children and themselves. It promised to be a long, cold and uncomfortable journey.

It was less than 20 minutes later that Tom had his encounter with Macey and Madeleine in their inflatable raft. He felt blessed that he had been in a position to help these people, otherwise he might not have come across them, and he might have been stranded on the island himself.

The motorboat chugged on, surrounded by the other boats fleeing the island. It was a fair distance to Anjouan, which normally would take about 2 hours. With the circumstances and overcrowding on the boats, the journey would take at least twice as long as speed was limited and there was a danger of capsizing.

Macey and Madeleine were becoming faint and dizzy due to lack of water and food. They were tightly wedged between a man, his wife and their two children, who seeing their plight offered them some of their precious water, for which Macey and Madeleine were very grateful. At least they were all safe for the time being. What a miracle that they should bump into Tom.

The fog lifted as they moved away from Grande Comore. After over 4 hours they reached Anjouan. All the passengers were stiff, cold and very hungry, but they were safe and alive. The other seven boats were just a little way behind. Nothing disastrous had happened to any of them during the voyage, the sea being relatively calm as they journeyed towards the second largest island of the Comoros. As they clambered out of the boats, a little the worse for wear, they were welcomed by the inhabitants of Anjouan, who greeted them with warm rugs, hot drinks and wide smiles.

***

Tom, once again, started planning his escape, the thing that was always foremost in his mind. There was nothing he and Macey could do on Mayotte, since all the other recruits had gone down with the plane. There had been no contact with Corsica since they had left, as it was virtually impossible to get any connection between the two islands. He was, after all, a free agent on Anjouan. He could reach the airport without much difficulty, flying on to London and finally Sweden. All his papers had disappeared in the crash, so it would not have been too difficult to explain their disappearance and request new ones. However, his conscience was telling him differently.

After a week on Anjouan, Tom felt he should return to Grande Comore with the natives to help them get their lives back together. He felt responsible for the islanders of Grande Comore and had vowed he would take them back to their homes and help them. He was optimistic. He felt strangely protective of these generous and impoverished people, who needed help to build up their lives again. He did not know what Macey was feeling on this issue. He was pretty sure he felt the same but Macy had become quite attached to Madeleine, and Tom was not totally sure of what was going on in his mind. He felt it might be better to handle this on his own until Macey told him otherwise.

"On reflection," he thought, "It would be wiser to broach the subject with him tonight and ask what his plans are." When he did, Macey was quick to respond.

"I am with you Tom. We can do nothing for the inhabitants of Mayotte but we can do something for the islanders of Grande Comore." Macey had echoed Tom's sentiments exactly.

"We cannot stay here any longer." Macey continued. "We have overstayed our welcome as it is, even though I know the islanders of Grande Comore would do the same if the boot were on the other foot! Two-hundred-and-three extra people cost a lot to house and feed. It's time that we went. I will talk to Madeleine as soon as possible and ask her what she wishes to do. It depends a lot on her commitments back in Corsica. She has been unable to contact her family, who must be in a terrible state wondering if she is alive or dead.

"We must also try and get through to Corsica again tonight. Headquarters should really be acquainted with the situation here and be advised of the terrible tragedy of the young recruits so they too can pass this information on to their families. They might order us home, but I will not return until I have resolved the situation on Grande Comore." Tom had reservations about contacting the Foreign Legion, but held his tongue as he considered the recruits' loved ones.

When Macey spoke to Madeleine a little later on, she too said she would prefer to return to Grande Comore to try and bring some sort of order back to the island.

The next day Tom, Macey, Madeleine and the Grande Comorian islanders bade fond farewells to their very kind hosts and motored towards their homeland. The sea was calm, the skies blue, and the sun shining warmly down upon this large group as they travelled. They were naturally very apprehensive about what to expect on their arrival. It was not going to be a particularly pleasant homecoming but at least they were all alive.

Three and half hours later they reached the shores of Grande Comore. The lava was cool and dry near the shore. The beautiful land had been ravaged and supplanted by a landscape that looked as though it had come out of a horror movie. Everything looked bleak and grey.

The small houses on top of the cliff had been flattened by the hot lava, the gardens obliterated. How long would it take to get the gardens and farmland producing food again? Horror was written all over their faces. It was not possible to cross over to the other part of the island as a lava field lay in the middle.

A plan of action needed to be made immediately. The main priorities were to provide food, shelter and bedding for the islanders, and preferably before nightfall. This might prove a little optimistic but not impossible. Tom put the young men in charge of collecting wood and straw to build houses for approximately 35 families, mostly consisting of two adults and four children. Since most of the families came from farming stock, they needed to build the houses on high ground to access the pastures. Luckily the ash had not polluted all the water from the wells, public tanks and private fountains, so there was a sufficient amount of water from everyone. As time wore on, the younger children were getting fretful and needed food and sleep. The islanders had been given something to eat and drink to tide them over when they left Anjouan, but this had been consumed some time earlier.

Since the islanders had the motor boats standing in their harbour, Tom suggested that some of the older, stronger members of the community take five of the boats and motor around to the other side of the island, pick up as many food supplies and blankets as possible, and gather tools for erecting the houses and utensils for cooking. He chose ten men who had a knowledge of boats for this task. He had no idea how much the men would be able to collect, as the inhabitants of the other side of the island, although not being displaced by the eruption, did not have much in the way of surplus goods.

As the island was 42 miles long and 16 miles wide, it would probably take about 2 hours to get to the other side, gather supplies and return. It would be getting dark by then, so the sooner they returned the better. The remaining men and women concentrated on removing the rubble in order to provide an area on which to build temporary shelters.

About 2 hours after they set off a great cheer went up as the men returned with all the necessary requirements. The materials were now ready for building the dwelling places. Everyone went to work to help erect the simple wood and straw houses which were done in about an hour and a half – record time! It was June and the air was pleasant, without being too humid.

The people filled themselves with the simple food that they had received from their fellow Grande Comorians on the other side of the island and got ready for bed. Everybody was exhausted, but Tom, Macey and Madeleine stayed up a little longer to help the women and their offspring get organised in their new houses. It would be some time before they would have a real home again and proper life style, with furniture and beds. It would be longer before they could continue with their work creating beautiful embroidery and weaving raffia from which they made baskets, mats and purses. The men too would be unable to settle down to their livelihoods, which involved making intricate jewellery out of mother-of-pearl, silver and gold. They lived in a changing world, which was unpredictable.

The next day dawned beautifully warm with patches of blue sky showing through the thinning ash clouds. Everybody was in a wonderful frame of mind, but Tom and Macey were unsettled and needed to think about returning to Corsica. They still had not been able to contact headquarters. Madeleine had not managed to make any contact with her family either. There were no newspapers or any form of media through which they could receive news or send any messages out.

Discussing this with Macey, Tom knew that they had to come up with some sort of a plan. "How does one make a radio?" Engineering was not one of Tom's strengths.

"I used to tinker with radios when I was a boy and derived a lot of pleasure from it. Maybe one of the islanders has an old, forgotten ham radio that is not too badly damaged which we could do something with? Some of the older guys who collected the supplies seemed to be quite au fait with the mechanics of the boat, so they might have some kind of knowledge of radios too."

Moses, a tall strapping man in his early 40s who had steered one of the motorboats, appeared to be an especially cheerful and approachable person. He always looked on the bright side of everything. When Tom asked him whether he could speak to him about radios, his face lit up.

"Have you ever had, or do you have any knowledge of someone owning a ham radio?"

"I did have one," Moses responded, "not that long ago, but I have no idea where it went. It was in my kitchen just before the eruption, but of course everything disappeared as well as my radio. It was extremely useful as I used to get the most fantastic music from Johannesburg, and also a feeling of how things were outside this island." Without saying anything more except to ask them to follow him, Moses suddenly got up and with large strides ascended the hill where his temporary home had been erected.

It was fortuitous for Macey, Tom and Madeleine that Moses' new house had been built on the same plot of land as the previous one. This gave them all a better chance of finding the buried radio. The walls and roof of the original house had been obliterated by the weight of the ash and the inside was covered over with debris.

"If only we had a metal detector," murmured Macey, "I have never felt in so much need of one as I do now!"

With the various tools Moses had received from the helpers who had aided him in building the temporary house, he gave both guys a spade and a fork. He used a hoe to try and locate any metal object under the earth that had not been melted or burned by the heat of the ash.

"When I return to civilization," Macey said under his breath, "I will send these good people a metal detector to help them find their metal belongings in a very much shorter time. How can they manage without the simplest of tools?"

They searched every possible spot near Moses' home for the next hour but had no luck. Perhaps it had been covered up by the hot ash and gone forever? Tom and Macey carried on hunting for it over the next few days but all to no avail. On the fourth day while the young men were helping the islanders create a new vegetable garden, as Madeleine was at a loose end she decided to venture up the hill to view the houses, being most interested to see how they had been built. The houses were very simply constructed, having straw roofs, wooden frames and beaten earth floors but no running water or electricity. The kitchens were usually built at the back of the house. When Moses mentioned that the radio had been in the kitchen, she thought she would scout round the area with the hope of finding Moses' floor under the debris. As the floor had a beaten earth surface, it was not too difficult unearth and check for hard objects nearby. As the kitchen was so small, it took her only 5 minutes before she did, in fact, feel something. A little beneath the surface of ash, she found something that seemed to be of a rectangular shape. Realising she needed a spade, and without asking for help, she ran outside to find one propped up against the wall. On returning she immediately began to dig around this rectangular object only to discover the much needed radio. It was almost unrecognisable, being covered in ash, sand and dirt. She was thrilled! Calling out to the lads who were on the way up the hill, she caught their attention by waving the radio high above her head like a flag. Breaking into a celebratory run they reached Madeleine in great excitement. "Where did you find it?" asked Macey.

Madeleine proudly explained, "Moses mentioned that the last time he saw the machine it was in the kitchen so I thought I would give it a go and try there."

"What a clever girl you are, Madeleine," Macy said giving her a big bear hug. "This puts a completely different slant on the possibilities of how and when we can return to Corsica. That's marvellous." Meanwhile, because Moses was trying to catch some fish for supper, Tom and Macey had to bide their time until he returned. After all, it was his radio. Regrettably for the islanders, the coastline of Grande Comore was so narrow that was totally unsuitable for a fishing industry. The men really hoped Moses would not spend the rest of the day trying to catch some fish. He turned up 1 hour later. Not only had he caught some cod for his family, but he was absolutely delighted to hear that Madeleine had found the old ham radio. Macey had been studying the old ham equipment to see how damaged it was. It was not that badly wrecked but needed a bit of cleaning up, an antenna and, of course, electricity or a generator. Macey asked if it would be possible to get these things, but Moses did not think there would be any problem. Apart from anything he was so thrilled to have his radio back that he would do whatever was necessary to get it in good working order again.

The next day Moses once more motored round the island to visit his friends and ask them if they could possibly repair his radio and get it working again. They were pleased to oblige and Moses returned with a very happy expression on his face carrying the now extremely valuable and working radio. Tom and Macey were delighted that at last something positive was going to happen.

"Thank you very much Moses for going to so much trouble. Would you please tell your friends how much we appreciate what they have done."

Since it would only be possible to get short wave on the radio, Macey thought the best place to contact anyone would be Johannesburg in South Africa. Being a relatively civilized place they could perhaps ask for a seaplane to pick them up from Grande Comoro and fly them to Johannesburg. They then could return to Corsica on a scheduled flight.

It was now up to Macey to contact somebody by surfing the airwaves and giving them the metre number and details of the radio frequency so that the call could be returned. The metre band that was currently most often used was the 31 metre one, the frequency range being 9,400–9,900 kHz. With the antenna, a pair of transceivers and electricity there would be no reason for them not to be able to get a message through to someone who then, hopefully, could pass it on to the necessary authorities.

It was now 6 pm; a time Macey felt was a good time to call. Twirling the knob and hoping that he would tune into the right wave band, he began to speak into the microphone, willing somebody to hear him. At first everything seemed muffled with a lot of background noise. Then a person responded. The language was not that obvious at first, but then somebody asked if any help was needed in English. Macey, putting his ear to the receiver, relayed the information to the listener through the microphone, giving him the radio's frequency and asking him if he could pass the information on to the right authorities. He mentioned that he was stranded on Grande Comore and needed a seaplane to transport three of them to Johannesburg. The listener seemed to understand the message and confirmed that he would pass the information as soon as possible.

Macey thought it unwise to give more information than was necessary. Any newspaper would have a field day printing stuff about those who had survived or died from the aeroplane crash in the Indian Ocean before anybody else. This would be devastating for the families and friends of the deceased.

The next day Macey, sticking to the repaired radio like glue, received a call early in the afternoon. An Afrikaans accent floated over the radio, asking if he was the gentleman in question who wished to have a seaplane flown over to Grande Comore. Macey was delighted that his call been returned so quickly, and asked when it would be possible for the seaplane to pick the three of them up. He replied it could be in 24 hours. Tom was most surprised at the speed of this response. A day later the Legionnaires, bearded and looking very rugged and tanned, waited on the beach at the south side of the island with Madeleine. They were wearing some old clothes provided by Moses, their other clothes having seen better days. Madeleine was wearing a long and colourful dress, called a chiromani, belonging to Moses' wife. Instead of a small seaplane turning up a much larger aircraft arrived at the appointed place, several white Afrikaners descending the aircraft with pads and pens in hand. Tom, Macey and Madeleine looked horrified. How had they got hold of the story?

Tom went forward to meet them holding out his hand as a sign of welcome. "Thank you very much for coming so quickly to our aid. We really appreciate the speed at which you have come. However, we did not expect such conscientiousness and consideration, and regret that as we still have commitments on this island we will be unable to come with you at this particular moment."

The leader, a tall blond Afrikaner, seemed nonplussed and did not reply immediately but after a moment retorted angrily. "We have come all this way, at your request, to help you and to fly you back to Johannesburg and you refuse on the basis that you have not completed your business here. Why didn't you explain this before we came?"

Tom was taken aback by his vehemence. "I am very sorry to bring you out so unnecessarily. It was a complete misunderstanding on my part. As I said before, we are very grateful but with all the tragedy and disaster these poor folk have gone through we do not feel we can leave them before we have completed our mission, which is why we are here."

The leader became confused and turning on his heels without another word to Tom. He called his compatriots to return to the seaplane. "We should leave. We have come on a fool's errand and are not wanted here."

Tom and Macey gave a big sigh of relief as the plane flew away. "Perhaps they do not come from Johannesburg but from some other large town and want a piece of the action. We will have to try again." The same day Macey tried again. After a lot of knob turning he heard the voice of a young woman at the other end. She spoke English with an English accent, so Macey was curious as to where he was connected to and who had picked up his ham signal.

"Hello, can you hear me? My name is Macey. Who are you and where are you speaking from."

The disembodied voice came over the radio waves. "My name is Meg and I am speaking from Johannesburg in South

Africa. Macey is a very strange name." Macey was not quite expecting such a response. "I suppose it is. My first name is John but everyone calls me Macey."

The girl continued. "Well Macey, where are you transmitting from and did you just want to have a chat over the wire?"

"It is good to hear a friendly voice and one that can speak English. However, the reason I am calling is because I am in need of help and would like to ask a favour from you. Two of my mates and I are stranded on Grande Comore in the Indian Ocean, and I was wondering if you could contact somebody to arrange for us to be picked up and flown to Johannesburg?"

The girl was quick to respond and seemed quite excited.

"It is much simpler than you think, for my Father has his own small seaplane business and he could pick you all up himself! I can come too for I have nothing to do at the moment coming into the school holidays, and I have never visited the Comoros Islands."

"That would be wonderful. Do you think you could ask your Dad to contact me on this radio wave when it is convenient?"

"I will do that with pleasure. What is your frequency?"

A couple of days later another English voice was relayed through the microphone, which Macey assumed was the father.

"Good-day, is this Mr Macey?"

Macey smiled, "Yes it is. I believe I spoke to your daughter the other day. What a competent young lady she sounds."

Macey sensed the pride in the man's voice. "Yes, she has been tinkling with radios since she was little. How can I help you? My name is Peter Chalmers."

"Two mates and I would appreciate it if we could charter your seaplane to this island to then fly us to Johannesburg. We are not in a tremendous rush, but would be glad to have some idea when you might be able to do this."

"I have a free slot in 3 days' time," responded Chalmers. "Would that be okay for you all?"

With relief Macey answered. "Yes, it would be ideal. Thank you very much. I suggest that we meet you on the south side of the island, which is the Mozambique Channel. You will notice that the coast line is very narrow, but I will be outside waving a red flag!"

"I will be you at around 10.00 hours in the morning," he explained, "as I have another appointment in the afternoon."

Macey signed off gratefully. "That will be fine."

All three felt a little sad at leaving the island and these gentle folk, especially Moses and his family. They had grown quite attached to them and their kindness.

Three days later Moses sailed them around to the beach to wait for the plane before turning round and heading back to the island. The trio heard the sound of propellers a short distance away as the plane approached Grande Comore. All the three were ready with the few belongings they had acquired, Macey madly waving the red flag hoping that he could be seen.

The seaplane came in low and skidded on the surface of the waves near the beach. "Is that you, Macey?" a deep voice called out from the plane as the noise from the propellers died away. "Yes it is." Macey called back, trying to make out the face. "Good, stuff," he shouted.

Macey, Tom and Madeleine introduced themselves to Chalmers and he went on to introduce them to a slim blond girl of about 15. She was beaming from ear to ear.

This was something she would have to tell her friends back at school. She was delighted that she had been able to meet Macey and friends, and pleased with herself for having been instrumental in arranging their rescue from the volcanic island.

CHAPTER 13

Françoise

Françoise was a very courageous young woman. Working for the underground movement in Belgium during the 1939–1945 war, she and her family helped the Jews escape to safety, mostly to England via Oostende and Rotterdam, by hiding them in their enormous chimneybreast. The family had a very comfortable house on the outskirts of Gand (Ghent as it is now named). Françoise came from a family of four: her father, mother, brother and herself. For all intents and purposes they appeared to be a normal family; that is if anything or anyone can ever be considered normal in time of war, when hardship is the "norm" and when one is never quite sure if one's neighbour is a quisling or just a genuine person trying to cope with everyday life occupied by the Hun.

One day in early autumn, Françoise was cooking in the kitchen when four SS soldiers burst into her house, without warning, demanding the identity of the woman whom they had just seen through the window.

"Where is that woman who was wearing a red garment?" demanded the leader of the group.

"It was I," replied Françoise coming out of the kitchen with greasy hands.

"You are not wearing any red now, are you?" he leered.

"No I'm not," responded Françoise, "I had to change as I did not want to spoil any good clothing whilst I was cooking."

"Go and get it," the SS soldier barked.

Françoise, without hesitating and with great fear in her heart ran upstairs and started rummaging through all her drawers to find something red. She did not possess any red blouse or dress. Finally finding a large red scarf she held it over the banisters crunching it up so nobody could actually see what it really was.

The Germans left, seemingly accepting this explanation. The reprieve was very short lived, however, for about a month later, and again without any warning, they marched back into the house grabbing her brother Carlos and her father. Throwing them into the waiting car, the SS soldiers drove Carlos and her father off to Headquarters for interrogation. Françoise and her mother were arrested the next day. Fortuitously, as it was the same day the Allies marched into Belgium; the Germans retreated to their own country and they were subsequently freed. The war was over.

Though it was fortunate that Françoise and her mother had been freed because of the intervention of the Allies, it was a tragic time for both of them. Having still not heard from her father and Carlos months after the war ended, it was presumed that the two of them were dead.

Françoise's mother died fairly shortly after the war from a sudden heart attack brought on, it was assumed, by the tragic circumstances of losing both her son and husband to the Germans. Françoise was devastated by this further loss but knew she had to carry on. Though very interested in studying medicine, she was unable to afford the fees. Despite this she did manage to get a grant to train as a pharmacist. It was during her studies that she happened to meet the man who was to become her husband at a restaurant during her lunch break in the city. Bernard was a tall and charming young man, whose mother was Belgian and whose father was Scottish. Bernard had grown up in Aberdeen, in the northeast of Scotland, and was a most enthusiastic person. Being an exceptional chemical engineer he had been sent to Belgium on a sabbatical to do research for his company. It was by chance one wet and windy day that he decided to visit the recently opened restaurant near his office, which had been recommended by his colleagues. Walking through the door on this memorable day, he noticed a young woman sitting on her own at a booth situated near the door. He was immediately struck by her sweet looks and calm demeanour and asked if he could join her. It was love at first sight.

The couple became engaged and were married within a few months, but they did not move to Scotland until after Françoise had successfully completed her studies, achieving the highest mark in her intake in her pharmaceutical exams. She had no regrets about leaving Belgium, for she was now the last surviving member of her family. They had all been executed by the Gestapo by one method or another.

***

The young couple began their new life in Scotland in a small town called Petercalter just outside of Aberdeen. It was a very cold part of Scotland but Françoise loved the sea and she was the happiest she could remember in years.

She was thrilled when she became pregnant and gave birth to a little girl, whom they named Constance. She was a great joy to Bernard and herself. Regrettably no other baby came along but they were content with each other and their wonderful little girl, who grew up to be a credit to both of them.

In 1970, when Constance was about to enter university, her father Bernard suddenly died of a brain tumour. She and her mother had exhausted all their resources on trying to find a cure for him, but to no avail. They were left with very little to live on and it was now impossible for Constance to take up her studies. While Constance was disappointed, she was more concerned for her mother and their finances. She managed to obtain a grant at Aberdeen Hospital to start nursing. Her mother, Françoise, at the age of 50, started to look for work, her English completely fluent now. Being so distant from the main town, it was practically impossible to find a decent job. She was and had been resourceful nearly her whole life, however, and on applying to a small travel agency near her home in Petercalter her work as a bookkeeper began.

The years went by. Constance completed her nurse's training and left for French Guyana. Françoise, bereft without her daughter, seemed to work longer and longer hours at the travel agency. The company expanded and increased its turnover a hundred-fold. It was beyond the owner, Mr McDougall's, expectations. Mr McDougall greatly admired this marvellous woman, though after almost 5 years he knew her no better than when she had first arrived.

One evening in March, when the agency was locked up for the night, a formal looking letter was dropped through the letterbox addressed to a Mrs Frances Murray. There was no postmark on the letter. When Françoise arrived at work the next morning and opened, it her face drained of all colour. Mr McDougall, who happened to be standing near her, was alarmed and wondered what the contents of the letter were for her to be so affected.

"Mr McDougall," she asked, "do you think you could be kind enough to excuse me for the rest of the day? I will explain my concern as soon as possible."

"Of course you may, Mrs Murray, you have worked flat out this week. Take a few days off. You deserve it."

With a nod of appreciation Françoise walked out of the agency, taking the 29 bus on the corner of the main road. The bus would drop her off very near her house. She entered her quiet and peaceful home, her heart thumping so loudly she felt people down the street must have heard it. She sat down and looked at the letter again. It stated in French: "I am alive, Françoise, please come and get me. Ring 0049-305-612, Carlos." Françoise knew the digits for Berlin without being told.

How could Carlos be alive? It had been over 30 years since he and her father were driven off by the Gestapo, never to be seen again. It is not possible. If he was in East Germany, the Stasi, the Secret Police, would not let him escape unless it was so that they could shoot him as he did so. What would be the point of that? She wondered whether they were trying to get to her through him. She had not been involved with Belgian Intelligence for 35 years and couldn't imagine how she could I be of use to them now. She just didn't understand.

An idea was beginning to form in her mind as she mulled this problem over in her head. She still had a couple of contacts in Belgium – perhaps they could enlighten her? She requested another day off work from Mr McDougall, who was happy to oblige. He knew that if Françoise wanted to explain she would do it in her own time.

The next day Françoise was able to contact her compatriots, Patrice and Marie, with whom she used to work. Having a photographic memory she was able to recall their telephone numbers, and though it took a few hours to get through she was greatly relieved that they were still alive, living in the same town, and were willing to help. She explained about the communication and asked, as she had been out of circulation for so long, if they could explore this strange note about her brother still being alive and see whether there could be any truth in it.

Françoise returned to work the next day, explaining to her boss that she had been trying to resolve a difficult family matter that had suddenly come out of the woodwork. She did not apprise him of any further information. Her own daughter was not privy to any of Françoise's past and she had no intention of her ever knowing either.

The contents of the strange message were thoroughly researched, but neither Patrice nor Marie could come up with anything that could explain why and for what reason it had been written. Why had it been delivered without a postmark, and who would have known where Françoise worked? Also, why had it not been sent to her home? So much intrigue and no discernible answers. Patrice and Marie did, however, have a colleague, Antoine Valerian, who had a contact in West Berlin for whom he had a great respect. He was an ex-Legionnaire who had only returned to Germany the year before, after having excelled himself as a soldier. He was also a lawyer and had offices in a prestigious part of West Berlin. A couple of days later the lawyer was approached by Valerian to request his help. Valerian had a tremendous respect for Colonel Ziegler and knew that he would get a fair answer to his query. Valerian explained that he had been approached by Belgian Intelligence to investigate a strange letter that had been received by a former member of the underground movement. Madame Murray had been informed that her brother, Carlos, whom she had not seen or heard from in over 30 years, was still alive and would she come and collect him. The Colonel frowned at this far-fetched story.

"This sound like a hoax; a very dangerous one. However, since I have immunity, which allows me to go in and out of East Germany as I please, and given that I am still in the German authorities' good books, I will take a look and see what I can do." He left his office, advising his employees to hold any phone calls until he returned.

He packed his bag and with the telephone number given for Carlos in his note book set off for the railway station, arriving at Berlin-Schönefeld station in East Germany on a late afternoon in early spring. It was getting dark, but since it had been a beautifully sunny day the sky was still bright with the twinkling stars shining down upon the city. Ziegler had already booked a room at his favourite hotel, Sorat Hotel Ambassador, which was located in the city centre only 200 metres from the underground station. He planned to visit the Belgian Consulate as early as possible the next day. Even though no one knew the reason for his visit, he needed to be very nonchalant about why he was there. On being asked at the customs desk located at the end of the station platform why he was visiting East Berlin, he told the official that he had a meeting at the Belgian Consulate, after which he was going to the book fair in Leipzig. In the 1970s, the communist regime was still as menacing as before and one had to be extremely vigilant in the face of the secret police. It was better that the Stasi not know what was going on.

After a comfortable night at the Hotel Sorat, Christer Ziegler walked slowly and sedately to the Belgian Consulate, which was situated in the centre of the town. He gave the impression that he was not in any great hurry. He hoped that he was not being followed. He was not totally sure whom he should contact, but his friend Valerian suggested he speak to an old colleague of his who worked there and who always had his eyes and ears open for any subtle change in the climate of espionage. Ziegler had not made an appointment on purpose, as it would have brought much more attention to himself than he would have liked. As it happened, Valerian's colleague was the head of the Consulate. When Ziegler mentioned that he had called to pass on complements from an old friend of his, Valerian, Monsieur du Pont was delighted.

He was a pleasant enough person, tall and athletic, with blond wavy hair and very open demeanour, which masked his shrewd brain. After half an hour discussing old friends and the state of the economy in the country, Du Pont abruptly ceased talking and very quietly asked Ziegler why he was visiting East Germany. Ziegler answered cautiously but confidently, "Since I have never visited the book fair in Leipzig I thought I would do so, being an avid reader. As we both have a mutual friend, I thought I'd also look you up whilst I was in East Germany."

Du Pont was sceptical. "I am sure that the Leipzig book fair will afford you much pleasure, but there must be a reason, apart from your sending greetings from my old friend, for this informal visit?"

Ziegler was slightly disconcerted by being asked such a direct question, but he was ready for every eventuality. "I am looking for a compatriot of Valerian's and he wondered if

106

you would be able to kindly check him out for me? As I have immunity in this part of the world I said I would combine the visit to the fair with seeing you at the same time and enlist your help."

Du Pont relaxed his features for a moment. "Please give me his name and as many details as possible and I will see what I can do."

Ziegler wondered how much information he should give. This du Pont was a sharp and suspicious and Ziegler did not altogether trust him. He certainly did not want to give away more information than was absolutely necessary.

Ziegler continued cautiously. "His name is Marc André. He visited East Germany 5 years ago and never returned, thus the reason for this enquiry."

"What would have been his address in Belgium?"

"He was living in Gand with his mother, who has since died, and the house has been sold. I am unsure of the address but I will get it if it is helpful to the investigation."

"No it is not important. I will look into it and let you know."

"I would very much appreciate any help you can give. Thank you very much Monsieur du Pont. I am staying at the Hotel Sorat for just a day, telephone number 30-7285, before carrying on to Leipzig so would welcome any news that you may glean from his disappearance." Ziegler could do no more.

CHAPTER 14

Marc du Pont

D u Pont was a bitter man. He had been a key figure in the running of the Consulate for the past 2 years. He had been demoted for his clandestine relationships with the wives of other dignitaries during his time in France and Algeria and had been transferred to Morocco, where he had met, fallen in love with and married the most beautiful woman he had ever set eyes on. Her beauty was outstanding. She had luscious dark brown hair that came down to her waist, her olive skin that shone like translucent glass, her body was slender and lithe, and her charm and talents were known in all the foreign embassies in that part of the world.

His romantic escapades had ceased altogether, but his notoriety had not been forgotten. Though now a respectable married man he was transferred to the Belgian East Berlin Consulate, where the work was tedious and the atmosphere in the country heavy and ominous. His wife, Claire, was dismayed by their transfer and reacted negatively to their new move. Despite there not being much one could buy in East Berlin, what was available was extremely expensive. Claire started spending large amounts of money on a regular basis. She became disenchanted with her life, and without her constant admirers she started a series of flirtations with the husbands of some of the Stasis to entertain herself. Du Pont was mortified when he discovered these pastimes. He was unable to convince his wife that not only was her flirting doing harm to their marriage and was a dangerous game to play, but that at the rate she was spending he was quite unable to financially keep her in the style to which she was accustomed. She did not listen.

***

A few weeks after this incident a very well dressed man approached him while he was having a solitary lunch at a nearby restaurant. Asking du Pont whether he had any objection to his joining him, du Pont assented with a slight nod. "You don't look very cheerful," the well-dressed man noted. Throwing caution to the wind du Pont replied, "Would you, if you loved a woman to distraction but could not give her what she most desires? My wife is one of the most beautiful women I have ever met, but regretfully is most dissatisfied with me as a husband. She flirts with all sorts of men. She hates this miserable state we live in, and despises my inability to support her in the way to which she has become accustomed. I cannot pay her bills and she will not listen to my protestations, no matter how much I beg her to keep her spending to a minimum."

"I cannot help you with your marital problems," replied the stranger, "but I can improve your financial ones."

Du Pont sat up a little straighter. "How?" he replied. "How can you help me and why should you?"

"I have contacts in the government who would benefit from information you might glean from any little indiscretion or subterfuge that might be discovered in or around the Consulate."

Du Pont was affronted. "You mean spy for the police?"

"If you would like to use those words, but I would say the benefits will outweigh the negatives and simultaneously resolve your financial problems. You'll no longer need to be concerned about your wife's financial frivolities."

Marc du Pont's face crumpled, desolation seeping through every pore of his body. How had it come to this, he wondered? It seemed as though he had no choice. The gentleman took his cue. "I will let you know how this will be implemented within a day or two. Just start by keeping your eyes and ears open. You are a bright lad: start earning your keep."

***

A year had passed. Du Pont had prospered through this new arrangement and was now able to support his wife and indulge her every whim. He did not try to stop her flirtations and liaisons with her lovers, he couldn't. The marriage was as happy as it could be under the circumstances.

When Christer Ziegler arrived at the Consulate asking for Marc André, du Pont knew immediately who he was looking for, even with Ziegler's attempt to dress up the name. Du Pont was also privy to why Carlos was a danger to the Stasi regime and why it was necessary to eliminate him, as well as the sister if she started making inquiries as she was a loose end. The day before the war ended, and without Carlos' knowledge, a microfilm had been inserted into the area of Carlos' head just behind the ear. Du Pont did not know what was on the film but assumed that it was defamatory to one of the leading members of the Party and that it was vital that either the film be removed, or that Carlos be assassinated while trying to escape. He did not think it likely that the sister would venture behind the Iron Curtain; she would likely think it was a malevolent hoax.

Du Pont was expecting a contact to turn up sometime, but was not prepared for the arrival of such a distinguished colonel from the French Foreign Legion, and recommended by his old friend Valerian no less. No longer could du Pont contain his betrayal of his country. He had been a strong patriot at one time, defending and supporting Belgium against the Hun. "What am I doing?" he thought, angry and disgusted with himself. "People like Carlos and his sister have risked their lives to defend Belgium and now I am no better than the Stasi. How can I live with myself?"

Du Pont managed to organise the exit papers for Carlos within a few hours of his nine o'clock morning meeting with Ziegler at the Belgian Consulate. He arranged for them to be delivered by special courier to Ziegler at his hotel early in the afternoon. The parcel also contained some of the books that they had discussed at his office earlier that morning, so that if the courier were to be stopped the papers would be overlooked, having being placed in a hidden compartment within one of the books. Since Ziegler had received no information about the next move by 2 pm, he was relieved to receive a message from du Pont very soon afterwards. Marc du Pont asked him if he would kindly pass by the Consulate on his way to Leipzig to return one of the books that he had lent him, as it did not belong to du Pont but to a friend of his. Ziegler promptly responded, sending the message: "I am hoping to catch a train to Leipzig around 19.00 hours so there will be plenty of time if I leave the hotel at 16.00

hours and drop off the book and then catch the train from Schönefeld Railway Station to Leipzig. I trust this will be convenient."

***

Carlos was living in a community home for foreigners. He was free as long as his movements were kept inside East Berlin, but was watched on a daily basis to see whether he had any special contact outside the city.

The same day du Pont sent the exit papers to Ziegler, Carlos received a message commanding him to come to the Consulate at 3 pm to talk about a serious misdemeanour that had come to the Consulate's attention. Carlos, now a thin, balding man in his 50s, was petrified by this directive but had no option but to obey. The Stasi henchmen who were watching Carlos were puzzled by this order but were not especially interested, as they knew that du Pont was one of their own agents who would report back to them if there was anything that they needed to know.

When Carlos arrived at the Consulate he was ushered into a private and rather dark room that was soundproof. "Carlos, before I explain what I am doing, I would just like to say how much I appreciate all the wonderful and courageous work you did during the war. You will be travelling to England tonight, with the help of a friend of mine, to meet up with your sister, who now lives in Scotland." Carlos could not believe what he was hearing.

"It is necessary to change your appearance though. Luckily I used to dabble in amateur theatricals and have a fair idea how I can transform the way you look. First I want you to change into the clothes that are on the chair over there in the corner – sorry there are no mirrors in the room – and I will be back with you in a second with various aids to alter your appearance."

Carlos sat as though in a stupor. What had occurred for this shift to have taken place? He did not know why he been kept alive for so long. Perhaps there would be another twist in this melodrama and his demise would come about in another way.

Du Pont returned with water, brushes, make up and different kinds of wigs, as well as fake eye brows, and a gum shield (this was not very comfortable but it would change the shape of the mouth). Within half an hour he had changed Carlos into a completely different person. A photo was taken and placed in the new passport that du Pont also managed source in a very short space of time. Being the head of the Consulate certainly had its merits. Du Pont felt happier than he had for years. He was actually doing some good; a wonderful feeling. It did not matter about the future any more.

***

Together with his suitcase packed ready for his trip to Leipzig and the book that du Pont had requested, Ziegler arrived at the Consulate fairly soon after 4 pm. Like Carlos before him, he was ushered into this dark soundproof room to meet Carlos for the first time. He had not expected du Pont to have conjured up Françoise's brother with such speed, and was very sceptical as to how he had done it. He was, of course, totally unaware of Carlos' real appearance and was confronted by a slightly stooped man with a mass of grey curly hair, a moustache and a small mouth that gave him an air of meanness. His eyes were very dark brown with long dark eyelashes. He spoke German with a hint of a Belgian accent, which was not immediately detectable but this was not surprising as many Belgians spoke Flemish, he recalled, which was a brother tongue to German.

Ziegler was intrigued by du Pont's interest in wishing to carry out this deception to help a Belgian compatriot, knowing that by doing so it could bring about his downfall. "It would be better for you not to know why or how I have been able to do this," he said, reading Ziegler's mind. "Everything will be revealed in due course. All that is needed of you this evening is for you to accompany Carlos to the railway station for the short journey to West Berlin. When you arrive, could you please assist him on his journey to England. He needs to take a plane from the Berlin-Brandenburg International Airport in West Berlin, which will land him at London Heathrow. He will be met by one of my colleagues, Michel Delhomme, who works in the Belgian Embassy in the city. With the help of his contacts in Belgium Michel will notify Carlos' sister he is alive and ask her to come and pick him up."

Ziegler, aware of the frightening consequences of du Pont's actions, asked him. "What will happen to you, Monsieur du Pont?"

He answered without fear. "I have been so very pleased to have been able to help one of my fellow Belgians and it is just one small contribution that I can make. Do not be concerned for me. I shall be all right. Thank you for coming here and do send my very best to Valerian."

Ziegler and Carlos reached the train station at Schönefeld in good time for the 7 pm train to West Berlin. At Check Point Charlie all the papers were found to be in order. No questions were asked as to why they had been in East Berlin or where they were going. Ziegler could not believe it.

Carlos was put on a British Airways plane at the West Berlin Airport leaving at 10 pm that evening to arrive in London at midnight. Du Pont's colleague, Michel, was waiting for him at Heathrow Airport as planned. Du Pont had sent as many details as possible of the circumstances through the Diplomatic Pouch, together with a fairly detailed description of what Carlos' appearance would be. Carlos was in a daze, hardly knowing what was going on. Even though it was well after midnight when he had collected his baggage, passed through arrivals and been found by Michel, he was given as much information as was available as to why he had been imprisoned in East Berlin for so many years and the reason behind Françoise being called to come and get him.

Michel was unable to get hold of Françoise's home number in Scotland until the following morning, when he was able to contact Françoise's compatriots in Belgium and ask them for her details. Meanwhile Carlos was given a comfortable bed where he fell asleep immediately.

***

Françoise was beside herself with joy upon being informed of Carlos' escape from the Stasi and dropping everything at the office took the first plane from Aberdeen International Airport to London to see her long lost brother. Her boss, Mr McDougall, was pleased that some of the mystery surrounding his employee had been explained. Carlos, meanwhile, had shed his disguise and the reunion between brother and sister was momentous and extremely moving.

***

In the meantime Marc du Pont, having finalised all the arrangements and knowing that Carlos was now reunited with his sister sat down to write a letter to his wife.

My Darling,

The joy and happiness at having met and married you was one of the greatest gifts in my life. However, through my own stupidity I hurt my own chances by being a frivolous human being, thus my transfer to East Germany. I realize things could have been different for you if I had been a more responsible person. Regretfully, because of my limited funds and not being able to pay for your needs, I made a deal with the Stasi police who paid me to become their spy. I very much regret my behaviour – it was a dishonourable thing to do.

When you read this letter I will have gone to another world where, I hope, I will be forgiven.

Please, my Darling, go home. Someday you will find a more suitable husband whom you will love with all your heart like I loved you.

Your loving Marc

CHAPTER 15

Constance

Françoise's daughter Constance had been a solemn little girl, quiet and studious. She loved the sea and would contemplate whether she would become a marine biologist or a doctor. As she was an only child, she had grown up in an adult environment rather than a child's one and by the tender age of ten had significant confidence and wisdom. She had taken her O levels one year earlier rather than the usual age of 16 and her A levels at the age of 17. Her parents had been so proud of her. When she reached 18 she decided that she would train to become a doctor and specialise in tropical diseases. But tragedy struck. Just as Constance was about to enter medical school at St Thomas's Hospital in London, her father was stricken by an inoperable brain tumour. Constance and her mother had sought out every eminent brain surgeon in the country but the tumour was inoperable. All their income had been used up with visits to specialists to help her father, so mother and daughter had been left with only the house they lived in and a small pension, which her mother received every month. Constance had applied for a grant to enter St. Thomas' but unfortunately she was turned down.

With a very heavy heart Constance had had to let go of her dream to become a doctor; instead she applied to a nursing school in Aberdeen and lived on the small grant that she was given. She studied very hard and qualified as a nurse after 3 years' training. She acquired the highest marks in her year, there being 70 pupils in all, and started working in the large general ward as a qualified nurse.

After a year in the general ward and because of her natural abilities, she was transferred to the neurology department. Constance had naturally been very interested in this field due to her father's last illness. For the next year she had studied hard, learning as much as she could about brain tumours. The specialists that she and her mother had visited when her father was ill had never been particularly knowledgeable or hopeful about his specific cancer. Perhaps Constance's father would have lived if she had possessed the knowledge that she had now, she thought sometimes, but it was not to be. "Is this the field I really want to pursue?" she reflected one day. "No, I still want to study tropical diseases and help all those poor people in areas where there are few doctors and nurses." Constance had become determined that one day she would be a doctor and it would be in the field of tropical diseases.

While she was extremely positive and always willed things to turn out all right, Constance wondered how much of it was pure luck that, after a year in the head injuries section, she was transferred to the tropical disease ward where she met Dr Duncan. Dr Duncan was of the old school, a veteran in his field, and expected every member of his unit to be as conscientious and hard-working as he was. Constance became ever more fascinated with the work she was doing, and though only a nurse Dr Duncan saw her potential and believed that she had much more to offer. One day while working on the ward with her, he had approached Constance and questioned her. "Constance, what are you doing here as a nurse when you could and should be a doctor?" Constance had then regaled him with the sad history of her father dying from a brain tumour and then not being able to pay the living fees to enter medical school as all their savings had been used up trying to find a cure for her father's illness.

"I very much admire your tenacity, young lady, and I have a very good suggestion for you if you are interested? It will take a short while to implement and I will have to pull a few strings, but there is an opening in French Guyana for a nurse who has knowledge of tropical diseases and their treatment. Why don't you go out there for a year, and in the meantime I will put the wheels in motion for you to enter medical school when you return?"

Constance was stunned. How was Dr Duncan going to do that? Was he so high up in his field of medicine that he could wangle a scholarship for her? "That would be absolutely fantastic," she replied with the biggest smile on her face. "I don't know how you will be able to do it but I would be the happiest girl in the world. But there is one small problem. I would not be able to pay the fare to French Guyana and my mother would find it very difficult to survive without my support and on just her pension and wages from the travel agent."

Dr Duncan answered confidently, "That will be taken care of as well, as the post is funded by the French Foreign Legion. When I see potential such as yours, I feel it is my duty to nurture this ability so the world will be a better place!" With this astonishing rejoinder he turned on his heels and returned to his office, a baffled Constance standing in the same spot, her mind in turmoil.

In 1975, within 3 weeks, after getting all her jabs for the tropics and saying farewell to her mother, Constance flew off to French Guyana in South America, landing at Regina Airport. She was met by another nurse, Sheila, who came from Ireland and who was there to teach her the ropes. Together they took the pirogue, the natives' and Legionnaires' form of transport, down the River Aprouage to the French Foreign Legion headquarters. Thus, Constance began to learn what it was like to live in the jungle, one of the most uncomfortable places on earth, with the heat, flies, snakes and all the unpleasant diseases that existed in that part of the world.

CHAPTER 16

The last mission

Tom and Macey were alive and back at Raffali. They and Madeleine were the only survivors from the plane crash in the Indian Ocean. Despite his feelings about settling down and finding an office job when he'd been undertaking national service, Tom found himself longing for a quieter way of life. He wanted to find a girl and put down some roots but he had another 2 years to go before he would be released from the Legion. Mentally and physically he did not feel he could take any more.

A special service was conducted at Aubagne by the Legion's senior colonel to mourn the 12 recruits who had laid down their lives for their company.

After a few weeks' rest he was called to the adjutant's office and informed that he was due to leave for French Guyana in a few days' time. "A permanent regiment of Legionnaires has been based there for years," the Adjutant informed him. "They are situated in the region to maintain surveillance of the borders with Brazil and Surinam, where civil war has been carrying on for several years. You, Macey and ten others will be flying to Regina later this week where you will attend a jungle commando's course. You will learn more about this on arrival."

***

Having had a most pleasant flight in an air-conditioned aeroplane, the arrival at Regina Airport came as a rather rude awakening. On stepping into the hot and humid air, the young soldiers felt as though they were entering a sauna, with not even the slightest breeze in the air. They felt as though they were on a different planet. It was 33°C but with the humidity seemed more like 40°C. None of the recruits had read up on the vagaries of this assignment and felt rather stupid and ignorant. Fortuitously the Legion had ensured that they had all received the necessary vaccinations at Raffali.

The lectures started early the next morning, the basic theme being survival in the jungle. None of the men had ever been in the jungle before so, rather unusually, there were no smart asses to interrupt the lecturers and disrupt their concentration.

The daily runs in the heat were draining, the recruits never feeling that they had enough drinkable water, which seemed so commonplace in Europe but was scarce in the jungle. Tom and Macey promised themselves that they would never waste a drop of water again in their lives.

As part of their briefing and education about the jungle, the men visited a park where a guide introduced them to a large number of dangerous reptiles, giving information on the reptiles' habitats, lifecycles, why they were dangerous and how they should be handled. There, among the inmates, was an anaconda, which they learned squeezes its prey to death.

Although slow on land, the anaconda is very quick to attack its prey in water. They were informed that if any of them were to find themselves in the presence of this creature they should walk behind it (on land) and protect themselves by grabbing its head. The boa constrictor was another very large constrictor that was to be found in the forest. To prevent an attack, an interesting experiment was carried out by the guide using one of the soldiers. The soldier held the snake's attention from in front and the guide approached the snake from behind and tickled its head. This caused the boa to immediately stop hissing and spitting and become calm and docile. It was an incredible performance but a clear message was given to all: be vigilant and always be quiet and when confronted by a boa, for one's behaviour will depend on whether you live or die. Tom and Macey were asked to demonstrate "head tickling" to the other rookies. Though scared to death, they approached the snake and under the demonstrator's guidance emulated what he had done. No one else had the nerve, so there was a round of applause for their apparent lack of audacity.

Though they could do little exercise in the afternoon due to the heat and humidity, they still continued to keep fit with the various assault courses that were designed to help them prepare for their mission in the jungle. These courses were some of the most difficult that they had ever experienced. They needed to learn where best to set up camps, how to avoid predators, poisonous animals and the worst of the insects, how to look after their feet (essential in such a humid climate) and how to make fires. Though the accommodation at Regina was Spartan, the recruits were warned that the facilities in the jungle would be even more so.

After 3 weeks of instruction the group took the pirogue, which is similar to a canoe and the only means of transport down the river to their training camp. They were to inhabit the camp for the next 2 months. The camp consisted of a remote and temporary shanty with no facilities, the dwellings or huts of which were rough and crude. These were primarily hired out to soldiers or mountaineers. They were built 4 ft off the ground in order to keep the scorpions and unpalatable creepy crawlies at bay while the recruits were sleep. Everything and everyone was constantly damp, either due to the humidity or courtesy of the torrential rain, which from time to time drenched them through to the skin.

The lectures continued. It was very difficult to concentrate with the perpetual onslaught of the various insects and leaches that enjoyed feasting off the rookies. No insect repellent seemed to work at all; they actually encouraged these venomous creatures to attack at any time without reprieve.

The few times Tom went to the medical tent to be treated for sceptic bites and sores from the beasties, he came across a practical and confident but enigmatic girl called Constance, who came from Scotland. He was fascinated by her but they never really had the opportunity to talk. She found him delightful, and whenever she encountered him in the medical tent she would initiate amusing banter while she attended to his ailments. Feeling she would be a good ally and wanting to prolong their conversation, he took a deep breath and told her his story on one occasion. She became enchanted by this strong but gentle and kind soldier. He was not like the others in the elite mercenary company.

On asking about Constance's background, the sergeant was amused but happy to oblige. Tom learned that because of her ability and interest in tropical medicines, she had been sent to Guyana and assigned to the post to gain knowledge of the tropics and to learn about the diseases and repercussions for those who dwelt there.

Being bereft of women's company for so long, Tom decided – after being bitten by an especially virulent mosquito – to try and get to know her properly. He made his way up the steps into the medical tent, approaching her with his charming smile. Since he had visited the tent on a number of occasions for her to treat his ailments, he hoped that she would be pleased to see him regardless of whatever complaint he concocted. It was on this particular occasion that Tom plucked up his courage deciding that it was now or never. "You're a great nurse. How long have you been one and what on earth made you come to this god-forsaken place? I did not have much of a choice as usually I have to go where I am sent. I just cannot understand why you would choose this place. Did you specifically wish to come here?"

"Yes," responded Constance as she examined his (rather minor) bite and tried to hide a smile, guessing he had come for company rather than out of necessity. "I have always been extremely interested in tropical medicine and treating the various diseases that only exist in this part of the world. I really want to be a doctor and specialise in this field, but since I could not get grant to attend medical school the doctor whom I worked for at my home town in Scotland suggested that I come here to learn as much as I can. Hopefully he will be able to get me a scholarship at the medical school in my home town when I return."

Tom found her honesty and openness endearing. He already knew from her general banter that she was fun to spend time with. For the remainder of his time in the tropics he was a constant visitor, contriving to create as many complaints as possible in order to see her.

With all his bites and afflictions having healed, the next mission for every recruit was to be sent out on a 3-day exercise, deep into the jungle, to reconnoitre a particular area. Tom's task was to paddle up the Maroni River (an assignment known as the "death march") to scout an area about 20 miles from the camp. As well as their FAMAS assault rifle, ten bullets and a knife, the rookies were only allowed to take minimal rations, which were made up of two bottles of water and three sandwiches with fillings of ham, cheese and tomato. The rest of their food would have been found in the forest. They were reminded that there were many untold delicacies in the jungle, the tastiest of all being the humble beetle, which was full of protein and goodness. If there was any doubt about any of these delights it was suggested that the creature be put against the lips and then wait a minute to see if there was any allergic reaction in the form of rash or spots. They would then know whether or not to brave it.

One of the guidelines was to act with great stealth so that the enemy would not be able to locate their position. Map reading was a great asset, a skill Tom had learned at school while orienteering, and had applied during his national service.

Wading up the Maroni River was no picnic, the river often being infested, not only by the rubbish thrown into it, but also by the many floating human corpses, a lot of them having died from disease or else shot by the various adversaries they had encountered. It was revolting and the stench nauseating but fulfilling his mission was essential. As Tom doggedly waded through the mess, clambering over half submerged tree limbs, his foot touched upon a body that had its face downwards in the water. Usually Tom, with his sights towards his goal, would have passed on by, but something odd seemed to stop him in his passage. Gingerly turning over the body with his foot, he nearly shrieked with distaste and horror for it was a young woman, still clad in flimsy clothing but with half of her face having been eaten away, probably by fish. He knew that he could not do anything about the woman, so with minimal hesitation his mind went back into gear and he moved on. It was his duty. He would leave the corpse where it was and continue on up the river. If he survived this course, which he had every intention of doing, he would notify the military authorities when he returned. Even though he did not want to remain any longer in this area than was necessary, he felt the most honourable thing to do was to mark the spot by making an indentation on the tree just opposite the spot on the river bank. This could be identified at a later date. He could not do much more. Being in a very calm part of the river and tangled in branches, the chances of this female person being found again were not as remote as it might have seemed. He then made a mental note of exactly where he was, how many trees there were in the clearing and the distance between them, as well as the width of the river.

With mixed feelings he went on his way. He needed to erase this incident from his mind and concentrate on his mission, but found it very difficult. What on earth was a woman doing in the jungle all by herself, he wondered? Had she been travelling alone? Why had there been no search parties looking for her? How long had she been in the river? Of course there was the possibility of her dying or being killed somewhere else and dragged into the water. The perpetrator could have thought that by throwing her into the river her body would have been hidden forever, her corpse sinking in the water and being picked clean by the jungle's fauna. He might not have realized that this was a very shallow part of the river and if thrown in at night might not have seen the other bodies. If he had, he would have surmised that this attempt at duplicity had many pitfalls and chosen a deeper part of the river to hide the crime. From the actions of the attacker it would seem that he was an amateur, not really thinking out his strategy carefully enough.

Of course, thought Tom, there is always the possibility that it could have been completely innocent and the woman could have been there as part of her work, perhaps as a biologist, exploring and taking samples and specimens of the French Guyana jungle. She could have accidentally tripped, knocked herself out cold and fallen into the river. But then, of course, there would have been a search party. There had not been a whisper of anything except the cacophony of birds and buzzing of the copious number of mosquitoes that infested the air wherever one went.

Tom waded on, the river widening a little, but it was still not very deep and he therefore was able to keep his frame above water. He became very hungry and thirsty as lunchtime approached. He had his three sandwiches, but having still another two and a half days to go he reflected on whether he should capture and eat one or two of the beetles he had learned about during his jungle training. Then he would take a morsel of one of his sandwiches to hide what was sure to be a repulsive taste. He took the plunge, and stepping out of the river onto the bank spied a couple of regular beetles burrowing into the ground. With an ease he was not aware of, he picked up the beetles, throwing them into his mouth, crunching them a few time to ensure they were dead before swallowing them as quickly as possible. Then, taking a large chunk out of his first sandwich, he washed everything down with just a drop of water. That was not so bad but will that fill me up, he wondered. Since he had never encountered anyone who had partaken of these insects, he was really none the wiser. He carried on, feeling slightly better and with most of his rations still intact. He was quite pleased with himself for being able to use some of his training techniques.

With the light of the day coming to a close he knew he had to find shelter, and preferably on high ground or on a slope. This was not so easy to find but luckily, just as he was about to give up, he spied a small clearing a few feet away from the river. He built an A-frame shelter using the wood around the forest. With the poncho, which was one of the requisites all soldiers carried, he managed to make himself relatively comfortable. He took another small portion of his first sandwich after eating another two beetles, followed by another sip from one of his water bottles. Being absolutely exhausted, he soon fell into a dreamless sleep.

He awoke at first light, ravenously hungry. He removed himself from his poncho hammock and picked up another two beetles, gulped the last remaining morsel from his first sandwich, drained his first water bottle, and started once more on his way. The rest of his journey to his destination was uneventful, though his strength started to diminish with the lack of food and water towards the end.

On his arrival he checked on the area, and noted its size was approximately 270 square feet. The opening to this place was only accessible from the river, and the one structure there was a corrugated shack that stood in the corner on the far right-hand side. The area was surrounded by dark and very large trees, which were impenetrable. The only route from the camp would be by pirogue, though this would be a little difficult due to the shallow water, or by paddling, which Tom had been doing the last couple of days. He would not recommend this area for manoeuvres. He realized that his journey had taken half a day longer than intended, but this would not go against his record as long as he fulfilled his mission.

He found a good place to build his A-frame and tied up his poncho/hammock, ready for the night. As night falls almost immediately in the tropics, he was aware that he only had another 20 minutes before the dark cover of night fell over this part of the world. He had to dig up a few more nutritious beetles and consume them quickly. (He promised himself he would never denigrate a beetle again or look at them with disdain, but give them the respect they deserved. They had been his lifesavers.) He took half of his second sandwich and drank half of his second bottle of water before lying down on his hammock. Again he slept his dreamless sleep.

He awoke at sunrise, around 06.30 hours, and pondered how he would wend his way down the river. He had never been so hungry or thirsty in his life and had dropped one trouser size in this short space of time due to dehydration. Thoughts of food and water were becoming an obsession. Tom looked over his hammock and froze. A boa constrictor was slowly approaching his camp. It was nine feet away. The snake was unable to see Tom from where he was lying but he was sure he would be discovered in a very short while. Trying to remember what he and Macey had done during one of their courses, he calmed down just a fraction and thought rationally. This was the creature that could be disarmed by someone coming towards it and another from behind, tickling it on its head. He hoped it would work this time as well, but on this occasion he was totally alone. Jumping down very slowly and without a sound, Tom moved behind the shack with great stealth managed to manoeuvre himself behind the reptile. With courage he did not know he possessed, he came right up behind the head of the snake and began to tickle his head. Immediately the snake stopped its movements and became calm and docile. Though he always carried his FAMAS and knife close to his person, he had chosen the knife, for such a weapon would be much quicker and more effectual. Firing a gun might have alerted the unwelcomed adversaries to his whereabouts much earlier and he might not have been accurate. The possibility of then getting behind the creature to kill it with a knife would have been difficult. He cut off the head in one stroke, the blood spouting out all over the ground; then he sat down to recover from his ordeal, sweat pouring down his face and from every pore in his body. It was time to return. He ate his usual rations but taking a little more of his precious water than he should have done, he still being in shock. Packing up his belongings he started his journey back to the camp.

***

To his great relief nothing untoward happened on his return journey. The river still groaned under the masses of debris. Seven miles before he reached the camp he observed the tree on which he had etched a deep cut but the floating body of the woman who had been in the river was no longer there. All was still and calm, not even a breeze. Perhaps the woman's body had sunk further under the water. He gently turned the few bodies floating around him but could not find her.

Now it would be doubtful if the authorities would drag the river to look for her especially as it would be considered an accident or an incident of misadventure. It was possible too that he would not be believed. Making a mark on a tree did not prove anything. "Anyhow," he thought, "I should report it whether it is believed or not. Only then will my conscience be clear, I have nothing to lose."

With a fairly untroubled mind, but slightly puzzled by the missing body, he arrived back at the camp intact, having successfully completed his mission. Macey was waiting for him, but before being able to relax he needed to report to headquarters. He also wanted to visit the medical tent to have his feet looked at, but mostly to see Constance. After three and a half days of bites and cuts his face looked absolutely awful. Constance, as usual, was there waiting for his return. She made no comment, being professional as usual, but bathed and saw to his wounds, her heart going out to him. Although all 12 recruits had come in looking just as bedraggled and she was sorry for them, none meant as much to her as Tom. Tom longed to tell her about the dead woman and ask her advice but was unable to do so. Perhaps he would be able to speak to her when there was no one around.

He returned to have a coffee and a smoke with Macey and exchange news. Macey seemed to think that nothing could be done about the woman as she had completely disappeared, and suggested that he forget about it. However, this feeling of repulsion still persisted. Since nobody but Tom had seen his woman with only half a face, he could not expect anyone to understand, let alone sympathise with his feelings of inadequacy at not being able to do anything to solve the mystery.

He decided to speak to his commanding officer that evening, a Colonel Pradier, who was Swiss French. He was a pleasant enough guy but Tom did wonder if he had that much of an imagination. Tom ascended the steps that led to Pradier's rudimentary headquarters, his appearance slightly improved from when he had first returned but still looking as though he had faced all the elements in the universe. He knocked.

"Enter Fredriksson, what can I do for you?"

Tom took a deep breath. "Sir, I have something strange to report, and felt that it was my duty to do so."

The Colonel looked up from his desk. "Please continue."

"Sir, on my way up the Maroni River to do my reconnaissance I chanced upon a body which was lying near the edge of the river close to the forest, 7 miles from the camp. The body was face downwards in the water so I did not look especially closely at it, for as you know there are so many bodies dumped in that area. Suddenly it hit me that this corpse looked different, so I gingerly turned it over with my foot only to discover it was a young probably local woman of about 25 to 30 years of age, clad in a flimsy cotton dress, missing half her face. She was obviously no fellow biologist and was clearly not meant to be there."

Tom paused for a moment, trying to gauge the Colonel's reaction.

"Please continue Fredriksson."

"I knew I would have to return to investigate the situation but given I had a deadline to make, all I could do at the time was to mark the spot by making an indentation on the tree opposite the river so I would know where to look on my return.

"There was no current. Everything was completely calm and still in that area and was the same all the way up to the locality where I did my reconnaissance. Nothing had changed on my return except that the corpse was no longer there. I examined the few bodies floating around me and wondered whether she had sunk further into the water, but she had completely disappeared and I don't understand why."

Colonel Pradier did not say anything but a strange expression came over his face. "Thank you Fredriksson. I very much appreciate your telling me this, especially when you might have thought the information you were giving to me was just a waste of time, given that the body has disappeared.

"It is dark now, but at first light I want you to show me this spot. I will ask one of my sergeants to accompany us. Please be ready at 07.00 hours. The examination of this area will probably take all day."

With a curt goodnight he saluted Tom, who did the same and walked back to camp.

Tom was even more puzzled than before, but was glad he had not been ridiculed and made to feel stupid.

At the appointed time Tom was waiting for Colonel Pradier and the sergeant. They both had plenty of water with them in preparation for the long day ahead. Tom was familiar with the route and wondered why the excursion would take all day. All he needed to do was to show them the area where the body had lain, as well as the tree on which he had made a deep mark.

Reaching the place Tom stopped, the etching on the tree still being visible from the river bank. The same floating bodies lay motionless in the water, their seemingly not having moved at all. They had putrefied even further and the smell coming from the area was almost unbearable.

By the tree another man was standing. Pradier greeted him with a warm handshake, full of bonhomie.

They definitely know each other well, Tom reflected. Who is he? He is not wearing a uniform so he is not in the army. What is he doing here and how did he know where to meet us? Perhaps the Colonel had already communicated with him. The new arrival was then introduced to the sergeant and Tom.

"Monsieur Poupin is a forensic specialist who has come from Regina to take samples of the water where the woman was lying. Fredriksson, do you think you could locate the spot where the body was discovered as accurately as you can?"

"I will do my best Sir. The other bodies do not seem to have moved. Her body was situated just near to the right side of the river, where I was hugging the bank, hence the reason my foot touched her as I was walking along."

The newcomer took out three large jars from his rucksack and walked into the spot in the river where the alleged body was meant to have been. Tom looked on, fascinated. Poupin filled the jar. Why on earth was he doing this? Perhaps he would be privy to this stranger's behaviour and to his findings at a later date. With the second jar the forensic specialist went a little further across the stream, parallel to where the woman had lain, and took a sample of water there; and then again on the other side. Tom was completely and utterly baffled.

The journey up river had taken about an hour and the taking of samples a further hour. The jars had now been labelled, Poupin returning them to his rucksack. With a wide grin and another warm handshake, Poupin started to walk up the river to where he had parked his car, which was in a clearing on a dirt road beside the forest. This road would ultimately lead him back to Regina.

Colonel Pradier, the sergeant and Tom started wading down the river towards the camp, taking less time to reach the camp than the upward journey. The colonel did not share any of the reasons for Poupin's appearance or information about his behaviour with Tom, who felt rather miffed at being excluded, especially as he had initiated the whole enterprise. After a while, Tom could not keep quiet another moment. "Sir, since I alerted you to this situation of the dead woman in the river, do you think you could possibly let me know what is going on?"

The Colonel hesitated for a moment, gave a little sigh and answered, "This is classified, Fredriksson, and all I can tell you, even though you did start this investigation, is that it is drug related, there being a large drug cartel in this area. We have to be most vigilant in keeping this under wraps. I cannot give you any more information and I trust that you will not discuss this with any of your colleagues."

Tom and company arrive at their base at around 14.00 hours, Tom picking up something to eat and having a small siesta before joining the other recruits for some more manoeuvres. Their stay in the jungle was coming to an end, the 12 having learned survival in one of the most challenging places on earth.

Later that evening Tom went in search of Constance. He hoped that she was home in her little shack for he was desperate to speak to her about what had happened. Even though he had been forbidden to discuss the incident with any of his mates, including Macey, he needed to find some answers to this quandary and was sure that she would be able to help.

Constance was sitting in her hut reading up on tropical medicine. She was delighted to see Tom, bidding him to come in and find a pew. "Hello Tom, may I help you or is this a social visit?"

Constance always made him smile. "It is both," he answered. "I'm always happy to see you, but I also have a dilemma that I wondered if you could help me with." He proceeded to explain about the dead woman in the water, her disappearance, and Colonel Pradier's need to have a forensic specialist collect specimens of the water. "Don't you think that is a bit strange?"

She looked slightly alarmed by this story, but realised that Tom did not have a clue what it was all about except for the fact that it was drug related. She was a little unsure as to whether she should tell him what she knew. "Tom, what I am going to tell you is classified and it must go no further than here. The woman in the river probably had drugs attached to her. She probably became dispensable to the drug lords, was eliminated and thrown into a much deeper part of the river, their hoping that she would not resurface in the near future. She must have been weighed down with salt. As she was slightly built they probably expected her to surface when the salt had dissolved, which would take about a week or 10 days at the most. Then having, or so they thought, estimated the correct time for the body to surface, the rest of the gang would receive a message to pick the woman's corpse up and remove the drugs. Unfortunately for them it appears things went wrong and the woman floated down stream to the shallow area where you found her. During the course of the 2 days you were on your reconnaissance mission, the perpetrators must have finally discovered the body, taken the drugs and removed the body."

"Why did they need to remove the body?"

Constance replied gently. "As you thought, a strange woman lying dead in a river is more than just a coincidence. No woman is ever seen in this area, except for those collecting specimens and fauna and myself. She would probably have had a companion with her as well. If she had gone missing there would undoubtedly have been a search party out looking for her."

Tom, taking in this information started looking at Constance in a different light, realising that there was far more to her than he had thought.

"How do you know all this?"

"I have been in this part of the world for quite a long time now and have collected quite a lot of data of the area as well as learning about the seedier side of it. I am a listener rather than a talker and people like to unburden themselves and tell me their problems."

Tom trying to piece all this together continued, "Why then was this Monsieur Poupin collecting water in three different jars?"

"As this is a 'fresh water' stream, rather a joke since the water is so horribly polluted, I believe he was checking to see whether there was any salt in it."

Tom began to realise the implications of it all. "That's why he was checking to see if there was any salt near the body and comparing it with the other areas too."

"Yes," she nodded.

"Then the forensic specialist will return to Regina and check each bottle."

"Yes."

"What then?"

"If there is salt in the first bottle they will know a crime has been committed, for it will not be the first time drugs have been hidden in this way. In fact the authorities are well aware that this has happened on many occasions. The criminals probably think they have got away with it, especially as there was no one around when they picked up the body."

"What do you think they did with the body?" he inquired.

"Probably dragged it a short way from the riverbank on a make shift stretcher and buried or dismembered and scattered it."

"Would that be easy to locate?"

"Probably not," she answered.

"Is there a chance that these men will be found and prosecuted?" Tom asked hopefully.

"The police will now look for tracks through the jungle."

"I noticed that Monsieur Poupin exited the jungle by road near the river."

"Then that is the way they probably left."

"The authorities must have a list of the men who deal in narcotics, so it could be narrowed down to just a handful. Couldn't it?

"I am sure that is a probability."

"Do you think I might be called to testify?" Tom pondered aloud.

"I doubt it. I don't think the Colonel would want the Legion to be involved."

"I wonder if I will ever know the outcome."

Constance smiled. "You might read it in the newspaper."

Tom burst out laughing. "How fatuous that sounds."

"Seriously Tom, you do not want to be involved. These men are very dangerous and if they knew you had anything to do with it their henchmen would come after you."

"Thank you. I know nothing! Thank you also for putting me in the picture. I would have been baffled for a very long time and never been any the wiser. You are a great girl and a lovely one too." Constance, delighted with the compliment, blushed a faint rosy colour.

"I must go, see you soon."

He went down the steps but not before bending down to plant a lingering kiss on her lips. Constance held her hand to her lips not wanting the feeling to disappear. Tom was bursting with happiness. What a wonderful person she was.

***

The next day, two days before returning to Corsica, Tom awoke exhausted and dehydrated, drenched with sweat from top to toe, shivering so violently that he could not move a muscle in his body and with a temperature of over 40°C. Every muscle in his body ached, and he was at the end of his tether. How was he going to be able to function and to be compos mentis for the remaining couple of days in this Guyanese jungle? He had been stretched beyond endurance with the heat, humidity, darkness, snakes and mosquitoes, not counting the incessant cacophony of birds and insects. The jungle was a place he never wanted to see again, let alone even talk about. Part of him, trying to be positive about the situation, had got to thinking it would be an interesting and challenging place to exercise his skills and perhaps receive his stripes. His biggest and greatest joy had been to meet Constance, but really could there be a future with her? He just did not know. The sergeant in charge soon became aware of Tom's predicament and asked Macey to take him into the hospital tent so that he could be thoroughly checked out for suspected malaria. Although the Foreign League is an extremely harsh organisation and pushes its recruits to the limit, a wounded or ill soldier is taken the greatest care of and receives the best medical attention.

It had been 2 and a half years since Macey and Tom had first met each other, and they constantly looked out for one another. Even though Tom had a very high temperature, he found he was still able to test the waters of their friendship. Now there was the real possibility of Tom being able to defect. He and Macey had often talked about this moment, and it was now time to act. Macey had promised himself that he would complete the 5 years regardless of the hardships as he had chosen to be a Legionnaire.

On arriving at the hospital tent, Tom knew he would be given a urine test to determine whether he had an infection. The hospital tent was a very basic construction, so the luxury of having a separate cubicle to oneself was unheard of, which made the act that much harder. Tom was given a receptacle by the doctor but was unsure whether he would be able to produce much urine, as being constantly dehydrated his kidneys had to work overtime. As it happened, he had been given more liquid since he had been brought in and had to wait a fair amount of time before he was seen. He managed to obtain a sharp needle when the doctor's back was turned and hid is on one of his back pockets, embedded in the material and undetected by his superiors. Tom dipped his finger into his pocket, piercing himself on the needle as he did so, and let a drop of blood from his finger fall into the container.

He made a concerted effort to hide his bloodied finger in case it was seen by any of the medical staff. After completing this seemingly mammoth task, he lay back onto the bed he had been resting on, exhausted, and fell into a deep sleep. Constance, seeing Tom lying incapacitated conjured up memories of her father during his final illness; he had always been the kindest and most considerate of people, and Tom reminded her of this paragon of gentleness. While Tom was receiving blood and urine tests for possible infections, the corporals decided that since there were only 2 days left of their tour of duty in the tropical forest, it might be wiser to pack up the camp and head back to Corsica.

The remaining 11 rookies who had been on the exercise were ecstatic and incredibly relived to be returning to civilisation after 2 months of such hardships. Not one of the recruits, including the colonel and sergeant, was dismayed at leaving the jungle 2 days earlier than expected, though they were most concerned about Tom and hoped that they would reach Corsica before his condition worsened.

While the medical team packed up its supplies in the makeshift tent, the company collected all of its gear, and headed up to the river where a few motorised pirogues were awaiting them. The recruits reached the River Approuage with great shouts of glee in anticipation of the journey home in an air-conditioned aeroplane. They were returning to civilization! It was 20 miles up the river to Regina, a much harder trip than on descent to this remote camp, which was close to the Brazilian border. These mostly fair-skinned novices, though skilled and well trained recruits of the League, had been pushed to the limits of survival without their being repercussions. There was not an inch of uncovered skin that had not been bitten by mosquitoes and other insects. Everyone's skin looked like a lumpy mass of open sores. These were impossible to treat in this moist and humid environment. The ingrained dirt in everyone's pores disguised them in such a way that not even their mothers would have recognised them.

Tom was carried on a stretcher and placed very gently in the bottom of one of the pirogues. It was very important that he be given the greatest care and safe conduct out of the Guyanese jungle and on the way back to Corsica. He, although weak, was feeling better, but had to continue with the charade. There was a fear on the part of those in charge that this soldier might die from a serious kidney disease, which would create an enormous amount of paperwork and lead to serious admonition from their superiors.

They reached the outskirts of Regina, where the main airport of Guyana is located, to be met by an ancient army bus that would take the soldiers to the airport. Even though they attempted to clean themselves up, it would take many more hot showers and masses of soap to remove the grime and filth from 2 months in the rain forests and to return to the pristine and immaculate soldiers of the French Foreign Legion.

Constance was anxious for Tom's safety as the army bus wound itself round the poorly tarmac roads, which led to the airport. Tom had always been a favourite with the medical staff, so she knew that he would be taken great care of.

The airport came into sight, a modern building of white stone, which belied the poverty and deprivation of the country's people. The members of the Legion alighted from the bus and in an organised fashion marched to the plane, papers in order, and soon they were on their way to Corsica.

CHAPTER 17

Return to Corsica

The recruits reclined their seats on the plane, a beer in one hand and a cigarette in the other. They were going home. The French Foreign Legion had been their family over the past 2½ years. They were secure in the knowledge that without any ties they did not need to concern themselves with wondering when the next meal was coming from or thinking about what clothes to buy or pondering whether or not they would be able to pay their taxes. They had no idea what their next mission would be. It did not matter. They had left the forest and all its mosquitoes, insects, snakes, noisy birds, heat, humidity and lack of amenities. Even though many of their missions had been tough and certainly not easy, this last one did not need repeating. If any of them had had a choice, it was an operation that they would prefer never to relive.

Tom was gently transported to the plane on a stretcher carried by two colleagues from his platoon. They were anxious that Tom should not suffer any more than he was already. Although Tom still had a high fever, he was enjoying the comfort and care he was being given.

On arrival at Campo dell Oro Airport in Corsica, Tom was the first to descend the aircraft steps, being carried to an ambulance waiting to drive him to Miserecorde Hospital on the island. He still had the needle embedded in his trouser pocket, and would use it whenever necessary. His concern was that that when he reached the hospital he would be undressed and placed in a hospital gown. For this reason, he knew that his needle would have to be hidden in another place.

Luckily, when he arrived at the hospital he was able to conceal the needle in his hand until he was able to plant it in a pocket of his hospital gown and thread it into the material. He had hoped that Macey would be able to accompany him, but Macey's responsibilities were at Calvi and he had no option but to return.

Tom was placed in a single room while two other patients, who were also waiting to be examined for blood-related conditions, were sat in another. One of these patients, Hans, was a close mate of his, being one of the recruits he had met on his first day in Marseilles.

Every day Tom had to give a urine sample, which he managed to contaminate each time by pricking his finger and dropping the fresh blood into the bottle. The doctors were becoming alarmed at not being able to diagnose the problem and kept a close watch over him. On the fourth day, after having already given a urine sample in the morning, a couple of male nurses entered the ward. "Would you please give us a further sample by peeing into this receptacle?" they requested.

"I gave you a sample this morning, why do I need to give you another?"

"Please do not be difficult. We are doing this for your own good so we can get to the bottom of your condition," one said.

Tom was petrified. How was he going to put some blood into the fresh sample when the nurses were standing by watching? "Can't I have a little privacy? It is not always easy to perform on tap."

"Don't be ridiculous. Don't waste our time." They were dismissive of his possible discomfort.

Suddenly there was a large crash from the next room, which sent the nurses running in to see what had transpired. In that split second Tom jabbed his finger on the pin harder than usual and at the same time peed into the cup. Tom had managed to give a fairly acceptable sample by the time the nurses had returned. Tom did not know what had caused the commotion in his friend's room. Either it was an extremely welcome coincidence, or Hans had realised that Tom was faking it and had created this charade to distract the nurses. He thought the latter was more likely and was overwhelmed by the comradeship of his fellow recruit, who had saved him from an extremely difficult situation. He had told Macey of his abduction a long time before but was not aware that anybody else knew of his desire to escape.

Unable to solve the problem of Tom's blood disorder, the doctor in charge intimated to the commanding officer that unless the Legion was willing to accept a very seriously soldier it would be better if he were sent to Marseilles to be seen by a haematologist specialising in blood disorders. Perhaps the haematologist would be able to diagnose this condition when the doctors on the island had failed. The colonel in charge, de Cannière, was sceptical of Tom's strange illness. Having observed him from a distance, de Cannière felt that once again this man wanted to abscond from the Legion. Despite this, he could not prove it or understand why. Tom was a bright and popular soldier, being very capable and brave. He could go far in the Legion, so why the need to escape? He had never had a conversation with Tom but had watched him on the side-lines, so was not privy to his thoughts and concerns. Perhaps his special mate, Macey, would have the answers; but this was an area upon which de Cannière could not intrude.

Colonel de Cannière had to sign the papers to release him from his duties at the French Foreign League until further notice and to allow him to board the Hercules military plane that would fly him to Marseilles for treatment. Arriving 2 hours later at Marseille Airport, the plane was met by an ambulance, which was to take him to the military hospital specialising in blood disorders. The build up of traffic and the stopping and starting of the vehicle en route to the hospital led Tom to initially consider bolting from the ambulance, but after a minute, realising that he had neither money nor any travel papers on him, he did not give it a further thought. A motorcycle policeman approached the driver of the ambulance, asking him whether it was an emergency and did the driver want a police escort to the hospital. The ambulance driver confirming that indeed he did want assistance, the policeman put on his flashing lights and siren and escorted the vehicle through the busy streets to Laveran Military Hospital. This hospital was especially adapted for military personnel. Arriving in record time, Tom was ushered into the haematology section and placed in a single room to wait to be seen. It was most fortunate that while Tom was being wheeled into his room he recognised the voice of one of his friends, Harry, coming from the next room. This gave Tom a sense of relief, for he was in great need of support and hoped that he would have some assistance in trying to escape. He was, however, a little sceptical about this. First of all Harry might not be strong enough to help him physically (he did not know why his friend was in the hospital), and second Harry could, by now, have an inbuilt loyalty to the Legion and therefore not want to aid and abet a deserter. Most of his colleagues must have been au fait with Tom's previous attempt at desertion, and he had to consider that they may not want to get involved.

Since this was a military hospital, the walls were built to a height of 10 ft. There was a link of barbed wire snaking around the walls of the compound, making it virtually impossible for anybody to climb over. Tom seeing this from the window in his room wondered what chance he had of being able to escape. A doctor appeared in the late afternoon to examine him, but thankfully did not ask any questions that could not be answered and did not give him any more tests.

During the period he had been in the Legion, Tom had had intermittent contact with his parents, though only to let them know that he was alive and well. Other than that he gave them little information about his escapades. They would be worried if they had known what had really happened to him and there would have been nothing that they could have done. With his papers being accurately forged, nobody would have believed him and he would not have been able to prove otherwise. Thus, he considered that escape was his only option and he was once again prepared to contemplate this regardless of the outcome. This time, though the plans were not fool proof: there was only a 50–50 chance that it might work.

That night when all was quiet in the hospital, except for a faint rush of water in the pipes and distant electronic bleeping from a machine in another room, Tom - with the few francs he had saved for such an eventuality (tucked into the sole of his left shoe) – crept down to the lobby where a pay phone was hanging on the wall. Nobody was around. He dialled his parents' number in Sweden and gave a quiet sigh of relief as the ringing on the line ceased as his mother picked up the receiver at the other end.

"Mamma, it's me, Tom."

"Tom, where are you?" His mother's voice was full of concern, so without preamble Tom explained exactly what had happened to him and where he was. "I shall try and get over the wall early tomorrow afternoon during visiting hours. As yet I have no idea how I will be able to do it. I am hoping there will be so many people milling around that it will not be too obvious that I am not in my room. I do not have a clue as to when this will be, but do you think you could be prepared to be outside between 2 and 5 pm? If I don't make it, could you repeat your visit every day between those hours until I do?"

"We shall be there and every day until you do manage to escape. We have arranged to stay with your Aunt Anna, who is renting a flat fairly near the hospital, so at least we shall have a base where we can stay for the moment."

"Thank you Mamma. Love to you and Pappa. Hope to see you both soon."

Tom slipping back to his room was not that concerned about being overheard: first he had been speaking fairly quietly and secondly he had been speaking Swedish, a language that not that many people were familiar with. Despite this, someone was awake and heard him sneak back into his bedroom.

CHAPTER 18

Christer Ziegler

Ziegler stood at the departure gate, his mind wandering off into the distance. Just watching Carlos go through passport control, still in his disguise, to board the plane to London gave him a sense of loneliness and emptiness. What had he done with his life except devote his life to the Foreign Legion and become a lawyer? His parents had died in their 40s, he had no siblings, and very few cousins with whom he had any contact.

After retiring and returning to Germany from Corsica the year before, Christer had had this persistent feeling of not belonging anywhere. The Legion had been his family for 30 years, rising to the ranks of colonel while studying and practicing law at the same time. He had been there a long time. He was now tired and needed to slow down a little. Germany was back on its feet after the war years but still had the East to contend with. What a shambles. He never understood how the USA, France, Britain and the USSR could create a situation where all the Eastern Bloc countries were captives behind a wall patrolled by men carrying guns. Having journeyed through East Germany recently, he felt the people's dissatisfaction and unhappiness at being closed in by patrolled guards, their poverty, and also their separation from their loved ones in the West.

He had not done much travelling since returning from Corsica, but now he had a strong urge to go to Scotland to meet up with Carlos again, to find out more about this man and to meet his sister, Françoise. He was fascinated by this woman who had fought with the Resistance during the Second World War as a young girl, but he did not know much more about her. The fact they had fought on opposite sides did not lessen the respect he felt for any adversary who had fought for his or her country – quite the opposite in fact. Any person who honourably fought so valiantly was an admirable person.

Before Carlos left West Germany for Scotland, Ziegler had asked him whether he could kindly pass on his new address, in case Ziegler wished to get in touch with either him or Françoise in the future. Carlos did this soon after his arrival in Scotland, saying that he would never be able to thank him enough for all that he had done. For the last year he had heard nothing further from him. Valerian had rung him to confirm that everything had gone to plan, which of course Ziegler knew from Carlos' report. He did not discuss du Pont with Valerian, but told him that he had been very helpful in locating Carlos, and assisting him in the escape from the Stasi police. He never knew what had happened to du Pont. He was pretty sure that he had been waylaid on a dark night and executed. The Stasi had no time for weaklings or people who were enemies of the State. He did not know what might have happened to the wife in such circumstances.

Ziegler made a decision to visit Scotland and contacted a couple of travel agents who gave him information on many of the beautiful places to visit in Edinburgh. It was summer and pleasantly warm. He had written to Carlos and Françoise asking them if he could visit them in Aberdeen. They were naturally delighted, Françoise especially, as she was intrigued to meet the man instrumental in helping liberate of her brother. She was, however, rather puzzled that he should wish to spend time with them. She knew that he was an ex-Legionnaire. This was an interesting fact, considering her daughter Constance was presently nursing the mosquito-bitten young Legion recruits in French Guyana. At least they would have something to talk about.

Ziegler took an early flight to London Heathrow a week later, stopping over for just an hour before continuing his journey to Edinburgh. He discovered the city of Edinburgh to be quite elegant, with wonderful historical buildings, interesting art galleries, and magnificent castle dominating the skyline from its position on top of an extinct volcanic rock. He also found the people charming and friendly. He felt he could live in this part of the world.

He stayed in the city for three days and nights before taking a train up to Aberdeen, which was situated right up in the north of the country in the Grampian Mountains. It was a long journey but he enjoyed the coastal trip by train instead of taking an aeroplane from A to B.

Ziegler was met at Aberdeen train station by Françoise and Carlos. Their little Morris Minor was parked nearby. With Carlos having shed the disguise that du Pont had so cleverly manufactured for him a year before, Ziegler was interested to finally see the real Carlos, who was unrecognisable from East Germany. He was of medium height, slim and extremely fit looking with an air of contentment written all over him. Gone were the moustache, fake eyebrows and the mass of curly grey hair. His hair was grey and he was balding. He still retained the large dark brown eyes and long eyelashes Ziegler remembered. The mouth, having been made to look small and mean to completely change his appearance, was now revealed as being warm and generous.

"Petercalter is a small village about 50 minutes drive from here. It is inland, so one does not get the biting wind from the North Sea so much. It is not the warmest of places to live but we are very happy here," explained Françoise.

Ziegler understood that the feeling of peace and tranquillity here was the complete opposite of what he was used to, but he felt happier than he had been for a long time. As they neared Françoise's home, he observed that the road was lined with green plane trees and there was a mass of summer flowers in the gardens that had recently come into bloom. The weather in this part of the world was a little behind the rest of the UK, but it was beautiful and serene.

As they approached the house he noticed that it was set back from the road with a semi-circular driveway, the only one in the vicinity. The small house was a picturesque vision of the old world, with high ceilings and wooden beams. The small cosy rooms were decorated in magnolia, the Chippendale furniture enhancing many of the rooms. The beautiful glass pieces, which had been passed down by Bernard's family, added to the effect. The ambience of the home and garden gave Ziegler a sense of belonging, something that had eluded him for a large part of his life.

The back garden, he later discovered, was in a realm of its own. It boasted about half an acre, with most of the garden covered with grass. Three magnificent ash trees, intertwined in harmony, stood proudly in the middle of the lawn. When warm enough guests would sit under the trees for hours, reading, drawing or just contemplating. Large spruce trees circled the garden, with a combination of annuals and perennials having been planted in the flowerbeds.

Ziegler stayed with Françoise and Carlos much longer than intended. They were delightful company. After just 1 year Carlos had regained the confidence that he had lost in East Germany and was full of anecdotes about the past. He also regaled them with funny stories of the Stasi. Ziegler realised what an amazing sense of humour Carlos had, added to the fact that he could so quickly open up to discuss his previous masters without any rancour or bitterness. Ziegler was most impressed, considering Carlos a remarkable man. One had to remember that Carlos had been a key figure in the Belgian Intelligence and had probably needed to be resilient, but nevertheless the way he was able to recall his time, and conduct himself after everything he had been through, was truly admirable.

Françoise had a lovely temperament, as well as being a handsome woman. She was in her early 50s but her looks and behaviour belied any of the toughness that she might have acquired from her experiences during the war and since her husband had died. Ziegler was taken with her the first moment he laid eyes on her. They spent a while discussing the French Foreign Legion and the repercussions of becoming a Legionnaire during the 1970s. Françoise mentioned her daughter, Constance, and proudly outlined her achievements and what she wanted to do in the future. Françoise explained to Ziegler, "I believe she has met a young man in French Guyana of whom she has become very fond. She has not said a lot about him, but I have a feeling from her sporadic letters that it is quite serious. She will be back at the end of this year, but he still has another 2 ½ years of service to complete. I do not know how it will resolve itself."

"Do you know his name, for I was in the League during this time?" Ziegler grabbed onto the possibility that he could help this woman in some way.

"She only mentions the name Tom. I do not know him by any other name."

"Love always finds a way. When you are young you can resolve anything."

"Do you really believe that Herr Ziegler?" He was a little taken aback but very pleased that she seemed to value his opinion. "Very much so, and please call me Christer. May I call you Françoise?

"With the greatest of pleasure," Françoise replied, smiling.

He spent just under a week in this serene area of Northeast Scotland, very much wishing that he could stay longer. Nevertheless, he knew that he should not outstay his welcome. He was also aware that the work at his law practice was piling up and he needed to return. He was given a delicious dinner on the eve of his departure and the following morning he took the train down to Edinburgh, from there catching a plane to London and then to West Berlin. He felt rejuvenated, sensing that something good was waiting round the corner. Ziegler had invited both Françoise and Carlos to visit him in West Berlin in the early autumn, when he could show them around. Carlos was not especially enamoured at revisiting Germany, even though it was on the west side, and very politely declined the invitation. He also thought that it would be good for Françoise to be able to have Ziegler's undivided attention. It did not seem that Ziegler had had many female friends over the years, having been "married" to the French Foreign Legion for so long. He had certainly been smitten by her, it was written all over his face, but Carlos was not sure whether his sister reciprocated Ziegler's feelings. Only time would tell.

***

Having a week's holiday due to her, Françoise travelled to West Berlin by the same route that Ziegler had done on his home journey in the summer. She was enchanted by West Berlin and how it had been renovated and reconstructed into this modern and thriving city after the terrible bombings it had received 30 years earlier. She felt slightly strange, being in the company of man other than her husband, but at the same time comfortable and content. She had not thought that she could or would have ever felt the same again with another man. She stayed at his comfy apartment in the southwest of the city. It was a typical bachelor flat, but very elegant with beautiful furnishings.

Ziegler's lovemaking was gentle and considerate, and she was surprised how passionate she could be after so many years. It had been a long time since she had given any thought to lovemaking, it having vanished with Bernard's death. They spent a week together, seeing all the sights during the day, taking walks around the parks and gardens, dining out at enchanting restaurants in the evening, and even going to see Don Giovanni at the Berlin State Opera (Unter den Linden). What a wonderful week it was.

With a heavy heart she returned home to Scotland to once again resume her bookkeeping job at the travel agent. Ziegler went back to work, his memories of the lovely Françoise Murray still fresh in his memory. He did not know when they would meet up again. Soon it would be Christmas and her daughter would be returning home from French Guyana. He would love to be able to spend Christmas with them all, but he did not feel he could intrude and as yet had not been invited. Apparently Constance had been devoted to her father and might not welcome a new man in her mother's life. Ziegler was intrigued to know more about this young man in the Legion that Constance was interested in and thought he might do a little research on him. If he was in Guyana, he could quite easily identify which branch of the Legion he was in by checking which one was based there at the present time. He rang through to headquarters in Marseilles and was informed that although no one was there at the moment, the second parachute regiment in Corsica had recently returned from French Guyana, having being on a commandos course to teach them the how to survive in the jungle.

That is interesting, he thought. Being my platoon I should know most of the recruits there but I don't know anybody named Tom. I only know the men by their surnames. He pondered over this for a while but did not come up with any satisfactory answer. Perhaps if he met the daughter he could get a better description of Tom and surmise who he was. He reflected from experience, however, that he should tread very carefully and not interfere in matters of the heart.

CHAPTER 19

The Brazilian rainforest

Due to the Foreign Legion returning to Corsica earlier than expected, Constance was unable to complete her 1-year study in tropical medicine in French Guyana. Since she still had another 3 months left of her contract, the chief medical officer in Guyana recommended that she be transferred to the forests of the Amazon in Brazil. She was due back in Scotland at Christmas, where she hoped Dr Duncan would keep his word and help her enrol as a medical student at the Aberdeen hospital where she had trained as a nurse. She hoped he had not forgotten. She had diligently sent him regular reports on the activities and accompanying diseases of the area, which she believed would be of interest to him.

Constance was disappointed that the placement in French Guyana had ended as early as it had done, as 3 months was not a very long time to get established in a new place and learn the ropes. Not only was it most unsettling, but Tom had suddenly disappeared from her life and been transferred to another land. She was not able to forget him; he was not a passing fancy that would disappear like a puff of smoke. He had made a lasting impression on her and she was desperate to know how he was and whether she would see him again. She knew his last name was Fredriksson, but not the name he was born with or where he came from in Sweden as he had kept that information from her. She sensed that there was something preying on his mind, which seemed to trouble him despite his often cheerful disposition, but she had never had enough time to find out what it was. She had a strong feeling that Tom might not return to the Legion and would then disappear into thin air. Would she ever find him? She made a decision to write to Macey at the Legion in Corsica when she reached Brazil to see whether he had any information about Tom, but she had a strong suspicion that he would not be there. With a heavy heart Constance packed her bags and took a pirogue alongside the other nurses up the river to the airport at Regina. The other nurses took a plane back to London, while she flew off to Brazil, her destination being Manaus, one of the larger cities in the north of the country and situated in the state of the Amazonas. Though Guyana was located next to Brazil, flying to Manaus was the quickest and easiest way to get there. She realised that she was the only nurse whose term had been extended, though some of them had arrived before her. She had been informed before she left that she had great potential and being transferred to Brazil was confirmation of this. As she was not au fait with the Portuguese language, it was suggested that she stop in Manaus to take a crash course, otherwise she would find it almost impossible to give advice and help to the Brazilian military when required.

Arriving at the Eduard Gomes International Airport, she took a taxi to a tourist hotel that had been recommended to her in the centre of the city. Her intention was to find a suitable language school she could comfortably walk to and from every day. It was a very large city with lots to do and apparently very safe, but being a single woman she did not think it advisable to venture out at night. She was not at all concerned about missing out on the night life, for she needed to master Portuguese as quickly as she could. After her daily lessons and the homework she needed to present the next day, she felt that she would be too tired to do anything else.

Almost immediately after her arrival she discovered a highly recommended language school, which was located only 15 minutes walk from the hotel. The lessons started at 8 am and finished at 3 pm as most Brazilians had a siesta in the afternoon, it being far too hot to work.

The hotel was comfortable and the food sufficient, but she was not expecting any more. The grant she had been allocated was not enormous but adequate for her needs. At breakfast time a couple of days after starting her course, while checking on some verbs she was learning to conjugate, a young and very attractive man approached her table. "Sorry for disturbing you. May I ask what you are doing?"

He spoke excellent English, his polite and charming manner and knowledge of English being a breath of fresh air to a woman in a strange and foreign environment.

"Please join me. I have been bereft of speaking my language since I arrived and learning Portuguese is harder than I thought."

The man smiled. "Would you like me to help you?"

"That would be so helpful. I do have a very good knowledge of French and a working knowledge of Spanish, but Portuguese eludes me with its different sounds. My tongue keeps getting tied up in knots."

"May I introduce myself? My name is Clemente da Silva and I am staying here for a short while before proceeding into the rainforest," the man said as he took a chair opposite Constance.

"Are you really? I am going in that direction too, but I need to stay here until I have endeavoured to master this confounded language. Are you an explorer?"

"No, no," he laughed kindly, "I'm heading there to meet up with some military personnel. The base I'm headed to is stationed about 9 miles from the centre of the city." He gently took her exercise book in his hand as though to study it and noticed her name on the cover.

"Don't worry, Constance. May I call you Constance? Your name was written on the front of your exercise book. I shall help you with the pronunciation and you can speak to me with that wonderful English lilt you have. The notes of a sonata seem to resonate from your throat every time you utter a word." Constance realised that he was flirting with her but she was totally unconcerned.

"I am Scottish not English. I have lived in Scotland all my life, but by birth I am Belgian." She smiled back at him and continued, "Are you always so profuse with your compliments to young strange women or is it just part of the charming characteristics that you Brazilians seem to have?"

"No, I am struck by how you look, the way you speak, and very much admire your tenacity for travelling alone in this part of the world. Are you planning to venture into the rainforest?"

"I have just come from French Guyana, so I am familiar with the landscape of the jungle and all its idiosyncrasies. Except for trying to explain myself in Portuguese to the authorities and help the wounded, I do not have any concerns about myself."

"What do you intend to do on your return to Scotland?" queried Clemente.

"I am hoping that the doctor who recommended me for this mission has made arrangements for me to enter the main hospital in Aberdeen as a trainee doctor. That is what I would really like."

Changing the subject Constance inquired. "What do you do then and what is your interest in the rainforest?"

"I buy and sell life-saving products to be exported to developed countries. Do you know much about the Amazon and what a fascinating place it is?" he asked.

She thought for a moment of how little she knew about the Amazon. "I studied a little at school, but there was no chance of doing any extra study in French Guyana. My time was taken up looking after all the attendant ailments that the soldiers managed to accumulate, as well as studying all the various diseases in that part of the world."

He responded earnestly. "If you wish to be an expert on tropical medicine, working in the Amazon will be a perfect eye-opener for all future studies." He went on to give her some facts, being an enthusiastic advocate of the area. "Did you know that 80% of the developed world's diet originates in the rainforest, which includes 3,000 different kinds of fruits, vegetables and many types of spices and nuts? One-hundred-and-twenty-one prescription drugs that are currently sold worldwide are based on substances discovered in the rainforest. A fifth of the world's fresh water is in the Amazon Basin. The rainforest also recycles carbon dioxide, producing 20% of the world's oxygen." He seemed extremely passionate about the subject.

"There is so very much more, but I will leave you to read up on this yourself. I have a very informative book, in

English, in my room, which you might find illuminating. I will drop it off at the reception, if you wish me to?"

She liked Clemente but was not prepared to enter into a new relationship. She also feared that he was not quite what he appeared to be. She had always been an independent person and had become discerning about the people whom she had met over the years. He was far too charming and she did not trust such men. She decided she would watch him. Constance was not beyond believing that he had already researched her moves and had bought a book on the Amazon to get closer to her. People could be so conniving.

During the next 2 weeks she worked hard at mastering the Portuguese language and in the end had a reasonable grasp of it. She was quite pleased with herself. Clemente continued to join her at breakfast and help her with the grammar and pronunciation, but otherwise she saw little of him during the day; she being at school and he going about his business, whatever that was.

Clemente invited her out in the evenings on more than one occasion but she had declined on the pretext that she had too much work to do, her real intention being to keep as much distance from him as possible. On the Thursday, the day before they were both due to leave the hotel and travel by boat up the Negro River to the military compound, she developed a very unpleasant stomach bug. She rarely became ill but although not enjoying the symptoms, Constance was relieved that she could refuse his persistent suggestions of a night out on the town.

She did not feel 100% the next day but was relieved that on passing her room after breakfast, Clemente offered to carry her heavy case down to the lobby. "Thank you, I would appreciate it. I just have to check a few things to see that I have not left anything behind and I will be down in a minute."

Clemente, however, had another agenda. Walking very quickly to the nearest gentlemen's cloakroom, which was situated just near the lifts, he moved into the largest cubicle taking the two cases with him. Removing some very valuable papers from the bottom of his case, he transferred them into Constance's case. A maid coming into clean the men's room nearly bumped into Clemente as he was moving the papers, for as the cubicle was too small to accommodate two open cases he was unable to completely close the door. Clemente gave a little start on seeing the maid but, being able to turn the charm on at a moment's notice, gave her a very warm smile and walked slowly out of the cloakroom to the lift as though nothing untoward had happened. Not actually seeing that anything improper had happened, the maid felt there was nothing to report and forgot the incident.

Clemente arrived in the lobby just before Constance, who paid her bill with the cruzeiros she had brought with her. With Clemente still carrying the two cases they left the hotel, winding their way towards the Negro River to hire one of the outboard powerboats that would take them into the rainforest where the air-force base was stationed. These boats were specially constructed to combat any obstacle, whether getting through swamps or under overhanging trees in the forest. This form of conveyance was the least expensive and Constance and Clemente were quite content to take this means of transport, Constance herself having become familiar with the pirogue in French Guyana.

The military compound they were heading for was situated in a jungle region where the Brazilian Army's 12th military region was located. By boat it would take approximately 30 minutes, depending upon the various obstructions en route. As the boat motored on up the River Negro, Constance thoroughly enjoyed the scenery and the gentle breeze that caressed her face as it sailed along. It had been so humid in the city that this was a wonderful change and she was relieved that she had finally reached this place and had, in fact, learned enough Portuguese to communicate with any native of Brazil, though she was not as yet fluent. That would take a while.

Thoughts of Tom still plagued her, but the pain of leaving him dimmed as the days passed by. She would resume her search for him on her return. She had written to Macey to ask whether he knew anything about Tom's whereabouts, but Macey had not received any news from him. He only knew that Tom had been transferred to Marseilles, where there were more qualified doctors with knowledge of blood disorders. Macey did not tell Constance of Tom's plan of escape. He would let Tom tell her all of this when he was next in touch with her.

As predicted, the journey did not take much longer than half an hour. On arrival a car was waiting to take them to the airfield where they were both checked out for any illegal contraband. This particular base had been created in 1970 but there had been a terrible accident there only a year later when one of the engines had burst into flames and 16 people had been killed. No other disaster had occurred since then. The military's responsibility, due to the vastness of the area, was to protect the borders, patrol and defend them. A lot of funding was needed to carry out this objective, as well as a lot of manpower. "This is going to be on a much larger scale than in Guyana so I do hope that a great number of nurses have been employed for such a considerable enterprise," Constance thought to herself.

At the compound she was introduced to the senior laboratory technician, Raphael Fonsceca, who took her on a tour of the area as well as introducing her to the other nurses. They were all Brazilian except for one slight and wiry nurse, called Claudine, who was French. Constance was pleased that there was at least one person with whom she could communicate in her second language and at a fluent level. Claudine seemed a happy person and greeted her with a very warm handshake. The other nurses looked on rather warily. There are always problems when the language is alien from one's own, but Constance was determined to spend these last remaining months gleaning as much information as possible about the miraculous plants that grew in this immense and lush forest.

While Constance was getting to know her nursing colleagues and exploring the vast military compound with Raphael Fonsceca, unknown to her Clemente was in the process of bargaining for a very important piece of merchandise with Miguel Amorim, who had been the sales manager on the compound for the past 10 months. Clemente had met up with him on a few occasions and their business relationship had flourished with the wares that he, Clemente, had managed to unearth from his dealings with the less than upright individuals he dealt with. With every valuable discovery he would visit Miguel on the compound and negotiate a price. Of course Constance had no idea of Clemente's association with racketeering and would have been horrified, though not specially surprised. It was for this reason that Clemente had arranged to meet Miguel to discuss the latest medicinal formula he had obtained, hoping that that they would come to some satisfactory agreement. It was one of the best pieces of merchandise that Clemente had ever managed to acquire and he wanted a very good price for it.

Bargaining with Miguel, he thought, would take time. Since the sales manager knew that he himself would receive an even higher price from his immediate boss for the formula of the active compound and how to extract it from this particular life-saving plant, which was usually sold on the black market, he did not mind. Miguel had not as yet been caught out in a shady transaction, but time was running out for him and his superiors were just waiting for him to put a foot wrong before they pounced. Miguel was a small, portly man around 40 years old, with a crooked nose that had been broken on more than one occasion, and a lopsided mouth that only smiled after having had a good meal and several drinks. His only redeeming feature was a pair of large and beautiful brown eyes that gave anyone he came into contact with the impression that he was a kind and gentle man. They were very mistaken in this; Miguel was a calculatingly cold human being who thrived on getting what he wanted and did not care how he did it.

Clemente, on the other hand, was quite a different individual. Though dishonest and conniving, he was not as tough or as cold-blooded as Miguel. He was charming and very good looking, with soft wavy brown hair and hazel eyes. He was of medium height but very well proportioned and extremely athletic. He too was aware that he was sitting on a time bomb and needed to finalise these arrangements and remove himself from the base as soon as he possibly could.

On entering Miguel's office soon after his arrival, Clemente was confronted with an impatient and irate sales manager. "Where is the formula you were meant to bring with you?"

"I don't have it with me."

"Where is it then?"

"I put it in the case of my woman companion to avoid any suspicion falling on me if I were to be caught."

"All right, go and get it."

"I can't, not now. I will have to wait until I can get into her room, which she is probably sharing with another nurse, and for all I know she might have already unpacked and wondered how these papers could have got into her case. She is not dumb and I don't want to implicate her in this transaction."

Miguel snapped at him, "You are getting soft. What a stupid thing to do. How were you planning to remove these papers if she is in another part of the compound?"

"We are good friends and I had intended to meet up with her when these transactions were finished today and then slip into her room when she wasn't there."

"I thought you were going to stay here for a couple of days?"

"I have changed my mind and feel it would be better if I cut my trip short and leave as quickly as I conceivably can."

"That is wise. All right, I will give you until this afternoon but if you have had no success by then I will hunt her down and get the formula myself."

"Please don't do that. It could cause disruption and she could very well go to the authorities."

"Do you think that there is a possibility that she should she discover it she would be unaware of the importance of this formula?"

Clemente shook his head. "I doubt that. She is a very bright young lady. She has learned Portuguese in the 2 weeks she has been here in Brazil in order to communicate with the doctors and nurses and to learn about the plants and their properties. Don't underestimate her. I have a feeling she has already deduced that I am not quite as I seem."

The sales manager smirked. "I thought that you, with your charisma, could charm the pants off any woman, young or old."

"Not this one," Clemente frowned, thinking back to Constance's excuses not to join him on evening excursions.

"Well anyway, do not leave it much longer or we will both be in the shit house: you with me and I with the people who wish to buy this valuable piece of information."

Clemente walked out of the office and strolled into the coffee shop on the base to reflect on what he should do. He was extremely worried. How was he going to get into Constance's room and retrieve the formula? He had not thought this through at all. He had no intention of her ever seeing this unsavoury side of his nature. The best way to find out whether she had unpacked was to visit her in her room on the pretext of finding out how she was settling in, and then somehow break into her room later in the day and get the papers. He genuinely hoped she would be happy to see him. He felt that they had left each other on good terms and she had even suggested that they meet up before he left.

He walked towards the nurses' reception area, asking very politely if he could be given the number of the hut that the new nurse, Constance, was staying in.

"Regrettably sir, we are unable to give out that kind of information," the receptionist informed him.

"I am leaving the base very shortly and I do not know when I shall see her again. Can you suggest how I can get in touch with her?" Clemente turned on the charm. The receptionist was only too happy to help in this respect. "If you give me your telephone number I can ask her to ring you." Clemente thanked her and wrote down the telephone number of the room he had been allocated (which was always the same one, arranged by Miguel).

The phone call came through from Constance at around 4 pm that afternoon. She sounded furious. "Clemente, what on earth have you put in my suitcase? The papers you placed there look very important. What are they and how dare you plant them in my case, for I could very well be implicated in your murky dealings. I am taking them to the senior laboratory technician who will know what to do with them."

His heart sank. "Please don't Constance, if you do that I shall be a dead man. Could you please give them to me so I can pass the papers onto the persons concerned?"

"Don't be dramatic; nobody is going to kill you. No, I won't give them to you unless you can give me a very good reason as to why I should turn a blind eye to your shady activities. We should get together but I will not bring the papers with me. Let's meet in a public place, perhaps at the coffee shop at 8 pm tonight, and we can talk it through."

He answered quietly, "I shall be there."

Clemente, even more anxious than before, decided not to tell Miguel what had transpired, hoping that he might be able to win Constance over. At 8 o'clock promptly, Constance and Clemente met at the coffee shop. There were only a couple of people at nearby tables having a nightcap before they left for their huts. To Clemente's horror, as he ordered the two coffees for Constance and himself, Miguel walked calmly but purposefully into the coffee shop with a very ugly expression on his face. In a low menacing voice, heard only by Clemente, he said "There is a pistol in your ribs. Give me the formula immediately or I will kill you and then your girlfriend."

"We don't have it with us," he stammered as he felt the cold muzzle of the gun move and press up against his kidneys. Looking at Constance, in the same low and menacing tone he repeated his threat. Clemente, in an act of courage, leaped to his feet to protect Constance. At the same time, he tried to grapple the gun out of Miguel's hand. He was much the taller and stronger of the two but the gun discharged itself and Clemente fell to the ground, blood pouring out of the gaping wound in his chest. Miguel ran out of the coffee shop in fear of what had taken place, due not so much the shooting but being implicated in the theft of the formula. Constance ran over to Clement, bending down over his chest and putting pressure on the wound. She shouted to the girl behind the counter, who had been drawn back into the café by the ruckus, for a tea towel, with which she attempted to stem the flow of blood.

The next few minutes seemed like hours as Clemente bled to death on the floor. The shot was heard by the military police, who were on the scene within a few minutes.

Constance sat back on her heels, her face drawn to a chalky grey colour. She was distraught and not very rational. "If only I had given the papers to Clemente when he asked he would be alive. It's my fault," she mumbled. A policewoman gently pulled her away from the body as the ambulance crew arrived. They placed Clemente's body on a stretcher to be taken to the morgue.

Constance excused herself so that she could change her blooded clothes but a policewoman accompanied her back to her room in order to collect the clothes she had been wearing for examination. Constance was then ordered to go with the policewoman the station for questioning. Anxious and feeling responsible for the situation she was in a terrible state. She had no friends in Brazil, and though she might have a better knowledge of Portuguese than 2 weeks ago, she would not be to explain her side of the story as clearly as she would like; the reason for the murder and why the papers containing the formula were still in her case. She could very well be considered an accomplice of Clemente's. She was unsure what to do. The worst of it was that nobody else had seen Miguel in the coffee shop: the other couple had left just before he entered and the girl behind the counter was in the back of the shop packing up for the night.

As she was about to be questioned, she would not have the time to remove the papers from her suitcase before her belongings were searched. If only she could find a way of removing the papers and giving them to her boss, Raphael Fonsceca. But how? Should she ask for a lawyer or would that be an indication of her guilt? As it happened she knew no one directly who could help her, although her mother had recently started writing to her about a friend who was a lawyer and lived in Germany. What should she do? Exhausted by the emotion of Clemente's killing and her so-called involvement in the she was nearly ready to collapse, but she knew that this would not resolve any of her problems. Her only course of action would be to be absolutely truthful and explain what had really happened.

On arrival at the police station her fingerprints were taken. She was then taken to the interview room to be questioned, the policewoman accompanying her. After waiting for about 10 minutes, the police chief entered with various papers in his hand. She was relieved to see that the papers containing the formula were not among them. He began to question her about her relationship with Clemente and how she came to be bent over him when the police walked in.

Constance answered honestly. "He had been shot and since I am a nurse my first responsibility is to try and save the patient. I had only known him for a couple of weeks. I came to Brazil to nurse and to study the plants here and their medicinal properties.

"On arrival from French Guyana it was recommended that I should fly to Manaus, take a crash course in Portuguese for a couple of weeks, and then proceed to here to continue with my mission. I met Clemente at the same hotel. He used to meet me at breakfast and help me with my studies, pronunciation and grammar. After breakfast I went off to school and returned in the afternoon to study, have something to eat and go to bed. We did not communicate in any other way. Except, however that we did travel to this base together by boat. The rendezvous at the coffee shop was the first time I had seen him since our arrival. He only needed to spend a short time in this camp so he rang and arranged to meet me for coffee and to say farewell. I do not know who killed him. Some man came in, shot him and ran out, taking the gun with him."

"This does not shed any light on the motive for this shooting, Miss Murray. Is there something else you wish to tell me?"

Constance bit her lip agonising over whether she should fill him with the facts. She proceeded cautiously. "Yes there is, but the information I shall give you could be incriminating."

"I will be the judge of that." Her interrogator seemed less than impressed. Constance resigned herself to the fact that she would have to tell him everything.

"When I had been introduced to all of the personnel and been escorted round the base I returned to my room to unpack. Tucked in the side of my case lay some papers wrapped up tightly in a plastic bag. I have no idea how they got there but I suspect that Clemente planted them just before we left for the boat; I would have noticed them if they were there earlier as I only packed that morning. They are still in my case; I have not removed the packet. When we spoke on the telephone around 6 in the evening we arranged to meet at the coffee shop two hours later. He asked if I would bring the papers with me so he could pass them onto the prospective buyers and forget that I had ever seen them. I declined and said it would be better if I handed them over to my boss, but Clemente would not hear of it. When we were at the coffee shop, as I mentioned before, this crazy guy marched in and turned a gun on Clemente, threatening to kill him unless he presented the papers. It all happened so fast. I was threatened too. Clemente turned around and grabbed at the gun, which went off. The shooter must have panicked, as he ran off."

"All right, Miss Murray," said the police chief, "we will go and collect these papers and see if they are as important as they appear to be and check them and you out as well. You are to stay here."

"Look, I haven't eaten since I had a snack at midday. Could I please have something to eat?"

"Yes, somebody will bring you some food." He paused on his way out of the room. "I am a little baffled, Miss Murray. You have been in this country for only 2 weeks and you can speak Portuguese. It is not normal for any person to learn a language in so short a time. I am a fairly good judge of character, and though on the surface you appear genuine I do not believe you are."

With calmness that she did not know she possessed, Constance answered, "I cannot prove that I am innocent. I just know I am. My only crime, if you can call it a crime, is that I did not give the papers to the authorities when I found them in my case. But even then you might not have believed that I was telling the truth. I do not know anybody in Brazil and only met Clemente by chance at the hotel. He was very kind to me."

"Kind enough to get you embroiled with the theft of what must be valuable papers, more like. You are just interested in getting a share of the profits."

Constance was resolute. "Absolutely not!"

A woman carrying a tray of sandwiches and coffee entered the room and placed them in front of Constance. Despite her need to prove her innocence to this man, she ate immediately as she was ravenous.

The police chief turned to walk out of the room after the woman with the tray. "I am going to check the papers now and I'll be back. I suggest that you get hold of a lawyer; you are going to need one."

Constance leaned back in her chair, horrified that this had gone so far. She was in a middle of a nightmare. She must be. This could not be happening. Where was she going to find a lawyer? Her befuddled brain was in turmoil.

A short while afterwards the police chief returned holding some papers covered in chemical formulas, diagrams and scientific terminology. He had another man in tow. He laid out the contents on the table. "Is this what Clemente died for?"

"If you found these papers in my case they must be. As I said, I do not know anything about any formulas. I didn't read what was in the package and I have no idea what these papers are about."

Standing across from Constance and leaning over the table, the police chief gave her an accusatory glare. "Your thumb print is on the package, but not your boyfriend's."

Constance began to feel exasperated. "I don't know why not. He knew he could be incriminated so he might have worn gloves. I naturally picked up the package when I saw it. It was not meant to be in my case so I wondered what it was."

"Are you sure that is all you did? Did you know that this formula could be worth hundreds of thousands of dollars?"

Her eyes widened. "As I said, I have no idea what information it contains."

"Get a lawyer, young lady. None of this is getting us anywhere. For all we know you could have shot Clemente yourself."

Constance snapped back. "Don't be ridiculous, you can check my hands. I have no powder burns on them or on my clothes either, only Clemente's blood. You cannot charge me with the murder."

The police chief straightened himself up, brushing down his uniform and stepped back. "You are quite right. I can't. You can return to your own room but not before we go over your evidence one more time."

"Can I make a call?" she asked. "I need to contact my mother to let her know I have arrived safely at the base. I have not been able to get in touch with her since I arrived here and she will be concerned if I do not call her."

"Is she in Brazil?"

"No, Scotland."

"Then you can't call her." Taking pity on her crumpling expression, he went on to explain "We can't make any international calls from this station."

"As I still have to remain at this police station for still quite a while I would appreciate it if I could speak to my roommate, Claudine Marchant. Will that be possible?"

"I did not think you knew anybody?"

Constance explained. "She is French, I am Belgian. We can speak the same language and she was the first friendly face I happened to meet when I was introduced to all the personnel. She has suggested that she change rooms so she can be my roommate, which I thought was a great act of kindness. However, what I really need her to do is to ring my mother to tell her how I am and what's happened."

"All right, I shall arrange for her to visit you."

"Where shall I meet her?"

"She can come to this interrogation room."

"That will be fine. Thank you." Half an hour later Claudine entered the room looking very worried and went over to Constance, giving her a hug.

"What has happened, why are you here?" asked Claudine.

Constance looked distraught. "I have been accused of stealing a formula that I found in my suitcase this afternoon. Clemente, the guy I travelled on the boat with, must have put it there for I have never seen it before."

"What can I do to help?"

Constance took a deep breath. "I wonder if you would be kind enough to ring my mother in Scotland, do it collect. She will be very happy to pay for the call. She is Belgian, so you will have no trouble in communicating with her. Would you please tell her what has happened. I will fill you in with all the details. She is a marvellous woman and will work something out for me. Give her the telephone number on the base. There is a possibility that the phone will be tapped but I have nothing to hide, neither has my mother."

Constance was so relieved to have at least one friend she could rely on. She gave Claudine as many facts of the situation as she knew, which Claudine wrote down. Constance continued. "Do tell my mother that I am fine, but because I have learned Portuguese in such a short time I am much more of a suspect than if had no knowledge at all. They have such warped minds. The inspector assumes that because I am relatively proficient in his language I must have studied it beforehand and have also been in the country much longer than I say I have. He assumes that because of this I must have been conspiring with Clemente for a much longer period. The powers of deduction he purports to have must be limited, for he only has to see my passport to see how long I have been here and that I was working in French Guiana just before I came here."

"He believes that I am a thief and came to Brazil to negotiate this transaction and, with this in mind, studied Portuguese beforehand. What miserable minds these people must have. Why must they always think a person is guilty when perhaps only a simple honest explanation is needed?"

"Anyway, I really appreciate what you are doing. I have been told that I can return to our room later on tonight. I do not know what time it will be and I must come back here tomorrow. I have not been charged, as yet, and am hoping I will be able to get out of this mess before it goes to trial. This guy who shot Clemente will need to be found before anything more definite happens."

"If you ring my mother as soon as possible I would be so grateful. Scotland is approximately 4 hours ahead of us so it will be quite early in the morning there. I am sure, however, that my mother will wake up as soon as she hears the telephone. The sooner she knows of my predicament, the sooner she can start to act."

Claudine was most impressed with the calmness and clarity in which Constance had explained her plight. Feeling an innate trust for her new friend, she was more than willing to help in any way possible. "I will get on the case immediately."

Constance could have cried with relief at hearing these words. "Thank you very much."

At midnight Constance returned to her room, shattered after her long interrogation and distressed that she still had to return to the police station the next day for more. Claudine was fast asleep but had put a little note by her bed to the effect that she had got hold of her mother, who would be ringing the next day. She was comforted by this. Now she knew that her mother was on the case, she fell asleep as soon as her head touched the pillow.

Constance was allowed to do some nursing the next day, but no research. She was called in for the next interview at 3 pm. She was absolutely drained and knew she could not add anything more to her testimony.

Her mother had called her earlier in the day to get the full details. In her distress, Françoise found she wanted to turn to Ziegler for his advice but was embarrassed in case he thought she was taking advantage of him. Her daughter came first, however, and she took a deep breath and made a call to Germany.

***

Françoise called Constance back early the next morning, when luckily she could answer without being overheard.

Having spoken to Ziegler in Germany, he had got in touch with another Legionnaire, Sertorio Ortega, who was Portuguese-speaking and whom he had known and served with in Corsica. Sertorio, as it happened, had been born in Brazil and was very familiar with the northern part of the country. Constance gave a great sigh of relief. Her mother always came up trumps.

"Christer and his friend, Sertorio Ortega will be flying to Brazil tomorrow, landing at Eduard Gomes International Airport in the early evening and then taking a taxi to the base so that they can reach you as quickly as possible. They will want to speak to you immediately, so please be as meticulous with your answers as you possibly can for everything you say will be germane to your case. Christer's friend, Sertorio, has already contacted the military air base and asked for some digs for both of them, so you do not have to concern yourself with finding them accommodation."

"Thank you Maman, you have been wonderful. I do not know what I would do without you."

"It is thanks to Christer and his network of friends and colleagues that has got us this far. I shall stop now, darling, as there is not much more I can tell you and it is getting a little expensive. I look forward to hearing from you when things are a little clearer. Love you lots."

CHAPTER 20

Escape from Marseilles

Arriving back in his room, Tom thought he heard the floorboards creaking. Moving into the shadows he believed he saw the outline of a person walking towards his room. Thank goodness it was only Harry, whose voice he had heard in a nearby room. Harry was one of the English recruits he had met at the beginning of his training in the French Foreign Legion and whose company he enjoyed. He was of average height, with sandy hair and a wicked sense of humour. Like most of the rookies who had been in the Legion for the same amount time as Tom, he was extremely strong and very fit. Tom therefore wondered why he had also ended up in this military hospital. What was wrong with him?

"Are you there Tom?" Harry called out quietly from the cover of darkness.

"Yes Harry, please come in." Harry walked into the centre of the room.

"What on earth were you doing earlier?" he asked. "I heard you creep down the stairs as though you were planning some clandestine meeting with a married lady of dubious character." Tom burst out laughing. "Now, that would be interesting, but no, I was speaking to my parents."

Harry gave Tom a cheeky smile. "Then why so hush hush?"

"Oh Harry, it is such a long saga. If you have a few hours free I'll fill you in."

Harry settled himself in the green armchair opposite Tom's bed. "Carry on, I am all ears."

Tom then regaled him with the long tale about being press ganged into the Legion and how, for the last 2 and half years he had been trying to get out. "There now seems the possibility that I might be able to do it here in Marseilles, but I can't do this on my own. I need help. I have no right to ask you to take such a big risk for me, but as a friend can I count on you? Your room mate may need to get involved. This will therefore depend, on his willingness too and on how physically well you both are at the moment."

"Come on Tom, what's on your mind?"

Tom lowered his voice to a whisper. "My parents are flying over from Sweden as we speak, staying with a member of the family in the vicinity. Their intention is to wait, for however long it takes, outside this compound in order to whisk me away to an unknown destination. They will have a car in preparation for this getaway, and I hope some kind of disguise with which to alter my appearance so I will not be identified. What I want from you both is help to climb over the wall."

Harry stood up. "I'll help in any way I can and will speak to my roommate Benedict. He's a stalwart guy and I'm sure he will also be very happy to help. I'm guessing you are intending to execute this operation during visitors' time?"

"Yes, I am. Harry, I will never be able to thank you enough if you could do this for me. Are you sure you are well enough to help me?"

"I'll manage and so will Benedict. It would be a pleasure." With a wide grin on his face he continued, "I shall enjoy this. It is a little too dull staying in this comfortable place. I need some exercise and a diversion."

"You're a real pal. Well I'd better try and get some shut eye now for I do not know what tomorrow will bring."

With another chuckle to himself, Harry returned to his room to talk to his companion about the plans for the next day.

***

The morning dawned bright and clear, with just a hint of mist in the air. It was October, after all, and the sun took a little longer to break through and the air was cooler. Tom did not have a lot of warm clothing, having come from the tropical heat of Guiana, but luckily found an anorak in the cupboard in his room, which he put on.

He was brought breakfast at the usual time: 07.00 hours. Since he was meant to be ill with an unusual blood condition, he had to continue to play out the parody of a sick person. A doctor visited him in the middle of the morning to check up on him and asked him whether any other symptoms had manifested themselves. The doctor seemed so preoccupied with the many demands in the hospital that thankfully he stayed only a very short time.

Lunch came at midday. He knew he had to eat but had no appetite. He drifted off to sleep for a short while and woke with a start when the hospital began to buzz in preparation for the visitors that were due to arrive shortly. This was the highlight of the day for patients. Twenty minutes before the visitors were allowed in, Harry and Benedict walked quietly into Tom's room in preparation for Tom's escape. They sat at the small table in Tom's room and played gin rummy to pass the time. When the courtyard clock struck three o'clock, the three young men slunk down the back stairs to a door that led out into a garden that was green and lush, with the last red roses of summer still blooming, their heads full and heavy.

The visitors began streaming in through the large gates and through the garden. The guards with revolvers checked to see all the comings and goings and note who was visiting each patient. Tom, Harry and Benedict meanwhile meandered among the incoming crowd while they directed their attention towards the 10 ft walls that were covered with barbed wire. It took them 10 minutes to reach the edge of the compound. Checking that nobody was looking, Benedict, the taller of the two, stood on the level ground while Harry jumped onto his shoulders. Without taking his eyes off his objective Tom managed to climb onto Harry's shoulders, reaching the top of the barbed wire without too much trouble. Taking off his anorak he placed it on the top of the barrier and jumped, just missing one of the barbs that jutted through the fabric. He left it on the top. Shouting a goodbye and thanks to the lads, he landed on the hard ground outside in the street. He sustained a few bruises but nothing else. Looking up and down the street he spied an innocuous looking black Volkswagen Polo moving slowly towards him. Did it contain his parents? Yes it did!

Jumping into the car, he gave them a big hug; he was so overjoyed that they had actually found him. They sped off to Tom's aunt's flat just a few miles away. Tom's parents were so happy to see him, his father, who never usually expressed strong emotions, had to wipe away the tears in his eyes. Tom had actually managed it. It was now a matter of getting out of France and trying to get back to Sweden without being discovered.

"Where did you get the car? You didn't drive all the way from Sweden, surely?"

"No, of course not, but we will be driving all the way back in it. We flew into Marseilles this morning and bought this second-hand car in Anna's name near the airport. We were lucky. It's only got 80,000 km on the clock and has had just one previous owner. It will be a run around for a while when we are back in Sweden, and when Aunt Anna returns to her holiday flat here in Marseilles she will drive it back and leave it here."

Tom smiled at his parents. "You know that I will not be able to set foot in France for about 30 years?"

"Yes, but there are many other beautiful and interesting countries to visit, you do not need France."

In the meantime Harry and Benedict, having removed the anorak from the top of the wall, immediately ran back to the hospital and to their beds. It was necessary that the authorities not be alerted to the fact that one of the recruits had absconded. It was also imperative that Tom be given as much time as possible before the military realized that he had left the hospital and the base for good.

With the visitors sat chatting at the bedsides their friends and relatives, the hospital retreated into a quieter state. Tom had received no visitors since he had arrived but had occasionally left his room to use the bathroom, orient himself, and look for books or magazines to read. He had pulled his door shut on the way out, so it was not obvious that he had gone missing and no one was concerned that Tom's bed was empty.

As the day moved into evening, however, the nurses began to question why he had not returned. His absence was passed on to the doctors and the administrative service. The alert went out. Where was Tom? The whole hospital and compound were searched but Tom had vanished. The guards at the gate had not noticed any strange person coming or going. He had not passed through the gates. Perhaps he had climbed over the wall. The guards wondered how. He was tall, but not tall enough to vault over such a high obstacle. Had he dug out or found a hole somewhere and got through like that? They checked and found no holes along the boundary. It was mystifying. It did enter their heads that he could have had help, but they dismissed it as most of the inmates were quite ill and would not have had the strength to lift someone 6ft 3inches tall weighing 15 stone. Added to this, Tom was a newcomer, having just arrived the day before. He would not have known anybody.

A message was sent out to all airports and ports to stop any young man that fitted Tom's description. Tom would not get away.

***

Tom and his parents raced along the road in their little black polo towards Aunt Anna's flat, which she rented every year when she visited Marseilles. They knew that they did not have much time before Tom would be missed and the authorities would be after him. Stopping at Aunt Anna's for the shortest time possible, Tom attempted to change his looks so that he appeared closer in likeness to his brother Anders, whose passport his parents had brought with them. This was not going to be especially easy, as none of his family had needed

186

to develop such skills. His parents had nevertheless brought some hair dye that was the same colour as the picture in the passport. Anders' skin was a shade lighter than Tom, so with the makeup that his mother had found in a local shop Tom was able to apply a small amount to his skin to improve the resemblance to his brother. Tom was taller than Anders by three inches, but this would not be noticeable unless the car was halted and he had to get out. Also the police inspector would be looking for a passport with the name Fredriksson on it, not his family name Sandberg, as written on his brother's passport.

Quickly grabbing a sandwich and a cup of coffee at Aunt Anna's, Tom and his parents left by a side entrance where the car was parked, their first port of call being Grenoble, which would take approximately 4 hours to reach. Tom's parents naturally had no idea how long it would be before an APB (all points bulletin) would be put out for their son's arrest so they had to avoid demonstrating any strange behaviour, such as erratic driving, that would alert a law enforcement officer into thinking that something suspicious was taking place.

Tom's father, Nils, carefully manoeuvred the Polo onto the main road, gently driving out of the city. If only they could get out of France before the alarm was given they could then cross the borders into Switzerland and would be home free, or nearly. Of course it would be a very long journey through Switzerland, Germany, Denmark and Sweden, and he prayed that they would not be picked up by the authorities. He knew that trying to escape from the French Foreign Legion was considered a crime and he would be prosecuted if he was caught abetting a fugitive, but was sure that his son would not be arrested for desertion once he was out of France.

Hoping that his escape had not yet been discovered Tom sat in the back of the car, his head spinning with the outcome of the day. Was he really free? Not quite. There could still be unforeseen dangers ahead and he had to be vigilant and prepared. He did not believe that anybody had seen him jump over the wall and into the waiting car, but one can never be sure. In case the APB put out had contained a description of what he had been wearing when he left the hospital, he had changed into the clothes his parents had brought with them. With his hair dyed and his new complexion he knew he looked different, but was it enough?

His mother kept on turning round in the car to look at him. Her shining eyes and the new lines on her face gave Tom an understanding as to how his parents must have been feeling during the years he had been away. He had not given a lot of thought to their anxiety and fear during this time and felt slightly ashamed. Seeing his parents' happiness at his return gave him once again a feeling of belonging in the real world; one in which he wanted to stay. He had never managed to say goodbye to Macey. He had been a great friend and someone whom he would not have survived without. He would contact him on his return to Sweden. Constance was another person whom he needed to see again. She must have left French Guyana at the same time as he did, but where did she go? When he became ill the whole unit packed up to return to Corsica, their only having a few days left of their operation. She still had to complete a further 3 months study in South America if she was to return to the UK to study medicine, but no further designated country had been discussed between them. He only knew her name and that she came from Scotland. Tom quietly muttered to himself in the back of the car.

For the first time in months he was able to sit back and contemplate things. They were not home and dry yet, but as all the memories of the past began to crowd into his mind he began to think of the future. He was 25. He did not want to join any fighting force, although he was very well qualified to do so. As he had mentioned to Ludi many months earlier, he was still interested in obstetrics. It would take quite a few years and would involve a great deal of study before achieving this, as he would have to qualify as a doctor first, and then specialize in his chosen field. Where would he do that? His challenges over the years had been more than he had wished for yet he had met all of them and become stronger and more mature because of them. He had been rather a spoilt young man, not knowing what he wanted, but at the same time not really prepared to give of himself. His experiences had changed him a great deal.

The car gave a sudden jolt, his father slamming on the brakes just in time to avoid an enormous truck that was carrying, at first glance, some highly explosive material, from crashing into them. Tom was thrown out of his reverie. He was back in the present. They had another hour before they reached Grenoble. There were still no signs of any sirens or roadblocks. Apparently his absence had not yet been discovered, and if it had the APB had not reached the local police.

They did not stop, except for a 5-minute break to fill up the tank. They had sufficient food and drink in the car to tide them over until they were in Switzerland. Grenoble was reached without any incident, but Tom knew that it would not be too long before the sound of police cars would be making their presence felt. Eight miles before the Swiss border, Tom and his parents saw a queue of cars in front of them, each car being stopped and searched, as well as passports being checked. Each car seemed to be stationary for about 5 minutes while the occupants were questioned about their time in France and their destination. Tom's parents suggested that the less Tom spoke the better, as he was so fluent in the language that the police would be aware that he had been speaking French for a very long time. Tom's parents' French was adequate but not fluent.

"Just to be sure that we relay the same information I suggest," said his father, "that we say we have been staying with my sister Anna, who lives in Nice from time to time, and came to celebrate my retirement with her and the family. We are now returning to Sweden, where we live. Anna will be flying back in a week or two. If you have to talk and answer any questions, it would be better to speak in English. If you are asked what your occupation is, say that that you are working in the same engineering company that I used to work for. Let's hope he does not order you to get out of the car."

"I hope he doesn't either."

His father continued. "If the police do not understand your English it does not matter, for I can always translate for you."

As all the cars gradually moved forward along the road, their car was told to halt.

"Good evening, Officer," said Nils politely, "Is it possible for you to tell me why you are stopping and searching all these cars?"

The officer answered freely. "We are trying to apprehend a young man who has escaped from the military hospital in Marseilles."

Jonathon played along. "Why do you think he did that?"

The officer continued. "I have no idea, and nobody else has either. It is a waste of time as far as I am concerned and it is hindering people from arriving at their destinations in time to make connections. Everybody is frustrated with the situation."

The officer quickly got back to the business at hand. "How many are there of you and may I see your passports?" he asked. Nils answered for his family.

"We are three, my wife, son and I. We have been holidaying with my sister in Nice to celebrate my retirement and now we are on our way home. We come from Sweden."

"Oh Sweden, that is a lovely country," he responded, with a cheerful smile on his face. "I went there once, to the south of the country, near Malmö, and would love to return. Here are your passports. They all seem to be in order. May I ask why you are driving? It is a very long way to return to Sweden by car. Why didn't you go by air?"

"This car belongs to my sister, Anna, who would find it too arduous to drive such a long distance, so as she wants to use the car as a run around in Sweden we are taking it back for her. She will fly back in a couple of weeks' time."

"May I have the insurance papers?" he asked, holding out his hand.

"Of course," answered Nils handing over the papers.

The officer took the longest 2 minutes to review the documents before handing them back to Tom's father. "Everything appears to be in order. Have a good journey back."

They gave an enormous sigh of relief as they were waved on. Nils looked in the rear and side mirrors to confirm that they were safe. The little black Polo continued on its journey.

Tom turned to his father. "Well done, Pappa. Distracting him as you did about other things certainly kept his mind off me."

With the tension and fear of discovery over for the moment, Tom and his parents drove to the Swiss border. Nils presented the three passports to the official to be checked. These were returned without incident or comment. Driving into Geneva, they chose one of the touristy hotels in which to stay the night. Tom still had to pass the borders of Germany, Denmark and Sweden, but all they wanted to focus on now was a good meal and long sleep.

CHAPTER 21

Return to Scotland

When Ziegler had received the emergency call from Françoise in the early hours of the morning asking him if he could help her daughter who was stationed in Brazil, he was awake in seconds, his mind galloping to find a solution to the predicament that she posed him. "You were the first person I thought of Christer, and also the only lawyer I know. I understand that specialize in criminal law. Please help me," she had pleaded.

How strange, he had thought that Françoise should call me to ask if I can help her daughter. He had not heard from her in a while; in fact since the week they had spent together in Germany. She had not rung or asked how he was or if they could meet up again. Women were so difficult to fathom. Perhaps she had returned home and thought better of having a relationship. Perhaps she had felt disloyal to her husband, despite the fact that he had passed away years before. Perhaps she was just busy with work. He wondered what she wanted from him.

She explained how Constance had got mixed up in a murder and the theft of some valuable documents. "Of course she is innocent" protested Françoise. Although his heart went out to her, until Ziegler had all the facts in front of him he did not feel it wise to comment. He had never had children, so he did not understand the bond between parent and child; that a parent would do anything to protect his or her children, even die for them. He would never know.

At least he would get to meet Constance. He would do his best to resolve the situation and try and get her acquitted. After all, this was what he was best at and his prowess as a defence lawyer was one of his strengths. He did have doubts, however, that being a foreigner he would not be able to practise as a lawyer in Brazil. Let's hope that Françoise will appreciate me a little more if I manage to get her beloved daughter out of the dilemma she has become involved in, he had reflected.

Ziegler had a very good friend called Sertorio Ortega who had also left the Legion at approximately the same time as he had. Because Ziegler had an extensive network of contacts and was such a likable person, he was able to call on his friends and colleagues when he was in need. This was one of those occasions. Sertorio lived in Portugal with his wife and twin boys of 18 months. "There is a lot of crime in the rainforest," he conveyed to Ziegler on the telephone, as they discussed the crime that Constance had been accused of. "With the fantastic amount of wealth that can be made from drugs, there are many unscrupulous scavengers who will do anything to make money. It is very possible that this girl had no idea that the papers in question were planted in her case."

Ziegler explained, "Apparently she had no knowledge of any Portuguese before she went to Brazil, so it is highly unlikely that she entered into any collusion with anyone except Clemente da Silva who, I have found out, was fluent in English. We have to prove she did not know Clemente before she arrived in Brazil and was unaware of his illegal business interests. The sooner we get to Brazil, the sooner we will get answers. I have booked a flight for this afternoon to arrive at Eduard Gomes International Airport around 6 pm. Is it possible, Sertorio, for you to join me in this case?

"I'll have to make some calls but, if my wife is happy to take the helm at home, I am sure I can."

"If we can synchronise the time at which we arrive, we can take a taxi to the base together and hope to see Constance immediately on arrival."

Sertorio managed to get a flight arriving at the airport 30 minutes after Ziegler's. Hailing a taxi outside the airport they reached the military compound within half an hour. The military guard checked their credentials and waved them through to the nurses' quarters. At the nurses' station they were again required to show their identification and were led to Constance and Claudine's hut.

Constance sat alone waiting for them, Claudine having decided to go out for the evening. On opening the door Ziegler was immediately struck by a petite young woman with startling blue eyes surrounded by large dark circles. She had a very determined look on her face as to say, I am innocent, now you prove it. Constance was impressed by the man who had cast everything aside to rush over to South America to help her. He must really care about her mother. She was pleased to see Sertorio, standing just behind Ziegler. She considered him a life saver if he could explain and argue everything in Portuguese.

Constance welcomed the gentlemen into her quarters. "You must be tired after your flight and also hungry. I have prepared a small meal for you both and of course you must taste some of the excellent wine, which is produced in the region. We can talk over dinner and I can fill you in with all of the details that you need to know."

Ziegler found Constance coherent and very clear in her explanations and answers. Although this was only the first encounter with her, she seemed pretty up-front and did not seem to have a hidden agenda.

"Not only did I not know any Portuguese before I came here, there was no need to know any. I was sent by a Dr Duncan to French Guyana where I worked for 9 months. The intention was that I would complete the full 12 months in Guyana but one of the recruits became very ill, which resulted in the whole unit packing up and returning to Corsica."

A rather sad expression flitted over Constance's face, which Ziegler observed and wondered about. He would make some enquiries later on.

Constance continued. "I still had another 3 months to go so it was suggested by the chief of the medical staff in Guyana that I transfer to Brazil for the remaining period. I had to leave as I was no longer needed to attend to the recruits. I kept Dr Duncan informed."

"I met this charming and attractive young man, Clemente da Silva, while I was staying at a tourist hotel in Manaus. I do not know if he was a plant, but I don't think so. He seemed genuinely interested in me but since I did not reciprocate his advances he probably guessed that I would not want to get involved with his scheme. He was right. But he still created a difficult situation for me by transferring the papers to my suitcase in case his was searched. This did not benefit him at all. He never managed to retrieve the papers.

"I am not sure about when and how he transferred the papers to my case. I wonder whether anybody saw him but did not register that something was amiss. He offered to carry my suitcase and his down to the lobby while I finished tidying up in my room. He would not have had much time to transfer the papers if he had returned to his room, as he would have had to backtrack and would not have been down in the lobby before me." Constance tried to recall the layout of the hotel. "He must have turned right out of my room towards the lift, stopping somewhere to make the exchange. My memory tells me that there is a gentlemen's cloakroom just before the lift. Perhaps he made the exchange in there. I wonder if anybody saw him.

"Do you think you can ask around at the hotel to find out whether any member of staff saw anything unusual?" she asked. Constance found that speaking her theories out loud helped her determine whether or not they were plausible.

Ziegler was impressed by her thought processes. "If you give me the details of the hotel, we'll start making enquiries as soon as we've finished here."

"I do hope this doesn't go to trial and we can resolve this before it gets to that point." Ziegler continued. "As I am not Brazilian I will be not be able to represent you as I am not entitled to practise law in this country. In the unlikelihood that it does, we will find a suitable defence lawyer and Sertorio and I will be by your side to assist and advise you."

"Thank you. I appreciate all you and Sertorio are doing."

Ziegler got to his feet and turned to Constance. "It is late. We should go. We shall see you tomorrow."

Constance retrieved their jackets from where she had hung them on the back of the door. "I'll point the way to the visitors' quarters, which are about 10 minutes walk from here."

The gentlemen thanked her for the meal and took their leave.

Constance slept fitfully that night. It was marvellous that Ziegler and Sertorio had come to help but there was still no proof that she had not been involved. If only a witness could be found in the hotel who had seen the exchange taking place. They also had to locate Clemente's murderer. Was he still on the base? He could have left, but at the same time she was unsure as to whether anybody would have been allowed to do so in the circumstances. At least forensics had confirmed that she had not been involved in Clemente's homicide.

***

Soon after breakfast the next day, Ziegler and Sertorio took the boat downstream to the centre of Manaus and walked to the hotel where Constance had been staying. Although Clemente had also been at the same hotel, they did not know how long he had been there. They hoped that the staff would be accommodating. As it was a murder investigation there was a strong possibility that the police had already questioned the staff and some of the guests.

They asked at the desk if they could see the manager. As the hotel receptionist was English-speaker, Ziegler initially asked the questions but knew he would get tangled up with the language when the subject became more complicated. The manager was busy but was most concerned about the murder of a patron and was most accommodating in answering the questions put to him.

"Yes, the police did come and question me about Clemente and the girl, who always had breakfast together.

I do not have any further knowledge on how they spent the rest of the day. I never saw them together other than at breakfast. I did see the young lady on the odd occasion when she took an early meal in the evening."

"Did he seem interested in her?" Ziegler asked.

"He was very pleasant and flirted with her, but she did not reciprocate," the manager responded. "I remember overhearing one conversation in which she declined his offer of diner. All this young lady appeared to want to do was learn Portuguese. She and I touched on various topics, on the few occasions on which we spoke. She wanted to practice her Portuguese. She was doing very well. A lovely girl, always very pleasant and cheerful."

"Signor," said Ziegler tentatively, "I must ask you another question pertaining to this case. Has any member of your staff approached you about something strange that happened? Possibly in the men's cloakroom, the one located by the lifts on the first floor? It was on a Friday, 2 weeks ago."

"No, not that I can remember. What unusual happening are you talking about?"

"The murder victim planted some very important papers, a formula, in the young lady's case while she was finishing up in her room. He offered to take her case along with his own down to the lobby. On route it seems likely that he stopped somewhere and planted the papers in her suitcase, as he didn't want to be found with the papers in his possession if he happened to be searched. On the floor she was on, is there anywhere that he might have carried out such a task?"

"Certainly," said the manager. "There is a men's cloakroom, but it is very small in there. It would be difficult to make an exchange like that without having to leave the door open. You are welcome to examine the room and form your own opinion."

Ziegler thanked the manager and continued. "Do you think you could check the roster for that day and see which members of staff were working in that area of the hotel. I'd like to ask them whether they saw anyone behaving strangely."

"Yes, I can do that," replied the manager, "I'll show you to the cloakroom then start making some enquiries. If you would like to have a complimentary coffee in the Blue Room while you wait for me to assemble the relevant staff you are very welcome."

Though the manager spoke fairly good English, Ziegler thought, it would be easier if Sertorio did the bulk of the talking during the staff interviews and he could relay what needed to be asked. Several individuals were interviewed but were unable to help. The manager returned confirming that one member of staff, a middle-aged woman by the name of Sophia, had been on duty at that time but was off duty for the next few days.

"Could you please give me her address and telephone number so we can get hold of her?" Ziegler requested.

"I hope she will be at home so you can speak to her. Often when she has some time off she visits her elderly parents who live in the country." The manager explained.

"Do you know where that is?"

"No, I don't," said the manager. "I regret that you may have to wait until she returns, which will be next Tuesday."

Ziegler knew that time was of the essence. "In the circumstances it's worth trying to contact her. Sertorio, could you kindly ring Sophia and see if she is at her home. If not we shall have to return to talk to her next week."

Sertorio telephoned the number he had been given but there was no answer. They asked whether the manager would contact them as soon as Sophia returned. The manager was eager to be of assistance. "Of course I will. I want this resolved as much as you do, for this kind of publicity only gives the hotel a bad name."

Shaking hands with the manager and thanking him for the coffee and his cooperation, Ziegler and Sertorio sauntered out of the hotel to return to the military compound. They were at a stale mate and would not be able pursue this line of enquiry for another 4 days. They could, of course, investigate Clemente's background, but they would have to be a little careful not to interfere with the police's enquiries.

On returning to the base they had a quick word with Constance, filling her in on what they had been doing. Constance was disappointed that no one at the hotel had seen anything. She was a little happier when she heard that there had been a maid on duty on the day that she and Clemente had left the hotel that was yet to be interviewed.

***

Ziegler and Sertorio spent the next day checking the layout of the compound. It was enormous. Everyone appeared to be present and correct except Miguel, the sales agent. They discovered that he had left the compound and had not been seen since the night of the murder. They came to the conclusion that he must have left just after the killing. The police had been informed and had gone to his rented flat. He had taken just a few necessary items – his wallet and some papers – and had walked out of the gates without being asked any questions. Knowing that Miguel had done a runner, Ziegler hoped that as Constance's representative he would now be able to search the apartment. Arriving at police headquarters with Sertorio as his interpreter, he requested to see Miguel's flat. Permission was granted on the condition that they did not remove anything from the premises. Ziegler was still unsure how thoroughly his flat had been searched. There was no other proof there that he had killed Clemente and no witnesses had come forward to corroborate Constance's story about him entering the coffee shop. He had not sat down or taken a drink. There was nothing to indicate that Miguel had been there or that he was guilty of any crime. His only suspicious action was the fact that he had left the base at around 20.15 hours on the night in question and had not been seen since. Before leaving the police station and heading to Miguel's flat, Ziegler wanted to know what Miguel had been wearing. He put through a quick call to Constance hoping that she would be free to speak.

"I don't remember much of what he was wearing except for a very bright red long sleeved shirt. He had a gold chain dangling from his neck," she responded.

Ziegler thanked her for the information. He and Sertorio went on to search the small flat, which lay on the second floor. It was neat but with very few mementos and pictures, giving little idea of the individual's personality. The flat held no surprises and Ziegler felt that he was at a deadlock. The two men walked downstairs and wandered to the back of the flat, where six large green bins belonging to the flats were situated. They were not numbered so Ziegler and Sertorio were not able to connect any particular bin to Miguel. Always prepared, Ziegler had brought two pairs of plastic gloves as well as plastic bags on the off-chance that they might need them. One after the other of the bins was turned upside down in the hopes of finding the murder weapon or other evidence. Having gone through four of the bins they were getting frustrated. Was this going to be a complete waste of time? They turned the fifth bin over, which was filled with rotten tomatoes, eggshells and cans empty food cans. At the bottom was a bright red shirt. Holding his breath, Ziegler grabbed put it in a plastic bag while Sertorio made a further search of the rubbish hoping to find the gold chain. It was there too! Ziegler was sure that Miguel's aim was to rid himself of any evidence that might connect him to the crime. Ziegler was pleased at their discovery but disappointed that the police had not thought to make a more thorough search of the area.

After returning to their accommodation to clean up, they checked in with the police and handed over the plastic bag that contained the bright red shirt and the chain. Both were splattered with blood. The items were entered into the system as evidence and forms were filled out so they could be passed onto forensics. They knew it was a long shot due to the shirt having been immersed among the putrid contents of the bin, but they hoped to find evidence of gunpowder residue and determine whether the blood type matched that of Clemente. The gun had not been recovered so it was presumed that Miguel had either discarded it, or else he still had it in his possession.

Within a few days it was confirmed that the red shirt definitely contained powder burns and that the blood group was the same as Clemente's. Taking fingerprints from his flat, the police had since identified him as someone who had been suspected of carrying out various crimes in different parts of the country but had avoided conviction. Not being able to catch up with him, the police assumed he acted under various aliases. A thorough check of his references had revealed various holes in his supposed background.

The other five residents from Miguel's block of flats who had been interviewed were not able to add anything of further use to the police or Ziegler and Sertorio, who carefully combed their statements.

As soon as the police had discovered that Miguel was not who he appeared to be, a national APB was put out with his photograph and a request that any sightings should be reported to the police station on the military compound in Manaus. It was advised that he should not be approached at any cost as he was dangerous. Since Brazil is an enormous country, it was thought doubtful he would ever be found. Nevertheless, as he was wanted in connection with a number of crimes, the police considered offering a reward. There was always the chance that a substantial reward could induce a person to disclose information that might lead to Miguel's arrest.

***

The Tuesday after Ziegler and Sertorio's visit to the tourist hotel in the city, the manager rang to let them know that Sophia was back at work. He said that he would not speak to her about the incident until they arrived.

Pleased that Sophia had returned, Ziegler and Seriorio left the base immediately, arriving at the hotel in the middle of the morning. The manager was waiting for them in his office already having asked Sophia to meet him there. Sophia – a plump, matronly individual – stood up as they entered. She looked absolutely terrified, not having any idea as to why she had been called into the manager's office. She was worried that the foreign-looking men might have accused her of theft, and that she might lose her job. "There is nothing to be concerned about Sophia." Sertorio explained after being introduced. "We just need a little information and hope that you will be able to help us."

"I will do what I can," she answered nervously, her fingers worrying at the cuff of her blouse. He went on to explain why they were there and asked her to cast her mind back to the day in question. "Did you happen to see anything strange or unusual during the time you were cleaning the men's cloakroom?" Sophia looked puzzled. It was, after all, a few weeks ago and she hadn't noticed anything of note.

"I cannot remember anything of particular importance. What was I meant to have seen?" Ziegler and Sertorio looked at each other. They did not want to tell her what they wanted to know in case she agreed she had seen Clemente, just to please them. The manager intervened. "Did you happen to see someone struggling with two suitcases?"

"Oh yes, that's right, I did. I thought it a little strange for he could not close the stall door because he had both of the cases open. I did not see anything else. He was rather surprised at seeing me but gave me a pleasant smile as he walked out with them. I forgot about the incident a few moments later, for it did not seem that important."

"Thank you Sophia, you have been most helpful," said Sertorio gratefully. "Before you go I would like you to write down what you have just told us. I will then type it out for you to sign. I would appreciate it, however, if you do not mention this to anyone."

"Of course not. May I go now please?" She looked pleadingly at her boss.

The manager looked at the gentlemen who responded for him. "Yes you may. Thank you."

Ziegler pondered the statement Sophia had given them. Would this exonerate Constance from police suspicion? It could do, but he personally would only be completely satisfied when Miguel was caught.

***

The days went by, Ziegler and Sertorio kicking their heels on the compound, keeping Constance company but doing very little else. What else could be done at this stage? They could not go searching for Miguel; they would not know where to begin. Constance was relieved that a maid had been found who was able to verify her suspicions, but the police were not completely satisfied. Ziegler thought of flying home. There was a lot of work awaiting him on his return, but he did not want to leave Constance in the lurch. Apart from that, he had promised her mother that he would resolve the situation. Sertorio, on the other hand felt that he should return home to his family in Portugal. This was understandable. They had both been in Brazil for over 2 weeks and Sertorio's wife wanted him back.

Constance gave Sertorio a special farewell dinner before he left. He had been a marvellous ally to Ziegler and herself, giving up his precious time to travel to Brazil, leaving his job and family behind. She could not have got so far without him.

After Sertorio left, Ziegler felt quite bereft. How was he going to manage with the communication barrier? He had picked up a few words of Portuguese and could understand a certain amount but he would not be able to argue any point of law. Though it was not the best of solutions, Constance suggested that maybe her roommate Claudine Marchant could fill in when it was absolutely necessary. She had been living in Brazil for many years and her Portuguese was fluent. This would, of course, depend upon whether she would be allowed to leave her duties at any given time. Claudine was the only person Constance knew whom she could trust absolutely and translate accurately and honestly.

***

The days went by with no further news of Miguel. He seemed to have disappeared into thin air. The APB put out for him had produced a couple of sightings but nobody had been able to apprehend him, and nobody had come forward.

"I wonder how long this will go on," Constance thought. She had, in the last couple of days, been allowed to continue with her research on tropical medicine, which she so loved. Even though there was a cloud hanging over her, the joy of research distracted her from the plight she was in. She was optimistic that she would be cleared of the charge of stealing the formula and be allowed to complete her contract in the military compound, which would come to an end in 2 months' time.

Since the maid had verified fact that Clemente had exchanged the documents in the men's cloakroom she had written to her mother – I was very important to tell her how marvellous Ziegler and Sertorio had been to her. She hoped Ziegler would be able to join them at Christmas, discovering that he lived on his own and had no plans. She knew her mother cared for him and had an inkling that she might be able to bring them together. She wanted her mother to be happy, she deserved it. She had been through a lot. Her father had been dead for some time now. If her mother found another man with whom she could be happy, who was she to stand in the way?

***

At 6.30pm 2 weeks after her interview at the manager's office, Sophia was accosted on her way home. A man jumped out in front of her, dragging her into an alleyway. She was petrified but since he had clamped his hand over her mouth she could not scream. He twisted her arm behind her, pulling it until she thought it would break. Tears rolled down her cheeks. Growling into her ear, the man almost spat his words, "If you struggle, bitch, I will hit you. I suggest that you don't. I want some answers. If you scream I will hurt you. Do you understand?" She nodded.

"I was hovering near the manager's office when you were called in to talk about something to those foreign men."

He removed his hand so she could answer. "What do you mean, what foreign men?"

He gave her a sharp slap across her face, which made her reel. "I want a better answer. Who were these guys and what did they want from you?" He prompted her. "They had come to talk about the man with the two suitcases, hadn't they?"

"Yes, they had." Sophia hardly knew how to answer, was he going to kill her when he had finished with her? She was prepared to tell him anything and he knew that. "I said that the man had gone into a stall with two cases, but as both of them were open and the stall was too small and the door was left open."

"What else?"

208

She searched her memory for anything she could give him. "Nothing else. I did not see anything. I was occupied in cleaning the cloakroom. I had put a notice on the door saying cleaning was in progress, but he probably did not see it. He was a little surprised when I entered the room. What was I meant to see?"

He gave her another slap across the face. "No insolence. What did you do then?"

Tears were streaming down her face. "I finished my job and went home."

"So you did not report it?"

She was quick to answer. "No. I did not see anything. I told you."

Getting a little more confident Sophia asked: "What are you asking me this for? I am just a maid who cleans hotels and does as she is told."

"All right, piss off. But if I find you know more than you are saying, I shall seek you out and I won't be so lenient the next time."

He threw her away from him, she falling down on the hard stone. She was not seriously hurt, a little bruised from the fall, her face smarting from the slaps she had received, and her shoulder aching. Sophia rushed home, white with the horror she had just been put through. The only colour on her face came from the large red marks on her skin where she had been hit.

Sobbing, she put a call through to the manager as soon as she arrived at her flat telling him what had happened. The manager immediately rang the police and sent a car to Sophia's place to collect her. When Sophia and the police had arrived, he remembered the lawyer. He called Ziegler, who found it difficult to understand what he was saying. Since his friend Sertorio was not there to translate, Ziegler asked the manager in slow English if he could wait a few minutes so he could get a new translator. Claudine had finished work for the day and at Constance's request was able to come to Ziegler's aid more or less immediately. As Ziegler was fluent in French, he was able to communicate with Claudine quite comfortably. The manager told Claudine that an assailant had waylaid the maid in a dark alley, knocking her around a bit and asking her questions about the suitcases in the stall. The police, who were still talking to Sophia, had said they suspected that Miguel was in the area and responsible for the attack. They were on alert with road blocks and armed men at all the entrances and exits of every rail station and airport in case he fled the area.

Sophia was terror-stricken. After being interviewed by the police it was recommended that she either stay with a friend or relative or be put in a safe house until Miguel was caught. Sophia, knowing that she could not go to work until this was all over, opted to go off into the country to stay with her parents. She was escorted by the police to her flat so she could pack a bag and was then taken to her parents immediately.

***

Meanwhile Miguel was none the wiser about what he should do next and feared for his life. His bosses were hunting him down to obtain the formula that he was meant to have handed over to them. He had been paid up front and they were not the sort of people to let such insolence go unpunished. Realising that now everybody would be pursuing him, he thought it better to stay where he was until things had cooled down a little. He knew he should have killed the maid and not been so soft. He should have realised that she would have reported her run-in with him to the police. He thought of turning himself in but was still hopeful of escaping to Rio Janeiro. It would take a long time as he would have to travel across country, but there was still a chance. At least no papers were needed to get from one state to another. He walked to his rented room, reflecting upon his next move.

When he was only a few yards from his residence a dark figure suddenly darted out from the shadows, attacking him from behind. The figure slit Miguel's throat from ear to ear. It was done so quickly he had no time to cry out in the cool air. His body slumped on the ground was only discovered by a mechanic leaving for work at sunrise. A news bulletin was sent out reporting his death, which Claudine happened to pick up later in the morning. Claudine passed the news onto Constance and then to Ziegler, both of whom were relieved but still a little unsure as to how the police would take it. Would Constance now be vindicated or would there still have to be further investigation to prove her innocence? Checking on Miguel's room in the city, which the police located without too much difficulty, they found papers pertaining to the drug cartel that Miguel had been associated with. It clarified that Miguel and Clemente, as middlemen, had been involved in the theft and black-market sale of the chemical formula found in Constance's suitcase. There was no mention of Constance anywhere.

On consideration of the evidence, the case against Constance was dropped. Ziegler returned to Germany, his heart much lighter than when he had arrived in Brazil. He had received a very warm invitation from Françoise to stay with them at Christmas. He hoped that it was not only because of his assisting Constance.

***

Ziegler was still curious as to whom Constance had fallen in love with. Judging by her sad countenance when talking about the young recruit's return to Corsica, he felt it could be Tom, the man her mother had mentioned. He did not think it a good idea to talk about Tom while he was in Brazil, but maybe he could lead up to it when he visited them at their home at Christmastide.

With Constance's name completely cleared she was allowed to continue with her studies and have access to all the various files and information that hitherto she had not be permitted to have. Ten days before Christmas, Constance packed her bags in preparation for her return to Scotland. She was very sorry to have to say farewell to Claudine, who had become a close friend, but at the same time she had high hopes that Dr Duncan would have arranged for her to start her studies at the hospital in Aberdeen at the start of the next academic year.

Not having replied to Macey's last letter and not having heard a word from Tom, Constance began to wonder if her connection with him was a figment of her imagination. He might also be too ill to communicate. Oh, if only she knew! She could not put these ideas to rest so shortly before leaving Brazil she wrote another letter to Macey hoping that he had more knowledge of Tom's location. If he still had not heard anything then she would know that it was over, before it had begun. Still, she felt needed to give it another try. She wrote her Scottish address at the bottom of the letter in the hopes that it would be passed on to Tom.

CHAPTER 22

Back to Sweden

Tom took over as the driver on the long and tiring car journey from Switzerland through Germany. Before they reached Denmark, his father took over so Tom could rest. Tom drove back into Sweden, arriving at his parents' home in Eskilstuna exhausted, not only by the long journey but due to the fear he might have been apprehended at the borders.

Everything had gone smoothly, his parents going through the same charade at each checkpoint so no one would be suspicious. It would not have been a special concern to the authorities if he had been found to be fleeing from the Legion, but impersonating someone else and travelling under their passport was. He was so very grateful to his parents who had undertaken this mammoth task of rescuing him that it came as a surprise a couple of days after his return that he felt strangely flat. Reflecting once more on the past few years, he realised that he had not given that much time to thinking further than escaping, choosing to fill every moment with manoeuvres, peace-keeping missions, playing cards, joking, getting drunk with his friends or just trying to stay alive. It had been a challenging existence. He sorely missed Macey.

He had become a true friend and a rare one at that. He also missed Macey's sharp wit and great sense of humour. Tom's mind often drifted off towards Constance. He had no idea where she could have gone. He felt he needed to get in touch with both of them and provide some explanation of what had happened.

He decided to write to Macey the next day filling him in with what had happened and his escape from Marseilles. Although Macey still had another 2 ½ years in the Legion, Tom said he hoped that they would be able to meet up when he had completed his time there. Planning ahead, Tom knew that re-entering France would only court trouble, so proposed that the rendezvous be in Sweden or England. He asked what Macey had in mind when his period in the Legion was over: whether he would leave or stay and further his career. He asked him whether he had received any information on the whereabouts of Constance of if she had contacted the Legion to ask after him. Unfortunately, as Tom had not given any cause for Constance to think he was especially interested in her and she had not given him any either, it was a long shot. "What a waste," Tom thought to himself. "We were ideally suited to each other and yet I no indication about what I felt for her."

It would take a few days; maybe a week before Macey received the letter. It would also depend upon whether Macey had undertaken another mission. He had mentioned that he was interested in going to Chad before they left Guiana so he might not get Tom's letter for some time. Tom wondered if he should contact Madeleine if he received no response after a month.

Macey did reply. It took about 2 weeks in all. Tom was right. Macey was off to Chad in a couple of weeks and he would probably remain for about 2 months. He would be back for the special Christmas festivities the Legion usually offered to all their soldiers, which would take place at the barracks in Calvi. Christmas in the Legion was a very special affair and not comparable to any other unit. Festivities usually started on Christmas Eve with all the long tables mounted with the most sumptuous food possible, as well as a spectacular array of whiskeys and spirits, traditional ales from around the world, and a choice of the finest red and white wines. Everyone was equal on this special night, whether you were a rookie, a sergeant or an officer. The NCOs and officers were the hosts, treating everyone as honoured guests and personally serving each and every one of them.

At midnight each man was presented with a Christmas gift by an officer, followed by the Germans, who had the most harmonious voices, singing "Stille Nacht". It was always a most memorable night.

Macey had seen Madeleine on quite a few occasions and they planned to move in together when he had finished his tour of duty in the Legion. They were not quite sure where yet, but he thought he might join a parachute regiment in England and Madeleine was very happy to come with him. She hoped to join Air France as a stewardess.

***

There had been quite an outcry at Tom's desertion from Marseilles, nobody having any idea how he managed it. Harry and Benedict had returned to Calvi after their stint in the hospital but kept absolutely silent about their involvement. Knowing that Macey was a good friend of his, they nonchalantly asked him about Tom's escape and whether he had returned safely to Sweden. Macey confirmed that he had, which Harry and Benedict were delighted to hear.

"But life goes on," Macey wrote, "there are still quite a few recruits who try and desert, some succeeding but others who don't" Macey explained that he had received a letter from Constance, who had written from the rainforests of Brazil. She had addressed the letter to him, Macey, as she knew that he and Tom were such good friends that he might be able to shed some light on Tom's whereabouts. Unfortunately Macey could not give her any information, as he had not heard from Tom at the time he had received her letter. She told him that she would be in Brazil until Christmas, when she would be returning to Scotland. She had written her Scottish address at the bottom of the letter.

Macey ended the letter by saying that he hoped that they would be able to meet up, either in Sweden or in England, when he had completed his stint in the Legion. He ended the letter, saying "Keep well and please keep in touch. I know that 2½ years is a fairly long time and anything can happen during that period, but I shall very much look forward to catching up with you when I finally do leave."

CHAPTER 23

Chad

M acey knew that he would continue to be sent all over the world to protect France's interests. Much of the excitement of resolving the skirmishes in these foreign parts had waned for Macey. He and Tom had always met the challenges together with great enthusiasm, but with Tom's departure this had gone and he felt somewhat diffident and alone. They had always supported each other when one or the other had succumbed or fallen into a difficult situation, and they had probably survived where others might not. He had some great mates, Harry, Benedict, Hans, but they had not shared the same experiences as he and Tom had. He knew it was not very wise of him to reflect on what had happened so he forced himself to look forward to his next mission and the chance of adding one more achievement to his list.

He had requested to go to Chad, which was an African country situated south of Libya and nestled in between Niger and the Sudan. Chad had been plagued by unrest for years, Libya constantly making brief incursions with the help of Soviet agents in the north of the country. Chad had become independent from France in 1960 but Legionnaires were still sent there to help resolve problems with the rebels in the north and to try and bring some kind of peace and harmony to the area.

A unit of 12 recruits plus a sergeant left Ajaccio airport one autumn morning, their parachutes packed in preparation to jump 50–60 km away from the airfield. Dropping into the desert at the dead of night, the soldiers picked up their parachutes, adjusted their back packs and moved up into the hills, where they could not be seen. It was presumed that the rebels situated in another area had no idea that the Legion had been called in to provide assistance. Macey and his fellow soldiers crept up the hill and found a cave, not a very welcoming one, but one that would hide them and protect them from the cold night that lay ahead. It would also give them a base from which to reconnoitre the area and lay their plan of attack.

"Catch a couple of hours' kip," the sergeant in charge barked at them. "You Parker take the first watch. You are not going to have a lot of rest when the insurgence begins, so make the most of it. It is always very icy at night but luckily we are protected from the biting winds here in the cave. It is incredibly hot during the day, which I am sure you are all well aware of, so you will need to acclimatise yourselves to these extremes. Good luck to you all." Macey, Harry and Benedict made a point of lying very close to each other in their sleeping bags. It was one of the usual ways of keeping body and soul together.

Rising just before dawn, everyone except for the recruit who had been on guard for the last 2 hours, grabbed some rolls and hot coffee and started down the deep and rocky terrain in search of the rebels they knew were somewhere in the vicinity. From certain reliable sources they had been alerted to the fact that Libya had made many an invasion into Chad with the help of Soviet agents, and together with the bandits of the northern tribes had caused untold chaos. It seemed that various African states had become eternally divided by corrupt military dictatorship and centuries of animosity.

Among the soldiers, most of whom had volunteered for this mission, was a blond, blue-eyed Russian lad around the age of 22, called Nikita meaning unconquerable. Nikita Rusakov had joined the Legion about 6 months earlier and seemed very friendly and capable. He was a very strong 6-footer and none of the Legion's rules appeared to bother him. He had asked to join the mission in Chad, explaining that as it was his first mission he wanted to involve himself in a challenging assignment to get used to situations that might arise in the future. This reasoning did not go down well with the others. "Every mission is different and sometimes dangerous, and it would be unwise to compare one with another," responded Macey.

He did not seem to be bothered by the desert in the north of Chad or the effects of highly varying temperatures. He volunteered to be on guard the first night, not at all concerned that he would have little rest for the next 12 hours. Macey and Harry were slightly nonplussed by his disposition and thought perhaps it was due to his youth, vitality and lack of experience. No one was usually as enthusiastic as that. They had already forgotten their first time as new recruits and how enthusiastic they had been, how full of life. They were only approximately 3 years older than this young man, yet they were already hardened Legionnaires and extremely cynical.

Towards the end of the long day and after checking on a great many sites, they located another cave way up in the hills where they could stay the night. They had not discovered any special objects of interest that the rebels had left behind, only cans of beer, some clothing, food and water (always a bonus). No weapons. They were exhausted. With the night falling suddenly upon them, they needed to down some food, close up their sleeping bags and lie more on less on top of each other to get some warmth. The only poor bugger not tucked up warmly in his sleeping bag was the one on guard for the next 4 hours. Macey knew that his guard duty would soon come up.

Nikita continued as usual, carrying out his duties with the others in his usual manner. He did not appear to have much concern for himself but always seemed to watch out for the others. It was unusual for a newcomer to be so solicitous, and Macey was slightly baffled. Also baffling was the fact that in the week that they had been moving from one site to another, climbing over the razor-like rocks, not one single rebel had been spotted. He found it rather odd. He wished Tom had been there to discuss this somewhat unusual point at issue, as he always seemed to have insight into a problem that others may have overlooked. Unbeknown to Macey, Sergeant Greenfield, the officer in charge, was also puzzled. In all the time that they had been in the area the only thing spotted was the rubbish the rebels had left behind. The Sergeant wondered whether they had done this to put the Legion off their tracks, for it certainly did not give any indication as to the route they were taking.

Within the group there was another fairly new recruit called Dan, who had joined the Foreign Legion a year earlier. He was renowned for being an excellent tracker. It was hoped that he would be able to make some of sense from the oddments that were left behind. He spent a great deal of time checking on the footprints and to where the tracks led.

Two weeks after arriving in this desolate area, it was Macey's turn for guard duty. Four hours was a long period in which to stand out in the cold but he was prepared for the inevitable, he had done it on many occasions. As darkness set in he moved to the designated location. He would, of course, move around the camp to check that everything was in order and there were no unwelcome visitors, whether in the shape of a person or a wild animal. As he stood just outside the cave he heard a slight buzzing sound coming from the other side of the hill. It was so faint that it was hardly audible. He stealthily crept nearer to where the sound was coming from, holding his breath at the same time in case he could be heard, and almost tripping over a large boulder. It was Nikita, bending over a transistor sending out a message in code. What on earth is he doing, he thought, playing around with a transistor at this time of night? Who is he sending a message to? He hesitated for a moment but thought better of going any closer. It could put him in a dangerous situation. He would report it to Sergeant Greenfield immediately, even though in doing so it might mean having to wake him. It suddenly hit Macey that Nikita could be communicating with the rebels who were in contact with Russian agents. He was horrified at the thought. How gullible I have been to have thought that he was whiter than white, he reflected. He certainly seemed too good to be true.

Macey walked back as quickly as he could to the cave, hoping his absence from his vantage point as guard would not go against him as there was no one outside to protect his comrades in arms. He made immediate contact with the Sergeant, shaking him gently, urgently asking him if he could talk to him outside. Greenfield jumped out of his sleeping bag and stepped out into the cold night air, wondering what was so urgent that Macey had to talk him in the middle of the night.

"Sir, I am so sorry to wake you but before I proceed do you think you could ask another one of the rookies to stand guard for me for the next half an hour until I have finished talking to you." The Sergeant nodded his agreement and arranged for cover. This done, Macey squared his shoulders and without preamble reported his sightings of Nikita, whom he believed to be sending messages with a transistor on the other side of the hill. He ended by saying, "I do not know if he is back yet for I did not see him return. My concern was to report the incident to you as quickly as possible."

"I am glad you awoke me. It was the right thing to do. I shall just take a quick look to see if Rusakov has returned to camp. In the meantime, continue with your guard duty and tell the young soldier that he may return to bed. Tell nobody about this incident: that is an order."

The Sergeant returned 5 minutes later, not having seen anything suspicious. From the sleeping bags he was unable to make out who was who in the dark but it did not seem that there were any missing persons. If Macey was correct, Rusakov must have surreptitiously clambered into his sleeping bag when nobody was looking. He needed to check up on this recruit as well as asking the tracker to check on the area he had sent the message from. Even though he was wholly confident with Macey's report, he needed it confirmed by a more definite source. Maybe, just maybe, Rusakov was doing something else and not sending messages to the enemy. He really hoped that this was true, but with no sightings of the rebels at all there was a strong possibility that this was the reason for the lack of them.

Just before dawn and before the recruits had awoken and started their ablutions, Sergeant Greenfield pointed Dan, the tracker, towards the area Nikita had been in to see whether there was any cause to believe that he was really a Soviet agent. Dan, without a word, bent down to check the sandy terrain. To him it was quite obvious that somebody had been there the night before. There three pairs of tracks coming from the cave, one set being Macey's, one the Sergeant's and the other a person unknown. He was also able to conclude from the area that a heavy object had been laid on the ground. With a quick thanks to the tracker, the sergeant returned to gather everyone together to prepare for another gruelling day searching for rebels.

Macey was very tired after his guard duty but was also very disturbed at his discovery that Nikita could be a spy. When one joined the Foreign Legion one always felt one was joining an honourable group of soldiers who would fight to the death for the cause. It was therefore upsetting to encounter a person who had appeared to support the Legion but was actually working against them. Nikita, it appeared, was much more interested in aiding and abetting the enemy and creating disharmony in Chad. Macey wondered whether the Sergeant would enlighten him as to what his finding was and his next course of action. He had a feeling that he would not necessarily be informed. Perhaps there would be nothing to tell.

***

They moved onto a completely different area soon after consuming their rolls and coffee the next morning but just before leaving the Sergeant pulled Macey aside and in a very low voice said, "Macey, you are a very friendly chap. Please continue to be so in all aspects. Rusakov would think something was up if you behaved any differently. It is not easy to put on an act when it is against your nature, but it will be very helpful if you can watch his movements and report back."

"You wish me to spy for you?" Macey responded in a quiet voice, for the thought of spying on a fellow Legionnaire, even one suspected of contact with the enemy, was abhorrent to him.

"That's the sum of it. Just be normal and muck around with him and with your mates, Harry and Benedict, as you usually do. Nothing different. They are not to know what has been going on."

"I am not very good at acting, Sir."

"I am sure you will manage."

They carried on during the day, checking on various haunts where it was hoped that there might be some clues as to where the rebels were holed up, but again they only found some old clothes and remnants of rotten food that had been left behind. This time, however, Dan the tracker was able to determine, by checking the tracks on the ground, that these so-called clues were a ruse. Unfortunately there was not enough information to determine where their hide-out was. The tracker always made a point of checking the terrain when all was quiet, at the Sergeant's request. The less idea Nikita had of their suspicions the better.

"We'll stay here for the night," announced Sergeant Greenfield. "We have done enough trekking around for the day." There was the usual bustle as they set up camp. When everyone was asleep, Sergeant Greenfield kept his eyes and ears open. He waited for Rusakov to climb out of his sleeping bag and head for an open space where he could use the transistor and not be heard. A moment after Rusakov had left the cave, Greenfield clambered out of his bag and followed the soldier, hoping he would not lose him in the dark. There was no moon and the sky was overcast. About 5 minutes after rising, the Sergeant heard the same electronic buzzing sound that Macey had heard. It was so faint that Sergeant Greenfield had to listen more intently than he would normally have done to make out where it was coming from. Creeping up towards the grass hill, following the sound, he saw a dark figure bending down over what seemed to be a mechanical device. Greenfield kept well back so as not to be seen or heard. Nikita was not talking, but listening carefully Sergeant Greenfield suddenly realised that the message was being sent in Morse code, which was easy enough to decipher.

"They can't find the rebels; what is your next plan of action? Do you wish me to lead them into a trap?"

Sergeant Greenfield did not listen to anything else. He thought it better that he withdraw immediately before Rusakov returned and found him. Knowing that Rusakov was the enemy put a different slant on the situation. He would have to be considered the enemy; an enemy who would have no qualms in executing all of them if anybody got in his way.

The next day saw the group divide in half and move into two different directions. Macey and friends were in the group that included Nikita while Sergeant Greenfield was in the other. The Sergeant was anxious to receive advice as to the best course of action, given his new-found knowledge. Once the groups had separated, he called headquarters on the radio. It was suggested that he should not arrest Rusakov but wait and see whether Macey and the tracker came up with anything. The rest of the day was again taken up with searching for the enemy, which as expected resulted in nothing.

Each subsequent evening after the recruits had bedded themselves down for the night, Sergeant Greenfield would wait for Rusakov to leave his sleeping place and head for the hills to send his message. Most of the time the response was the same: bide your time and continue as planned.

A week later this changed. "They still have not located where you are and it seems they are getting restless and unsure as to how long they should continue their mission. They have a tracker who seems rather inept and who still cannot verify where the recruits should be heading."

This time Greenfield was luckily able to interpret the reply to Rusakov's message. "In a week's time we shall attempt to ambush the Legionnaires in one of the caves they are hanging out in and execute all of them. Keep your eyes open and make sure you keep to the plan, otherwise you will know what will happen."

Sergeant Greenfield ran back to the camp at full speed, throwing himself into his sleeping bag before Nikita returned. He now knew that the rebels planned to execute his group and would have to be on the alert. He had to establish as to exactly when the attack would be. He went through the message in his mind again and suddenly remembered the parting message Rusakov had been given. "Keep your eyes and ears open and make sure you keep to the plan, otherwise you will know what will happen." What did that mean? It almost seemed as if Nikita was being threatened, and if so what hold did they have on him?

The next day the sergeant had a quiet word with Macey when nobody was around. "Have you learned anything more from Rusakov?" he asked.

"Nothing, he has not slipped up once."

"I believe he is being threatened, so try and ask him questions about his mother, girlfriend, and sister when in conversation. He may say everything is fine but you can check his facial expressions, however, slight, when a loved one is mentioned. I could be wrong, but I do not see Nikita as a hardened criminal or a murderer. I suggest that you cajole Harry and Benedict as well as Nikita into having a game of cards, get the whiskey out and then start asking him about his personal life. Bring your girlfriend into the conversation and how you met her."

"How do you know about my girlfriend?" retorted Macey.

"It is my job to know about as much as I can about you all," Greenfield answered. "Your behaviour as a Legionnaire depends a lot on your frame of mind. I don't want a Legionnaire who is troubled and whose mind is only 60% on the job. It is dangerous for himself and his fellow recruits. Therefore talk about yourself, Madeleine, your sister and your family."

There was no time to talk about frivolities until 2 days later when Macey, his two friends and Nikita were sitting round the fire playing cards. "Oh," groaned Macey, "what I wouldn't do to be on a beach right now in the arms of my gorgeous Madeleine, with no mission ahead of me and none of your ugly mugs for company."

"You have a girlfriend, Macey? You've never mentioned her before," remarked Benedict,

"I suppose the subject never came up," answered Macey. "I had a rather distressing, but exciting adventure two missions ago when the plane we were flying in from Corsica crashed as it was coming into land on Mayotte in the Comoros Islands. The plane broke up on impact with the sea and sank into the ocean. Only Tom and the lovely Madeleine survived. She is the only one for me."

"Who is Tom?" asked Nikita.

"Tom was a great friend of mine and an amazing soldier, but he deserted and fled back to Sweden," Macey responded.

"How does he happen to be so 'amazing' when he dishonoured the Legion by running away?" Nikita retorted.

"It is a long story, which I will tell you someday. He did some remarkable things and was highly thought of."

"He sounds a strange man," Nikita remarked, wrinkling up his nose in distaste.

"Do you have a girlfriend Nikita" asked Macey?

"Yes," he answered. "She is back in Russian living with her family." A dark cloud seemed to pass over Nikita's face but was gone in a second. "I don't know when I will see her next, but perhaps she will be able to visit me in Corsica."

Benedict and Harry sucked in all this information but could not add any juicy bits of their own to the conversation as both of them had ended their relationships on entering the Legion, knowing that it would be very difficult to carry on a romance at a distance for 5 years.

Macey was unable to report his findings to the sergeant that night as Greenfield was once again outside trying to glean as much information as possible about the forthcoming attack. Macey was somewhat surprised that the young Russian had been bothered by Tom's defection, for it gave a different perspective on the man's character. How strange that he should perceive Tom as "dishonourable" for deserting without knowing why, and believing perhaps that laying a trap to capture and kill the Legionnaires was not. He felt, as a loyal friend to Tom, that he should not mention that part of the conversation to the Sergeant, but just Nikita's reaction when talking about his girlfriend. Only if he was pressed would he include Nikita's comments about Tom, which might help the Sergeant understand the Russian a little better. It seemed that Nikita had twisted and divided loyalties.

Sergeant Greenfield had gathered no more information from his last exploration and hoped that Macey had managed to extricate something he could work on. As soon as the Sergeant was alone, Macey approached him with his findings, a little unsure as to whether they may or may not be enough on which to act.

"Is that all he said?" queried Greenfield.

"He was surprised at the lack of loyalty of one of the Legionnaires who had deserted a short while ago," Macey added with some regret.

"Oh, you mean Fredriksson. Yes, it was a little mystifying, especially when he was such a fine soldier. Repeat verbatim what Rusakov said."

Macey proceeded to repeat exactly what Nikita had said. When he had nearly finished he remembered a rather unusual comment that Nikita had happened to say in passing: perhaps my girl friend will come and visit me when I am back in Corsica.

Sergeant Greenfield frowned. How did that fact fit in with the scenario, he wondered? Did Nikita really plan on executing them all and returning to the Legion as though nothing had happened? He was aware that it was going to be difficult, but he had to challenge this soldier when he least expected it and interrogate him. He did not have an office where he could conduct an interview, so the only way he could do this would be to confront him after he had sent a message to the rebels. He knew he had to be careful, for Nikita would probably be aggressive and prepared to use his fire arm if caught in the act. Even worse, he might be prepared to commit suicide if things did not work according to plan.

The night after the talk with Macey, the Sergeant once again followed the buzzing sound produced by the radio. Sergeant Greenfield waited for approximately 5 minutes until the young Russian had finished his message. When Nikita turned round to make his way back to the camp, he saw the figure of Sergeant Greenfield appearing from the shadows. "What you are doing, Rusakov?" he demanded in a sharp voice.

Nikita raised his FAMAS pointing the weapon at Sergeant Greenfield's heart. The Sergeant smiled in the darkness. "I should not bother, I have removed the cartridge."

Rusakov threw the rifle down on the ground burying his head in his hands. "You don't understand. I have no option but to do this. I have a good friend who will be buried alive if I do not do everything they say."

"What a charming way to die," the sergeant retorted sarcastically, waiting for the man to rise out of his self-pity.

"How dare you criticise the Soviet's efforts to clear the country of unnecessary forces and bring the country back to peace and stability," Nikita blazed out.

"You are so naïve, Rusakov," the Sergeant continued. "The rebels and the Soviet agents have a different agenda altogether. They know there are a lot of natural resources, such as gold, titanium and uranium, in the country. Their intention is to mine these valuable minerals, and with the uranium in particular manufacture nuclear devices. They are also capitalising on the death of President Tombalbaye, who I have been informed was assassinated yesterday. The Soviets are in league with the Libyans. They have no plans to bring peace and harmony to the country, only havoc and anarchy. They have hoodwinked you into believing that we are the enemy and have kept your girlfriend hostage to make sure you do exactly as they say."

"How do you know about my girlfriend?" asked Nikita, with surprise and fear.

"We have ways of finding things out. I do not know how you got involved but it is time for you to disentangle yourself from the rebels and join forces with us. Knowing us reasonably well after your time in the Legion, do we appear to be on the side of anything but honour, and courage?"

"I must say that I have been very disturbed by what I have to do and the thought of being instrumental in your deaths has been haunting me night and day. But how can I save my girlfriend?"

"You will continue to send the usual messages informing the rebels where we will be on the appointed day of the attack," Sergeant Greenfield instructed him. "We will be ready for them. Do you know how many there will be?" he inquired.

"About 20."

"I am sure we will be able to overcome them. What weapons do they have?"

"They have AK 47 rifles and hand grenades."

"I suggest," continued Greenfield "that you are not around when the attack takes place. In the meantime we will search for the rebels' hide out, find out where they are keeping your girlfriend and bring her back to you. Can you give us an idea as to where their location is?"

"Yes," responded Nikita, "it is about a 30-minute trek north of here, high up in the hills."

"I think you should also mention in your messages that having found no rebels in the hills the Legion are planning to retreat. Mention to them how discouraged and frustrated we are, and let them know that we have a feeling that there is nothing much more that can be done."

"I hope they'll believe me."

"They had better or your life won't be worth anything. I will not tell the other recruits what has transpired tonight. It could cause a lot of animosity between you."

"Thank you very much for putting things in perspective," said Nikita, giving a quiet sigh of relief.

They both retreated to their sleeping bags Sergeant Greenfield, exhausted by the last few weeks' subterfuge and night vigils. He still did not feel he was out of the woods. He would continue to watch Nikita until he was sure that he had definitely had a change of heart and come over to their side.

The following day brought no change. There was no action but the constant trekking up and down the rough terrain without any reprieve. At least the soldiers were getting exercise, though not in the most congenial of areas.

Sergeant Greenfield was glad that he had ordered Macey to keep his mouth shut, for it would have been impossible for Nikita to behave normally among the recruits if they had known of his treachery. He felt that he owed Macey an explanation after his confrontation with Rusakov the night before. He could not make this man understand the pressure Nikita had been put under and until he knew he could whole-heartedly trust the young Russian there would not necessarily be any thought of a future for him in the

Legion, if any at all. Macey would find it extremely difficult to act in any normal capacity if he had to keep this secret to himself for the rest of his stint in the Legion. The Sergeant informed Macey about the events on the hill soon after breakfast the next morning, and how Nikita had broken down with remorse about what he had had to do but was being coerced by the rebels. Rusakov knew that he had no option but to accede to their demands. Macey accepted this with equitable temper but found it difficult to comprehend how Nikita could ratify his conscience in believing that it would be acceptable to kill 12 people without compunction in order to save one.

Sergeant Greenfield with Nikita's help was able to locate the rebels' camp, which was situated way up in the mountains in a location obscured by bushes and protected by barbed wire. He felt it would be wiser to wait until the rebels had been terminated before trying to rescue the girl. He would be completely outnumbered if he was to make such an attempt. He had no intention, at the moment anyway, of involving the other soldiers. There would be time later on to explain what had occurred, if an explanation was needed.

Several days later Nikita received the news that their plan of attack was to take place in 2 days' time, which would, of course, depend on where the Legion was planning to rest for the night. He was to give the rebels the time and place so the operation could take place.

In preparation for the terrorists' attack, Sergeant Greenfield and his recruits took up their positions in the shadows of the bushes just outside the cave. Each was wearing the dark camouflaged clothes of the hunter, their FAMASs cocked and a number of grenades in their pockets. They had been advised that there were 20 rebels against the

12 of them. Sergeant Greenfield knew that his men were fitter, stronger and more focussed than nearly any fighting force in the world and felt they should have no problem in overpowering these rebels.

The enemy came slowly and silently down the hill, their AK 47 rifles cocked and grenades in their hands in preparation for a couple to be thrown at a moment's notice. Their leader, a tall, dark rugged fellow with a scar running down half of his face, led the way, only pausing to see if his entourage was close by. He was slightly surprised that there was no one on guard but suspected that the lookout was in another area, scouting for unwelcome visitors. It did not concern the leader too much but in fact made it much easier to gain a smoother entry into the cave where he expected the Legionnaires would be oblivious, cosily wrapped up in their sleeping bags. With a nod to two of his more reliable rebels, he ushered them to the edge of the cave where, with another nod, they threw the grenades into the entrance with tremendous force, causing a loud blast. A huge dust cloud to came out of the cave, followed by pieces of stone fractured by the explosion. The remaining terrorists rushed in afterwards, emptying their magazines on what they thought were the unsuspecting Legionnaires. The moment they saw their chance, the Legionnaires jumped the rebels, using the element of surprise to their advantage. They opened fire and overcame the men within 5 minutes of the start of the attack.

"Where was Nikita," Sergeant Greenfield wondered, "I told him to keep away from the rebels, but where did he go?" He moved back into the cave looking to see if any of the enemies were still alive. In the dim light he spied a body in the corner that did not appear to be moving. It was Nikita. He ran towards him trying to find a pulse. He was dead.

What a tragedy that a young man should die for no good reason. He sighed with regret. Why had he become involved with the rebels anyway? He would probably never know. Nikita probably thought that as he had betrayed the Legion he would never be able to return, so had effectively killed himself in enemy fire. Now there was no reason to explain the situation to the others, unless Macey felt that he needed to. The sergeant thought this unlikely.

I will search for his girlfriend, Greenfield promised himself, and get her home safely to Russia. The soldiers were delighted at the outcome of the attack. It had been a long and arduous mission, and until this last moment had been very dull. Sergeant Greenfield intimated that in the circumstances it would be wise to return to Corsica, having eliminated the local rebel cell.

Nobody had commented on Nikita's presence in the cave and the Sergeant was not ready to explain. That would be for another time. The Sergeant reigned in the soldiers' banter following their successful attack. As expected, the cave was no longer suitable for them to stay in. The men were ordered to move the corpses into the cave and to block the entrance with pieces of loose stone. Nikita's body was removed and placed on a makeshift stretcher with the greatest of respect, the Legionnaires mourning one of their own. This completed, he directed the troop to another sheltered area 3 km away. They uncovered their packs and supplies, which had been hidden in the sand nearby, and started walking.

On reaching the new camp, while the recruits celebrated with the cans of beer that had been given to them by the sergeant, he and Macey slunk away from the merriment towards the rebels' camp high up in the hills. Sergeant Greenfield was sure that there would be at least a couple of the enemy force who had stayed behind to watch over their camp. They would be waiting for their comrades' return. He was fairly sure too that they would be relatively complacent and not especially worried about the outcome of the raid on the Legion's camp. It was going to be a synch and they were looking forward to starting the celebrations.

High up on the ridge one of the guards, who looked rather like a tough gangster from a movie, was idly lighting up a cigarette and relaxing against the wall. He dropped the match as a bullet to hit him square in the middle of his forehead. He did not have time to cry out, his body slumping forward and falling over the ridge. Another rebel appeared having heard the thud and was somewhat surprised to find that his mate was not standing where he should have been. Another shot fired by Macey's silenced rifle went straight through the centre of his heart (he was an excellent shot), the rebel collapsing onto the sharp brush that surrounded the encampment. Nobody else appeared to be around, unless there were terrorists inside the fortress whose job was to watch the girl and who had not heard anything untoward outside.

The sergeant threw a grappling hook over the wall; it caught firmly on the side. Climbing up to the compound, he and Macey entered the rebels' den. They were able to creep downstairs without coming across any enemy soldiers, holding their rifles at the ready should they need to defend themselves. The stairs appeared to lead to a dark hovel under ground level. Again all was quiet. They were just about to step into the corridor when they spied a dark-haired man sitting outside a heavy, prison-like door. He was playing cards with another rebel. The men looked up hearing the scrape of a shoe on the stairs. They reached for their guns but Macey and Sergeant Greenfield were faster, shooting and killing them both instantly.

Perhaps they had been guarding the girl. Checking that they were dead, Macey searched all their pockets until he finally found a large key, which looked as though it would open the lock of this enormous door. Opening it with some difficulty they discovered a girl, barely out of her teens, sitting on a chair in the middle of the room with her arms tied tightly behind her so that she could hardly move. Her head was slumped forwards, suggesting that she was unconscious; her eyes were closed, and her skin was a mottled grey colour. Sergeant Greenfield immediately went over to her vital signs. Her breathing was very shallow but she was alive. Undoing the knots he picked her up, very gently putting her over his shoulder. He and Macey ran up the stairs to the ground floor of the rebels' den. No further enemies were in sight.

Attaching the rope to his middle, Macey swung down to the bottom of the hill. Undoing the rope he released it and the sergeant pulled it up. He made a sling in which he placed girl. She landed safely on the ground where Macey untied her. Sergeant Greenfield followed moments later. The operation took just under 15 minutes in total. Still carrying the girl, Sergeant Greenfield and Macey returned to the camp where the recruits were still celebrating.

Greenfield felt it would be wiser Nikita's girlfriend to be returned to her homeland as soon as possible. She was still unconscious but her life signs were a little stronger than they had been when they had first discovered her. He had radioed ahead for helicopter rescue, hoping that it would not take too long to arrive. They were situated in such a barren place and having no facilities to cope with her injuries there was very little he could do. The helicopter took about 2 hours to arrive. The soldiers had fallen asleep by this time, exhausted by their long and inebriated night. They were up as usual, however, at the crack of dawn in preparation for a new day and their return to Corsica.

CHAPTER 24

A new beginning

Writing to Constance immediately was Tom's priority. He told her how much he had enjoyed meeting her in French Guyana and how much she had come to mean to him. He said hoped that she had been happy in Brazil and would love to hear from her when she had time. Perhaps they could meet up again after Christmas.

He posted the letter the day after receiving her address from Macey. Day after day went by, but there was no reply. Tom was becoming frantic. Had she forgotten him? Had she met someone else? He could not talk to his parents. They did not seem to want to talk about Tom's experiences in the Legion at all, and brushing it all under the carpet they pretended nothing had happened. He felt so incredibly lonely. He missed the camaraderie that he had had within the unit and the support the soldiers gave each other. This was not how he envisaged life after escaping from the Legion.

A couple of weeks after he had written the letter to Constance it came back with "not known at this address" scrawled all over the envelope. Part of him was relieved that Constance had not rejected him, but he now had no idea how he was now going to find her. There was no one he could contact, either in Corsica or French Guyana. Macey had gone to Chad and would not be back until Christmas. Tom's only hope was to wait for Macey to return and contact him.

He wrote to Harry and Benedict to thank them for their invaluable help in Marseilles and to let them know that everything had gone well and he was now safely home in Sweden. As an afterthought, he asked Harry to forward any letters that came addressed to him to Macey.

The weather became very cold with biting winds and heavy falls of snow. It was the middle of December, only a short time before Christmas. Tom had registered at the prestigious hospital in Stockholm, where he hoped he could start studying medicine in the New Year. He had passed the prerequisite exams and was just waiting for an opening so he could start.

Just before Christmas a letter arrived from Brazil addressed to Macey at the French Foreign Legion in Corsica. Unfortunately as he was still in Chad the letter remained unopened until his return. Harry put the letter to one side.

***

Christmas arrived with the usual Swedish celebrations, which always started on Christmas Eve. Tom's mother, Margareta, was an excellent cook and provided the family with a magnificent spread of Swedish festive delicacies. These included Janssons frestelse, prinskorv, meatballs, smoked salmon, gravad lax, smoked eel, sill (herrings), boiled eggs, caviar, hard bread and cheese. All the Sandberg family were there to celebrate this auspicious feast, his brothers Björn and Anders as well as his sister Karen and her new husband

Rikard. Tom was very happy to see them all again but could not rid himself of this hollow feeling that continually seemed to persist.

Early in the New Year he received the news that he could start his medical studies in Stockholm on the 7th January. He was delighted.

***

Macey returned to Calvi after his mission in Chad just before Christmas, but did not see the pile of letters that had been put aside for him until after the festivities. It had been a gruelling mission and he was just glad to return to Corsica to unwind. He looked forward to catching up with Madeleine and wrote a list of all of the other people he wanted to call or write to.

He opened Constance's letter soon after the New Year's celebrations. He was pleased to hear from her and was glad to be able to forward it to Tom in Sweden.

***

Tom was over the moon at receiving Constance's letter, which his mother sent to his apartment in Stockholm where he had moved just a week before. With now having Constance's current address, he forwarded the returned letter, which he had not had the heart to throw away. It said everything he wanted in it. He just hoped that one day they would be together. He knew he would not feel truly happy until they were.

EPILOGUE

It took a long time for Yves Marchand to compile a dossier on Mr Z and his team, even with the information that Mr E from Egypt had given him 3 years earlier. With the profile completed he, with a number of his police colleagues, drove to Sampson House in the 21ˢᵗ arrondissement to shut down Mr Z's organisation and arrest the group.

Just as Marchand and his colleagues were about to enter Sampson House there was an almighty explosion, apparently coming from the tenth floor. Rushing up the back stone stairs, Marchand and his colleagues found that the tenth floor, as well as the whole of the eleventh and much of the twelfth, had been destroyed beyond recognition. From the debris they were able determine that there were a number of people who had been caught in the blast. They would have to be identified by forensic checks, such as dental records, and by elimination through missing person reports in cases where this was not possible.

***

It was unknown whether Mr Z had had survived the blast. No one reported anybody of his description missing and he was not spotted at any passport control checkpoints – not that the police were looking. He was presumed dead.

Marchand thought that there was always the possibility that Mr Z had set up the explosion to rid himself of the premises as well as his henchmen and surveillance team, who were on the same floor. In due course, Marchand surmised he would probably find himself another quorum, new premises, and start up his business again.

***

Tom, on his way home picked up a newspaper and read about the explosion in Paris. Not having any idea that this was the headquarters of the organisation that had press-ganged him into the French Foreign Legion nearly 3 years before, he frowned thinking about the loss of life, and quickly forgot all about it. He ran thorough the contents of Constance's latest letter in his mind and wondered how long he should wait before suggesting he travel to visit her.

***

A month after the explosion in Paris, after returning from a long day at the hospital he opened the front door, ascending the stairs to his first floor apartment totally unaware that two men were hiding in the broom cupboard opposite his apartment. They were watching his every movement through a slit of light in the door.

CPSIA information can be obtained at www.ICGtesting.com
Printed in the USA
BVOW04s1308260314

348831BV00001B/238/P